Before We Were Famous

Inspired by Emily Brontë's 1847 novel
Wuthering Heights

By Ally Adams

Atlas Productions

Before We Were Famous

Inspired by Emily Brontë's novel, *Wuthering Heights*

First published in 2022

Copyright © Ally Adams 2022

Atlas Productions
Greenslopes QLD 4102

 A catalogue record for this book is available from the National Library of Australia

Web: www.atlasproductions.com.au

This book is a work of fiction. Names, characters, places and incidents are either the product of the author's imagination or are used fictitiously. Any resemblance to actual persons, living or dead, or to actual events or locales is entirely coincidental. Any medical experiments or results cited in this novel have been fictionalised and any slight of specific people, experiments, research or organisations is unintentional.

Cover design by: Stefanie, Beetiful Book Covers. https://beetifulbookcovers.com/

Proofreading by: Penny Clarkson.

Beta reader: Sincere thanks to Simona Moroni for her insights.

This book is written in British/Australian English.

Respectfully dedicated to those talented Brontë sisters.

From one of the millions of readers over the centuries they have inspired.

Books by Ally Adams

The Saints' Team contemporary romance series:

Team Lucas
Team Tomás
Team Niklas
Team Alex

Spies in Love contemporary romance series:

My Boyfriend the Spy
I Spy my Guy

Parnormal romance:
The Dark Moors

PART 1

Chapter 1

THREE YEARS EARLIER

The director gave me a nod, the camera was rolling. I turned, bit my lip and gave the guy behind me the best sexy come hither look I could muster, and then lifting my ballgown slightly began to run across the moors, laughing and looking back at him until he caught me up and spun me around. He slowly put me down, pulling me against him, and leant down to kiss me.

'Hold that…'

And we did, like a kiss suspended in time while the wind whipped around us.

'Cut, that's a wrap, nice work Cathy and Liam,' the director called.

Liam cleared his throat and straightened, moving away from me.

'Nice work, Liam,' I grinned, teasing him.

'You too, *Wylde* girl,' he winked.

Several costume ladies raced over to lift my dress and help me back to the changing room, or tent in this case. The perfume commercial was done, my first ever.

I was the *Wylde* girl.

Chapter 2

GRADUATION DAY – NOW

There were two things I wanted out of life – to be a famous actor, and Heath, not necessarily in that order. It was graduation day. I pushed open the lecture room door and entered the theatrette; there was a buzz of excitement in the air. Heath's rehearsal was just about to start.

I sensed Heath before I saw him; I turned and watched him approach. Tall, solid, dark-haired and edgy; I know him better than I know myself. No words were wasted greeting me, he just kissed me; I'm not a PDA type of person but he had no problem with it. Heath grinned when I glanced at some of the first-year students who were sitting in the theatrette watching us and smiling; I knew my skin was flushed.

'Cathy, should I have you right here and now, give them something to really smile about?' he said, his lips close to my ear, his deep voice exciting me.

'No,' I pulled away, horrified at the thought which just made him laugh. 'That's not the performance they came here to see!' I exclaimed.

'They are probably going to have to do sex scenes somewhere in their acting career,' he said, wide-eyed as though his idea wasn't totally ridiculous.

'Yes, but that will be acting,' I reminded the man who took my virginity and was still the only man I'd ever been with. I wanted it to stay that way. There were lots of girls in our theatre company who wanted the chance to bed him too.

'Ladies and gentlemen, the cast of *Macbeth* on stage please,' our director called.

'That's me. Got to go,' Heath said, all serious again. He gave me a quick kiss and departed. It felt like he had never been a student, he's been an actor since day one of our course; he looked the part, he owned the stage, I'm an imposter trying hard. I watched him go and then I glanced at the same first-year girls to find them watching him too. Sigh, it happened when you loved a gorgeous guy. I made my way to my rehearsal group who were sitting in the middle rows of the theatrette.

'Hey, *Wylde* girl.'

Yeah boys, thanks for remembering. If I had a dollar for every time someone called me *Wylde* girl since I made that commercial three years ago, I would have made more than I did on the commercial, and I made enough from that to pay off my studies and Heath's if he hadn't got a scholarship.

Ryan, Jack and Emmett were in my class, they were stars in the making; Heath called them pretty boys. Unlike Heath who got in the first time, we auditioned a few times to earn our places. The guys were all about the big roles, the big bucks and the actresses they could bed. They thought

Shakespeare was a drag and wanted to do action roles, the occasional romance to get the chicks, and a major drama in the hope of clutching a few awards. It took all types.

I dropped down in a vacant chair beside them.

'Nervons?' I asked Jack.

'Nuh,' he said, all bravado.

Ryan leant forward. 'I'm shitting myself,' he said, and I laughed.

'Yeah, me too,' I confessed.

A couple of first-year students shuffled over and sat behind us; one of them leant closer to me.

'You're the *Wylde* girl, aren't you?'

'That's her but she's pretty tame most of the time,' Jack joked.

I smirked at him and nudged him away.

'I am. Cathy,' I said, introducing myself.

The two girls did the same – blondie-spiked and pink-hair. That wasn't their names but that's how I'd remember them because they looked so unique. They looked more model-type than actor-type – everyone else in the theatre was pretty conservative. I hoped they'd last the distance. I could see my three guy friends next to me appreciating them.

'What was it like, you know, making the commercial?' Pink-hair asked.

"Amazing,' I said, which was what they wanted to hear. They looked at each other and grinned, and then back to me for more detail. 'I loved it,' I continued. 'For two days I ran around in ballgowns; stood in front of wind machines; I jumped on the back of a motorcycle with a gorgeous guy, both of us head-to-toe in leather; and I dived into blue tanks of water in a white wedding dress … you know all the usual cliché stuff which was then cut down to a thirty-second perfume commercial!'

'Oh. My. God. I want that,' Blondie-spiked groaned. 'Your face was on television, billboards and in magazine ads. Everywhere.'

I still got a buzz from being recognised but I blushed at their gushing. It was a start-up fragrance company that couldn't afford a name and I got the gig. Lucky me.

'My boyfriend hated it,' I confided to them.

'He's gorgeous,' Pink-hair said. 'Didn't he like you being *Wylde* girl?'

'Oh no, he's fine with that,' I said. 'But he was bored stupid. He came with me and lasted two hours on set before he fell into a coma. He couldn't believe how often filming stopped and started, how long it took to do a few seconds, I thought he'd implode.'

They both laughed.

'Okay, quiet on the set, quiet in the audience please,' the director yelled, and I gave them a small wave and turned back to watch the stage.

My class—twenty other students including Heath, and Jack, Ryan and Emmett sitting next to me—had to choose to perform in one of three plays as part of our graduation week at the Manchester College for Dramatic Arts. Two of my best friends, Nelly and Lockwood, were studying here too. Nelly wanted to direct and Lockwood was into set building. We dreamed of being in productions together after we'd graduated.

I was pretty much thinking about my lines until Heath

came on stage, with his commanding presence demanding my attention. Sometimes I momentarily didn't recognise him on stage; he morphed into the character and drew you in. Heath's jaw locked, his dark eyes burned with intensity as he delivered the lines; he looked at me and I was taken hostage then, crash! One of the actors forgot their lines and the play came to a halt.

Ryan yawned and whispered, 'so boring.'

I tried not to laugh. We were both in *The Importance of Being Earnest,* Oscar Wilde's brilliant play; there wasn't an action-drama option to Ryan's dismay. I saw Lockwood scuttle off stage after doing a few adjustments to his set. Five minutes later the set was quiet and it kicked off again. Heath gave the actor who forgot her line an encouraging smile and she gave him a flirty smile back. *Whatever.* I was watching for any sign that it was more because I would be able to tell. I had known Heath since he was a kid and Dad arrived home with him – this angry orphan kid who didn't want to be rescued by Dad, or anyone for that matter.

My brother, God rest his soul – how weird was that saying, by the way? I can't imagine Hindley's soul resting for a moment, full of hate it was, especially for Heath. If there was a word stronger than hate I'd use it. But Dad loved Heath, I loved him, Mum put up with him, and now none of them was around anymore, except Heath and me and we were forever inseparable.

I was jolted back to the now thanks to the clapping going on around me. The scene had finished, the set was being changed and John called for a quick break before the next production—my play—began. I rose and followed Ryan and my rehearsal group. Blondie-spiked and Pink-hair wished me luck and told me to break a leg. So confident already those two.

'You got this?' Nelly asked, passing me.

'Absolutely,' I told her with a grin. *God, I hope so.*

Heath appeared behind me; he'd left his group to wish me luck.

Heath and Cathy. Cathy and Heath.

'You'll be fine, you know that,' he said, seeing me blink away tears.

'— it's not that,' I cut him off. 'I'm just being melodramatic. In a week we won't be here anymore and seeing our classmates every day. After three years together nearly every day, it will be over. And depending on our roles, where will you be, Heath?'

'With you, Cathy,' he assured me without hesitation. 'I will be with you always.' He leant close and whispered in my ear. 'I cannot live without my soul!'

A shiver ran through me. Was I the only one who wasn't excited about graduating and getting out into the world? I was like that at the end of high school too. Everyone was busting to escape school and break out into the world but I felt like the rug had been pulled from under me.

Again, now, I had a sense of foreboding as our graduation day loomed.

Chapter 3 – All the world's a stage…

LIFE AFTER GRADUATION

'She's beautiful, and therefore to be wooed; She is woman, and therefore to be won.' Every time Heath said his line with just a hint of determination as if he was accepting the challenge, he delivered it with a glance in my direction—just off stage—when he should be glancing at his leading lady, Margaret. I felt the eyes in the audience searching for me at the side of the stage where I had just taken my exit. I heard the titters and saw the smiles and nudges as though they had been waiting for that line. I felt myself blush which was just ridiculous, I've known Heath since I was six. I knew every fibre of his being and he knew all there was to know of me; he's more myself than I am! Not to mention Shakespeare would probably be spinning in his grave, but then again, he was a guy so maybe not.

If I were the director, I'd haul Heath's handsome butt into the green room and tell him to pull his head in, but our director encourages him! I suspect it was because the hashtag campaign that started about our romance was attracting an audience, and it was all about bums-on-seat. It didn't help that *Entertainment Weekly* might have mentioned we were living together in one of their trivia-gossip columns. So much for Heath's character—the Earl of Suffolk—and his co-star Margaret getting steamy!

God, I love the Globe Theatre – it was so exciting and authentic, so Shakespeare! It was Heath's favourite venue … he'd perform here forever if he could, but our theatre company did the rounds. Well, actually it's Heath's theatre company – he was a permanent player with a contract. I had to audition for every play, but I scored roles most of the time. I strictly forbade Heath from putting in a good word for me; I wanted to get the roles on my own. He promised me that he didn't say a word and lectured me about underestimating my talent, but yeah, not sure on that one.

I saw my best friend and fellow actor, Nelly Dean, approaching. There were not a lot of female roles in Henry VI's tale, but we both managed to nab one. We'd been in the same plays about half a dozen times since graduating. I loved it when that happened. She was playing the Countess of Auvergne.

'Oh Romeo,' she whispered, as she sidled up to me off stage and gave me a nudge.

I grinned. 'Shut up, and wrong play.'

'Nuh, you wait … I bet they'll be casting you and Heath in *Romeo and Juliet* next. I'm prepared to put my *Othello* program signed by Daniel Craig on that one.'

My mouth dropped open. Nelly loved that program. Nelly loved Daniel Craig. She flew to New York for the weekend to see that play and saw it twice.

I put out my hand to shake and offered my stake. 'My program for *The Audience*.'

'No! Signed by Helen Mirren?' Her eyes were huge.

I nodded. 'The Queen herself,' I said, recalling Dame Helen in the role at the Gielgud Theatre. She's my idol, well one of them, and there were a few. We shook.

Nelly turned away from the stage. 'When are you on?'

'Not for another fifteen,' I said, and we moved away to talk.

'Any news?' she asked.

'Nope. But Heath's been confirmed, he's off to Oxford after this for a short season,' I said.

We were both hoping to confirm our season would be continuing with this play and we would not be finishing up here in London. It was not the first time we'd performed *Henry VI* and I'd played Joan de Pucelle, or you might know her as Joan of Arc – yep, that's me … leader of men, maker of war, saving the country every night for a three-week season on stage, plus six matinees! Not to mention a bit of after-hours rehearsal and role play with Heath … he liked to get my armour off. Speaking of which, it was so uncomfortable. I adjusted it trying to find a better fit.

'I'd love to play Joan of Arc, you lucky bitch,' Nelly said, helping me.

My mouth dropped open. 'Why didn't you audition then?'

She shrugged. 'I don't think the world is ready for a black Joan yet.'

'Don't be ridiculous,' I said. 'You're fantastic, Joan should be so lucky. Besides, she was a 19-year-old French girl and

I'm a 25-year-old English chick … anything's possible. At least you've got a saucy role, I'm an armour-plated maiden who says she's knocked up to avoid burning at the stake!'

'Yeah, well we've all used that excuse,' she said, and we both laughed. Nelly continued: 'You know what I'd kill for … a regular TV role.'

I groaned. 'Me too. Heath wants to spend his life on the stage. He's already identified the awards he intends to win; the plays he wants to be in; the lead roles he wants to get before he hits thirty. He loves the adrenaline of knowing it is live and he can't stuff up,' I said, with a glance at him on the stage.

'Seriously? No film ambitions at all?'

I shook my head. 'Nup,' I continued. 'Call me shallow but I want to be a star and an actor. I want to be recognised and make huge money and have people doing my hair and make-up, and a director letting me do a scene three times if I forget the lines or if I'm not happy with it.'

Nelly grinned. 'Me too. I'm not a theatre tragic like Heath; I want to direct. At least you've done some screen stuff, *Wylde* girl.'

Ah, *Wylde* girl.

'I loved being the *Wylde* girl,' I said, reminiscing.

We stopped to listen to where they were up to on stage and then continued talking.

'I tease Heath that he can stay on stage and I'll go make the big money in film and keep us in the lifestyle we liked to imagine. He's not impressed,' I said, and shrugged.

I glanced at the clock and back to the stage.

'You're on in a minute,' Nelly said. She adjusted my

armour again for me, then gave me a wave and disappeared to go prepare for her next appearance.

'Decrepit miser! Base ignoble wretch!' I muttered. That was my next line, not a Nelly insult.

Deep breath. *I've got this.*

I moved closer to the stage curtain. I heard the audience titter again and glanced out to see what the excitement was about this time. Our production has too many hotties in it, seriously, it's Shakespeare … focus people, focus. Heath stepped off the stage and collided with me; he grabbed me before I fell backwards.

'Jesus, Joan, watch where you're saving the world,' he said, and grinned before giving me a quick kiss. He's always on a natural high when we were working.

He brushed his dark hair back and pulled away to let me breathe.

'Sorry,' I moved a little out of the stage exit area. 'Getting anywhere with Margaret?' I whispered, with a glance to the woman his character was wooing but supposedly to give to the king.

'Of course, … me or the king? C'mon, I'm the man.'

'That you are,' I teased, 'but go be manly elsewhere, I'm on in a second.' I gave him a smirk as I moved past him to wait for my cue.

He tapped my butt which I heard rather than felt through the metal plate of my armour. I gave him a look that said Joan was outraged by that and wagged my finger; I threw one of my lines at him: 'Thou art no father nor no friend of mine.'

'C'mon, who's your daddy?' he said and made me laugh again.

'Shut up, I'll forget my lines.' I ignored him, or attempted to, despite the fact he leant back against the set, crossed his arms over his chest and smiled at me with one of his winning looks. I'm such a sucker. I closed my eyes, breathed in deeply and listened to the dialogue on the stage to my left and then I heard my cue. I strode on and I'm straight into the character and in the moment. The Duke of Gloucester was about to give me a hard time before I'm burned to death, yep, nothing cheery about being Joan of Arc.

The rest of the play went so fast and before we knew it, it was over again for yet another performance. Three 'curtain calls' – that's huge! We were all beaming. We held hands as we bowed; Heath had wrangled his way next to me and took my hand on stage as we bowed and that increased the intensity of the clapping. When it was his turn to step forward by himself the applause was thundering. I almost expected to see lingerie flying toward him. It's good for me to see how other women desired Heath, it made him sexier. We'd been part of each other's lives for so long that I saw him as just my Heath.

That was it. The curtain closed, the lights went up, the crowds departed and we all chilled. It was a wrap, opening night done! Time to celebrate with the cast and crew.

*****

The morning after opening night was the worst. No, not because of the hangover, but because of the reviews. I died a thousand deaths. If mine weren't good, well I can live with that, even understand given my current acting instability …

I'd search around until I found kinder reviews and I would read those over and over. But I couldn't stand it if Heath got bad reviews when he was so much more passionate about it. My great miseries in this world have been Heath's miseries, and I felt it as keenly as he did.

But I needn't have worried about that. The next morning while I showered, Heath went and got the papers. He's forbidden from rifling through the papers and looking for the reviews until he comes home. I got out of the shower and dressed quickly. Moments later I saw his car, black and fast, turn into our driveway and the garage. From where I looked out, you couldn't see the changes to the building, just the original wall – that's what I liked about our place.

This was once a mansion, dark and sprawling, a huge estate. Now it had been converted into six townhomes. Heath and I lived on the second floor with our windows facing the moors – we couldn't see the subdivided section. Most of the other tenants preferred the view of the manicured gardens but not us. We spent most of our childhood on the moors, I knew it like the back of my hand and I needed to see it.

I heard his steps as he hurried in and the door closed behind him. There's a routine here … if the reviews were good, we'd go back to bed. He'd be passionate, rough, demanding, and then after we came down off our high, we'd walk down to the village for breakfast and I'd scroll through and read him the online reviews and the reviews that audience members had left on the company's social media pages. Heath didn't care too much for those, but I thrived on them.

But if the critic reviews were shit, then I'd take the newspapers from him and I would lead him to the bedroom.

I'd make love to him slowly, remind him there's more to life than the thoughts of one person sitting in the audience penning his vitriol. And then we'd both be morose all day and have to go back and perform again tonight.

God, please let them be good. Please.

'Got them,' he said and dropped down on a stool at the kitchen bench. He handed me two tabloid newspapers and he took the broadsheet. We discarded all the catalogues, weekend magazines and inserts, and cut to the chase.

We both read in silence and then I looked up and Heath's eyes met mine and he smiled; I grinned in response. *Phew, praise the Lord, it was going to be a good weekend.* This was what it must be like for actors, authors, artists, and even professional athletes and their poor long-suffering partners after a win or loss, a launch, or opening.

My small mention in the reviews was really good and I knew Heath was superb; the critics agreed. I read aloud the reviews from one of the tabloids:

'*Earnshaw owned the role.* You bet he did,' I teased. 'And more... *Earnshaw is a force of nature.* Or how about – *All hail Earnshaw, the Earl of Suffolk*'.

That got a laugh from Heath.

'Read me yours,' he said. I cleared my throat dramatically.

'It's frame-worthy,' I tell him. '*Catherine Earnshaw once again passionately delivered a defiant Joan de Pucelle.* Defiant, huh!'

I leant over and kissed him. 'You were brilliant.'

He exhaled as if he had forgotten to breathe.

'So were you, my love, listen to these ...' I watched him prepare to read out the reviews, his dark eyes lit with energy:

'*A fantastically lively Joan of Arc performance by Catherine Earnshaw makes her inevitable death that much more dramatic.*'

I laughed. 'That's cool.' We both knew we would read and re-read the papers a few more times yet, then cut out the reviews and keep them. Hey, we're still kind of new at this; after we've been doing this for a decade we probably won't bother. It made me sad for a moment thinking of how Mum would be clipping reviews and keeping them if she were alive.

I cleared my throat of emotion and returned to the now. 'Read me your reviews in full,' I insisted.

'They didn't say anything else about me,' he teased and folded the paper.

'What!' I tried to wrestle the paper from him but he only laughed and with so little strength required, held me at length.

'Okay, okay,' he gave in to me. 'How's this one: '*The Earl of Suffolk is delivered with intelligence by an actor who understands light and dark.*'

'Ooh, wow,' I said, taking in that review. 'That's impressive. Heath, seriously, you are on your way.'

He stopped reading and looked up at me with a hint of impatience.

'I'm twenty-six, you're twenty-five. We graduated over four years ago,' he reminded me. 'We've been hammering away at it for ages, we're well and truly on our way ... we should be there, wherever there is!'

Four years didn't seem like much time to be climbing the theatre hierarchy ladder but Heath was so impatient and such an old soul. Me, I was always surprised by my successes; I still can't believe I got the *Wylde* girl campaign. I think it appalled him a little that success to me was fame, funds and recognition. Success to him was credibility.

'You're right,' I said, not wanting to take away from the excitement of the moment. 'It's just that sometimes I feel like we're still learning, especially when we're some of the youngest members of our theatre group.'

He shrugged. 'True.'

'Shall I go online and see what the *Entertainment Weekly* had to say?' I asked. I valued their reviews even if Heath was on the fence about them.

'Nah,' he said, 'let's check out online reviews later.'

'Okay, but I want one more glowing review about you,' I insisted, sitting back in my chair.

He smiled and scanned the paper. '*Earnshaw's Earl is an intelligent, muscular performance.*'

I whooped. 'Brilliant, but I knew that.'

He laughed and put the newspaper down.

'Mr Earnshaw, I'd like my own *muscular* performance,' I said, giving him an encouraging look.

He rose and with a small bow delivered one of his lines: 'Gentle madam; I unworthy am, to woo so fair a dame – but I'll give it a shot,' he said, and picked me up. I yelped with surprise.

'I don't think that last line was Shakespeare,' I said and laughed as he raced towards the bedroom carrying me, my newspaper fluttering to the ground behind us.

That was the last week of our lives when everything was normal.

Chapter 4– An offer refused

NOW …

Entertainment Weekly

REVIEW: Heath Earnshaw and Emilia Blaese in *Cat on a Hot Tin Roof*, directed by Cordelia Lewis, at the Apollo Theatre, London.

Inventive, emotional and with a dose of humour, director Cordelia Lewis delivers a radical update of Tennessee Williams' classic with a blistering performance by Heath Earnshaw

By Marc Ferguson

Order three bouquets if you plan to give out flowers after this classic presentation of Williams' *Cat on a Hot Tin Roof* at the Apollo Theatre. Hitting her strides, director Cordelia Lewis continues to deliver and for my money she is the most bankable stage director in the UK.

But the accolades must be shared with its two estimable stars, Emilia Blaese and Heath Earnshaw. Ensconced on stage in the vast Mississippi mansion, we are swept up into the prison they have made for themselves, the desperation is palpable.

Earnshaw is superb as Brick, the star athlete who has retreated into alcoholism. His emotional intensity is raw and powerful, and his wife, Maggie (Emiliar Blaese) yearns for the sexual pleasure they once enjoyed – and make no mistake, they have sexual chemistry.

With Big Daddy dying and the inheritance of his estate looming like a ticking time bomb, we are introduced to Big Daddy's grandchildren – obnoxious spin-offs strategically played for maximum effect.

But of all the performers, all eyes are on Heath Earnshaw's Brick as we watch his obsessive decline play out on stage. A broken man with injuries, a denial of his love for Skipper and lack of love for Maggie, he is portrayed beautifully as a tormented shell of the man he could be.

The supporting cast is convincing and capable, notably Rhonda Berry as Big Mama and Ena Pattinson as Mae.

A fine production.

Cat on a Hot Tin Roof is at the Apollo Theatre, London, for a three-week season.

*****

Heath swore the *Entertainment Weekly* had sold its soul and become a gossip rag, but love them or hate them, they had been wonderfully supportive of Heath and his talent.

I suspected their theatre writer thought the sun shone out of him because every play Heath was in, not only got reviewed but very favourably at that. Nelly and I loved the *Entertainment Weekly* – it was the insider source of all information from roles that were about to open up, plus industry reviews, and sure, rumours too. It was compulsory reading and their website was updated daily so we found out about auditions.

They got the gossip right. Heath got a movie offer. It was after he did a brilliant job playing Brick in *Cat on a Hot Tin Roof* at the Apollo. On the final night of the production, film producer Edgar Linton was in the audience. It was Nelly who tipped me off. Off stage, I scanned the audience looking for him. It's not that easy in dim lighting to pick out audience members, usually.

'Where is he? Which one is Edgar?' I whispered to her.

'The shiny, gorgeous one sitting middle centre with the beautiful woman on either side of him,' she answered.

How did I miss that?

'Wow,' I muttered.

'Yeah, my thoughts exactly,' Nelly said.

It was like this guy had an aura around him – power and wealth and sexiness. We felt a presence behind us and wheeled around thinking we were in trouble for gathering backstage, which the director doesn't like, but it was Lockwood.

'Did you see him too?' he said, in a low tone. 'Edgar Linton! Oh my God, he's amazing.'

We nodded.

'Nelly spotted him first. Why do you think he is here?' I asked.

'To see the play,' Lockwood stated the obvious.

Nelly and I turned to give him the look. Lockwood shrugged.

'You think he's recruiting?' I asked.

'Could be,' Nelly agreed. 'Or he might have just read the opening night reviews and wanted to see the play before it closed. I wish I had a bigger part now.'

I laughed. 'Yeah, I don't think he'd be interested in me. He would have signed me up after seeing the *Wylde* girl in action,' I joked. 'But it's kind of exciting he is here and good for the theatre company, and good for Heath!'

'I'm going to ask Edgar for a pic with me, or failing that, get a pic with his sister,' Nelly said. 'It should attract more followers to my account. That's a brilliant self-promotion idea even if I say so myself,' she said, looking pleased with herself.

I knew his sister, Isabella Linton, like one knew a distant neighbour; we'd grown up near each other.

'Why would you want a pic with his sister?' I asked, and Nelly and Lockwood both looked at me like I had been living under a rock.

'Isabella Linton,' Nelly hissed. 'For the love of God, Cathy, what do you do in your spare time?'

'Um … read, walk the moors, learn lines, bed Heath,' I said and grinned.

Nelly chuckled.

'She's a supermodel,' Lockwood informed me. 'That's her on his left. The beautiful blonde one who looks just like him.'

I studied her. Yep, she was beautiful. I hadn't seen her for about fifteen years, I guess. Wow, and she would have been about ten then. She was a pretty girl … so she grew up and became a model.

'They have huge followings,' Lockwood continued, interrupting my thoughts.

'If I can get the photo, I'll tag them and then they'll remember me,' Nelly said, still developing her plan.

We heard the lines which meant the scene was coming to an end and we all scattered. The applause was thundering, and not long after we had to head to the stage for final bows. Heath got an amazing response. My heart could have burst with happiness for him; it was going to be a great weekend.

We always had an after-party on the last night, and the producers had booked out a very cool bar just around the corner for the cast, crew and VIPs. Everyone made their way there after they finished getting changed or doing whatever they had to do. When Heath and I arrived hand in hand, nearly everyone was there. We were all so pumped; it had been a great short season. Heath went to get us both a drink – I always had a champagne cocktail at the end of every production and traditions were important! I waved to Nelly from afar—she was chatting up one of the bar guys—shameless.

I saw people looking in my direction; most of them knew me and I wasn't the star of this show so no reason to be looking at me. Confused I turned around to find that Isabella Linton was standing just behind me talking to our director. Wow, she was something else, nothing like I remembered her. She was glowing, tall, and wearing this sophisticated sparkling dress that showed a lot of her lightly tanned skin, especially a lot of her chest. Someone must have gotten an invitation to them after spotting them in the crowd or perhaps the marketing team had that in hand weeks ago. I couldn't spot the other woman that was sitting next to Edgar in the theatre, probably his girlfriend … I wondered if she came along.

And then the director got pulled away and Isabella turned to me because I was the closest person to her.

'Hello,' she said, 'you were wonderful tonight.' Her teeth were so white and her eyes such a pale green. Nelly was right, the Lintons were shiny.

I almost laughed because it was such a sweet thing to say especially since my role was nothing; I wondered if she said that to everyone.

'Thank you,' I said, looking up at her, even with my heels on. 'Catherine Earnshaw' I said, offering my hand. 'We're neighbours on the moors, I believe.'

'Really!' She shook my hand but didn't offer her name – that's confidence. I was tempted to say that I hadn't caught her name but checked my bitchiness just in time.

'So, are you a regular theatre-goer?' I asked, raising my voice over the din. She leant in closer to talk with me and shrugged.

'My brother, Edgar, is a sponge for all things stage and screen, he's always looking for ideas, talent, different mediums to stimulate him,' she said, rolling her eyes. 'But I was very happy to come along to this performance. I saw you walk in with Heath, he was wonderful, wasn't he?'

'He was,' I nodded. 'He's amazing.'

Awkward pause.

I struggled to think of some small talk that didn't seem too intimate or too lame like, 'so you're a model?' or 'any exciting projects coming for you' or 'do you still go home to the moors?' Too try-hard, too stalker? I went to plan B – trying to plan my exit because the whole thing was so uncomfortable. But then Heath returned with our drinks and the two of them locked eyes.

'Hello, I'm Isabella Linton, and you were spectacular tonight,' she said.

Right, so she'll give her name to Heath so he knows it. Grrr.

'Thank you,' Heath said, with a smile and a nod, which said to me her thoughts weren't really important to him. Bless him. He handed me my champagne cocktail and turned his attention back to Isabella.

'Can I get you a drink or this glass of red, and I'll get another?' Heath asked her, offering his. So chivalrous. She won't drink red wine, look at those white teeth! Sure enough, she was just about to respond when Edgar Linton appeared at her side with two glasses of champagne and handed her one.

Heath and I were now standing talking with our moors 'neighbours', Edgar and Isabella Linton; it was all a bit surreal. I felt like we were street urchins next to them. We were both dark and casual, they were light and shiny. Heath and I had bar-hopping clothes on, but Edgar was in a very expensive suit and Isabella in a cocktail dress that defined glamourous. Aagggh.

I could see people taking shots of us on their phone cameras – really? Secretly I was thinking *'fantastic',* I hope they put them online right now, the more exposure for our careers the better. I've got to get my act together – for God's sake, I'm clever, funny and talented, I can make conversation.

'Good of you to come tonight, did you enjoy the play?' I asked Edgar. *Yeah, look at that, genius, I did it – formed a sentence!* I glanced at Heath who was nonchalance personified. He was subtly looking around the room to work out where the exits were so he could escape sooner rather than later – I knew all his moves.

'It was great, I last saw that play done in New York about five years ago,' Edgar said. 'But you owned the stage tonight,' he said to Heath and offered his hand in a sort of introduction and compliment.

'Thanks,' Heath shook his hand. 'Good to see you both here,' he said, looking from one to the other. I wasn't even sure if Heath knew or cared who they were.

'On your way to a theatre award for that performance,' Edgar said, continuing with the praise. 'Thought about going into film? Widening your audience and profile?'

My beautiful guy, Heath, didn't care about any of that. He didn't want fame; he wanted great reviews and respect. He already had that, but wanted to win a Laurence Olivier Award and a London Critics' Circle Theatre Award. Me, I'll take a BAFTA and an Academy Award, thanks.

'Can't say I've given it much thought,' Heath said.

Edgar laughed like it was the funniest thing he had ever heard. It probably was … I can't imagine too many actors saying to director, Edgar Linton, that he could take his medium and stick it.

Edgar continued. 'I was hoping we could have a word, it's work-related,' he said, with a small smile and a sparkle in his eyes. Edgar took a gulp of champagne, and Isabella touched his arm and looked at him fondly. They were like a performance in their own right, I couldn't take my eyes off them.

'He's all work, all the time,' she purred. Honestly, she purred the words like she'd delivered this sexy line for a lingerie commercial. The *Wylde* girl and the domestic feline standing together – Lord help me.

'Sure,' Heath says, 'now?'

Edgar nods. 'If that's okay with you? I was hoping we might talk about you taking a role in my next film.'

'Ah,' Heath said.

That was what he said, I swear to God.

Not "*Sign me up now*" or "*Lead the way, let's talk*" or "*Hell yeah, man show me the contract*". No, he said, *Ah*. And then Heath nodded towards the door, asked Isabella and me to excuse him and the two of them walked out to talk.

Isabella raised her glass at me and said, 'I'd better mingle then, good to meet you.'

I nodded. 'And you.'

Thank God for that, I thought I'd have to come up with some more small talk which was not my speciality. I can't imagine Isabella and I would have too much in common except that we thought Heath was hot. I stared at the door, wishing I could go put a glass against it and listen to the conversation but the cast moved in around me, filling the space left by the two men and for a brief moment I lost myself in the conversations, while never taking my eyes from the door.

Twenty anguishing minutes later after I had died a thousand deaths, the two men re-entered, Heath led the way. They said a few words to each other, shook hands and parted. Heath looked around for me and his eyes settled on mine. He gave a nod towards the exit and I agreed and followed. He was never one for after-parties, never one for mingling much, and I wanted to know what went on with Edgar more than I wanted to hang about the party.

I met him at the door, he took my hand and we left with a wave to a couple of fellow thespians near us. We headed to the hotel we had been staying at for the duration of the play; the production company got a good rate for the self-contained rooms and they were okay given we weren't there much. I bit my tongue to prevent blurting out a thousand questions about what Edgar wanted because I know Heath and he'd tell me more when he's ready to tell me. And then, because he's on a high post-production which I loved, he stopped and pulled me to him and kissed me.

When he released me, I wanted more.

'What was that for?' I teased him. 'Have you got exciting news?'

'That's because I love you, and because tonight was great, and I have everything I want and need and most of it starts and ends with you.'

I teared up like an idiot and he laughed. 'Come on.' He put his arm around my shoulder and pulled me into him. We walked along the street and it was so cool and lovely out now. A couple of theatre-goers at a nearby bar called out to us and Heath acknowledged their praise with a wave. I couldn't wait any longer.

'Tell me.'

Heath shrugged. 'He wanted to know if I was interested in a two-movie deal for a couple of his new productions.'

I stopped dead and threw my arms around him. 'Congratulations my guy, that is wonderful, how exciting.'

He frowned as he looked down at me.

'I thanked him of course but didn't accept. God, I'd rather eat grass than do every scene six times and have someone editing and controlling how I come across in the end. Where's the rush and thrill in that?'

My arms dropped from around him and I must have been standing there with my mouth open, because he put his finger under my chin, closed my jaw, grabbed my hand and we continued walking.

'But we do every scene in the theatre over and over too – every night for the length of the season and the matinees.'

He shook his head. 'It's different. You get out on stage and you do it with all your passion, totally immersed in the character,' he said, and watched me, expecting me to see the light. 'You are playing opposite other people and you only get one chance to do it right. You deliver that story once only, to an audience that has not seen the performance. They deserve your best and you feed off their energy. It empowers you. By the time you've got to do it again – the next night, it's like the first time, not five minutes after the director calls cut.'

'Right,' I said and thought about his reasoning for a few moments. Then I came up with my next logical reason for him taking the film.

'But …' I continued, 'it's Edgar Linton!'

Seriously. Edgar Linton – talented, rich, dynamic and not that Heath cares, but gorgeous too. Edgar Linton was the guy of the moment; he'd been that guy for a while now. His Indie film was a huge hit and then a studio offered him a budget and his next film was a blockbuster, both at the box office and scoring awards.

'Yeah, it was nice of him,' Heath said.

Nice of him! For the love of God, I can't get my head around it. Edgar Linton offers Heath a two-movie deal that no one in their right mind on the planet would turn down, except Heath. He's officially insane. I was beside myself. Give it to me. Give. It. To. Me.

I saw a small bar with a scattering of trendies in it and I nodded towards it.

'Want to have a quiet drink, just the two of us, like a date?' I asked, teasing him, which was a fair effort given my mind was racing a million miles an hour, but I wanted to slow him down and sit and talk about this.

'Will you come home with me afterwards?' he asked as if we didn't live together.

'Maybe.'

'Those odds will do,' he grinned and led me across the road. We sat on a bench seat out the front and ordered a drink from the waiter.

'Why didn't you tell him you'd think about it at least?' I asked. 'Give it some serious thought.'

'Cathy, I'd be doing it for you, not me. We don't need the money. We own our place thanks to Dad; we're doing what we love. Why would I do it?'

'Bigger picture stuff here,' I said and tried to make Heath rethink the offer. I tried to stay calm and not sound hysterical or pushy when I really wanted to shake him. 'The best and the worst thing about being on the stage is that nobody knows us unless they are theatre junkies and even then, we're only talking local crowds,' I said. 'Sure, people in our village know us, we've lived there long enough that they know we are actors. If they read the reviews or go to London or nearby theatres to see us in plays, they'll give us a pat on the back, but otherwise, we're kind of anonymous.'

I stopped talking while the waiter delivered our drinks and Heath paid. Then Heath raised his glass and we toasted again to good health and great roles – one of our regular toasts.

'Anyway,' I continued, keeping him on track, 'Imagine the size of the audience you could reach by acting in film and the profile you could build – hundreds of thousands. And if you wanted to return to the stage after making a couple of films, imagine the appeal that would have to stage producers and the audience you could pull in. You could pick and choose your stage roles!' That was a brilliant point, we both knew it.

He sat and thought about that for a while. Good, at least I got through to him. I kept quiet and watched the passing parade of night dwellers.

Then he shook his head and said, 'Nuh, I would be miserable. I'd ruin his movie; I'd be a pain in the ass to work with. You've got to know your limitations, Cathy. But you, *Wylde* girl, you'd be fantastic on the big screen. I mentioned you to him.'

Well, that's the dream to be on the big screen, if I ever got picked up.

'Did you? Thanks,' I said, half enthused and half devastated. If Edgar wanted me, he would have asked for me, and now I know for sure he doesn't.

'How did he take it?' I asked.

Heath shrugged. 'I don't know the guy but I think he was

seriously pissed off – I don't think anyone has ever turned him down before.'

'Yeah, well who would, except you,' I said. 'There are established actors out there throwing themselves at Edgar, and he offers a guy on the stage that hardly anyone has heard of a role in his next movie and that guy blows him off.'

We looked at each other and then we burst out laughing. It was so funny that it was tragic. I hyperventilated every time I thought about it. Later, I would come to realise that Edgar didn't take being turned down well ... not at all.

*****

Entertainment Weekly

RUMOUR FILE: Stage actor turns down film director

Rumour has it that Cordelia Lewis' production of *Cat on a Hot Tin Roof* (its season just finished at the Apollo) had several VIP guests in the closing night audience – film director, Edgar Linton (*Lost in Hate; The Journey*) and his supermodel sibling, Isabella.

The rumour mill is in full swing as Linton and stage actor Heath Earnshaw were seen talking in earnest and our sources tell us that Earnshaw turned down a role in Linton's next film. Now there's a man who loves to tread the boards!

Or is there more to it? Earnshaw and the *Wylde* girl, fellow actor, Catherine Earnshaw, are an item and perhaps a stage director has cast them in a future production as lovers on stage as well?

Chapter 5 – The separation

Now…

After reading the salubrious opening night reviews for our latest production, *Henry VI*, and after great love-making, we walked to the village for breakfast basking in our contentment. The morning was crisp and the walk beautiful and peaceful. No one was around. We crossed over the small waterfalls, along the foot-worn track enjoying the green surrounds. The sun was out but it was chilly; the moors were unpredictable – I've had sun, rain and treacherous wind all in one long journey.

I was so busy watching where I put my feet because the earth was slippery that I ran into Heath who had stopped in front of me and I hadn't noticed.

He straightened me up. 'Remember hiding here that time when Dad went out and *your* brother threatened to kill me?' Heath grinned like it was a big joke.

'Your stepbrother,' I reminded him. 'Hindley was always threatening to kill you. I was so scared he would succeed.'

Heath pulled me closer. 'I would have fought until my last breath just to stay with you. Truth be known, it's a wonder Hindley and I didn't kill each other – a fight to the end.'

'That's what Mum used to say,' I revealed.

His eyebrows shot up. 'That so. No wonder she wasn't keen on me sticking around.'

I could have said she loved him and defended her, but he was right. Mum never liked the disruption that Heath brought to the house; she rued the day that Dad brought him home. I thought about my poor 'real' brother, Hindley—blood brother—unlike Heath who was no relation except by adoption. Hindley was the poster guy for live fast, play hard, and die young. Too drunk to drive, he totalled the new car he got for his birthday and snuff, it was all over that fast.

I didn't realise Heath had been watching me. He must have guessed what I was thinking, who I was thinking about, and he sucked in a breath and changed the subject.

'I miss this air when we are not here.'

'Me too. Fresh and dry,' I closed my eyes and inhaled. I could be led here blindfolded from anywhere in the world and pick it first go as *my* moors.

'I miss the green and space,' Heath continued. 'I couldn't bear to live in a city forever, away from this.'

'We were so lucky to grow up here.' I broke free from him and kept walking. I crossed a small brook that bubbled over the rocks at our feet. The hours I had spent here with my feet in the water acting out parts and reading my books, I knew every rock by size and shape.

Heath followed me across the brook with one easy long stride.

'You're about to leave, aren't you?' he asked.

I snapped to look at him. How could he know? Did Nelly tell him? He studied me for a moment and then walked on, not asking anything more or waiting for an answer.

I hurried to catch up with Heath who glanced back and waited for me. My stomach churned but we kept walking, soon arriving at the village which was packed with a weekend crowd. We had our favourite place and they knew us. Our coffees were being made without us even having to order.

Once seated I took a deep breath and hesitantly studied Heath. His face was unreadable, his jaw was locked and I could tell from his eyes he was anticipating pain. He turned from me and then taking a deep breath, returned his attention to me. It was so much harder because he was all the family I had in the world and I was the only true family he had.

'What's going on?' he asked and reached across the table for my hand. 'Are you still pissed off I turned down Linton's film?'

I shook my head. 'No, of course not. Why would you think that?'

He shrugged. 'Since we finished *Cat on Hot Tin Roof* and started on *Henry VI*, something's shifted, you're … discontent,' he lowered his voice. 'You look at me differently.'

Straight to it then, I had practised this. I can do this.

'Not because I was angry at you or didn't respect your decision. But your conviction about what you wanted, made me think about my future. What I wanted … instead of just going along.'

'What did you come up with?' he asked.

'I'm not going to audition for the next play,' I said. I just put it out there. *Phew.*

His dark eyes ran over my face and he gave me the hint of a smile.

'That's it? That's okay, you have to do what you like and Shakespeare isn't your favourite, I know,' he said, and sat back as his coffee was placed in front of him. We thanked Jess, our waitress. 'So which production are you going to try out for?'

He raised his coffee to his lips and when I didn't answer immediately, he looked up at me. Then he knew what was coming because he knew me. He lowered his cup.

'No, Cathy,' he groaned.

I leant forward and began to talk too fast, laying all my justifications at his feet.

'Heath, you've got a role, you will always have a leading role with the company and you are doing what you love. Me, I want to, I mean I *need* to try something different.'

He was frozen waiting for me to say the inevitable – that I was leaving. I continued, getting my prepared speech completely out of order. God, I must have rehearsed this one hundred times.

'You have been my entire life. From age six to 25, every milestone of my life has been with you – my birthdays, my first kiss at 16, my first love, my high school graduation, losing my virginity to you at 17, the most important moments of my life have all been with you.' I drew a breath. 'Heath you will never know how much I love you and that is not because you're handsome—' I said, and he lowered his head and smiled, '—but because you are more myself than I am.'

He was still holding my hand and I watched him swallow the lump in his throat and then he looked up at me.

'And?' he asked.

'When this play's run is over, I'm going to London with Nelly. We are going to get an apartment for six months and try our luck – me with screen acting roles, Nelly with acting or production roles. I want to get an agent; I want to audition for films and television, even commercials.'

He nodded and held my gaze before speaking again. 'You've been planning this for a while then.'

I shrugged. 'Not long, but I've wanted to try for screen roles for a long time. And I wanted to be sure before I made this decision and told you.'

'Right, well of course, if that's what you want to do, then you must do that. I can try and get out of my contract and get work in London.'

I shook my head; I had anticipated this.

He looked stricken and then reined in his emotions, his expression strong and neutral. 'You don't want me to stay in London … with you?'

'You can't get out of your contract for another six months and you shouldn't,' I said. 'Besides, I can come home on your days off and we can have a catch-up and we can talk every day.'

'Cathy, I get two Sundays and two Wednesdays off in the four-week season. Not even two consecutive days. I could get to London easier than I can get to our village, but what if you're working,' he said.

'We'll make it work,' I promised him.

He said nothing and I waited. He needed time to process everything that I had just landed on him. For me, it had been months of planning.

Jess came back to take our breakfast order but we said we

weren't ready; our appetites were gone. Then Heath spoke in a low and measured voice.

'Those milestones, they've been the stepping stones of our life. I dreamt of kissing you on your 16th birthday and I'll never forget it. I ached to make love to you, to take your virginity and on your 17th birthday, we were truly one for the first time. You wanted to wait until you were 25 before we got married,' he said. 'That's this year … I've been planning my proposal,' he said, with a hint of a smile. I felt a rush of excitement and almost faltered. He continued 'I waited because I knew we were meant to be.'

I drew myself up and placed my other hand over his. 'Heath, you're driven to achieve more than most, so you know what it is like to feel that there's something you have to do, that there's another existence calling you.' I returned my attention to him. 'You know what I mean? That out there is more – things we should try, aspire to be, and understand. I need to do some of those things before we can commit to our lives together.'

'Oh, I get that, Cathy,' he said, with a growl. 'I just thought they would be discoveries we would make together.'

I bit my bottom lip. He moved his hand away from mine. I felt cold and I tore my gaze from him to look around. It was getting overcast; the weather was reflecting our torment.

'Call it what it is,' he said, then looked uncomfortable, realising he said that too loudly and we didn't want to attract attention. 'If you want out … want to break up, just do it fast, now. Don't drag it out until separation makes it easier to say,' he said, his voice faltered and he swallowed.

'No! Heath, look at me,' I said, demanding his attention,

making him look at me with his dark, intense eyes. 'It is a temporary work separation only,' I insisted again. He wasn't buying it. 'I don't want to break up, I don't!'

'Finish your coffee and let's get out of here,' he said.

The café suddenly felt claustrophobic but we bided our time and sat in silence as we drank and I thought over what had been said. I was preparing my lines for the next battle; I don't know what was going on in Heath's head or heart. He wasn't looking at me. He was looking outside at the passing people but not seeing them, his jaw was clenched, and his eyes grew shuttered. And I felt sick with anxiety. I didn't want to lose him. I didn't want to break up with him. I just needed to do this … and I didn't know what *this* was called.

I pushed my coffee away; Heath's cup sat untouched. He rose and paid, came back to the table to collect me and we walked beside each other not touching, not speaking. You could feel the tension between us, an ice wall that wasn't there an hour ago. It was getting darker and we hadn't brought any wet weather gear, but neither of us cared. Heath led the way and I knew where he was going – to our place on the moors, the place we had spent a lot of our childhood. It was an opening between two large rocks that provided shelter and an endless view of the green moors. My heart was thundering the whole walk; Heath walked as a man possessed.

I felt the chill rising, the paths getting hard to see, harder to navigate with the dark clouds amassing. I felt a little scared – not of the moors, I'm never frightened here but I don't like the lightning, the way it strikes and burns, the way it catches everything like a flash on a camera. I wanted to be under cover if it began. The moors sounded deathly silent, hushed and still – everything had taken cover from the pending storm, from us, and was quietly breathing, waiting. The land was reflecting our tension, it all felt so heightened. I tried to follow Heath like cyclists do when they are riding – in his stream. I grabbed for his hand but he pulled away.

When we got to our spot on the moors, he changed his mind and kept walking. I ran a few steps ahead of him and grabbed his hand again.

'Stop,' I panted. 'We need to finish this discussion. Let's talk in our place,' I said and nodded toward our rocks. He didn't look happy about the idea but he let me lead him in there. We took shelter and sat watching the weather change. The wind picked up and soon began to howl across the moors, the thunder boomed and I flinched with every crack of lightning. But we were cosy, high and dry and then the clouds broke and the rain began to come in sheets towards us, pounding on the rocks that hid us.

I was still holding his hand and I tried to explain.

'I just want to do all the normal things.'

I waited in case he wanted to ask a question or interject; he didn't so I continued.

'I've never really stood on my own two feet because you've been my rock. And I want to know what it is like to get a part on my own merit—'

'—every part you have played has been won on your audition,' he interrupted me.

'Heath, that's not so, and if you don't know it, everyone else in the company does.'

He turned to look at me. 'So I've got the reviewers in the palm of my hand as well?'

'No.'

'Right, so even if you somehow got a role because of me, you earned the review, didn't you?' he asked.

I nodded reluctantly, he was right about that.

He took a long breath and exhaled. 'Okay, I understand.'

'You do?' I smiled, relieved. 'Thank you, Heath. We can talk every night and we can catch up on any days we both get off either in London or here, or I can come to you in Oxford, it's a quick journey,' I said, gushing.

But Heath shook his head. 'You need to do what your soul tells you to do, I understand that. But as for us, the separation won't work Cathy, we'll just grow apart.'

'What! We won't,' I stammered. 'Trust me, Heath.'

We sat in silence, cocooned in our hideout as the wind and rain wailed around us. And then Heath nodded.

'Okay, we'll do this your way but … if you don't want out—'

'I don't,' I quickly interjected.

'—then be careful.'

I didn't really know what he meant but I nodded, not wanting to push the mood into darker tones. I squeezed his hand and breathed with relief.

But I could tell from Heath's expression that the storm was not outside, it was inside with us, in our hearts, battering our spirits and this was only the edge of the tempest.

Chapter 6 – The nightmare

Outside a gale was blowing, rattling the window panes, rapping to get in. I liked the wind. I liked the way it filled your head with noise and sometimes you couldn't think for the howling, but I've grown up with it, not everyone was a fan. You can't live in our village and not be a friend of the wind – some days it whistled, some days it roared, and since Heath left – the wind sounded as if it moaned. I lay in bed waiting to fall asleep. I wanted to pick up my phone and check my messages again but I wasn't going to because I did that ten minutes ago. Nope, I'm sleeping, any minute now. You are feeling sleepier…

It was my first night truly alone in my Wuthering Heights apartment. There had always been Mum, Dad, Hindley or Heath here, but now, in this huge apartment, I was alone. Sure, Lockwood and my other neighbours were on the other side of the building but I couldn't see or hear them. I may as well be alone in the whole building. Heath left first thing in the morning. He said he had auditions starting in Oxford the next day and had to get settled. I knew he just needed out, he was hurt and angry and scared of what he might say, or what I might say.

'Lockwood's here for another few days if you need anything,' he told me. I nodded. Still looking out for me even when he's pissed off at me.

Lockwood had scored a four-week stagehand contract with Heath's next play and then he was going to visit Nelly and me in London and crash with us for a few days. I was heading to London mid-week, meeting Nelly to move into the small two-bedroom apartment that we had rented for six months in Bethnal Green. It was a little more than we wanted to spend, but we had enough for the first three months and we were expecting to get work – we'll be busking or borrowing if we don't! Nelly's dad was happy to employ her to do social media for his business if she needed dollars, so having his company listed as an employer nailed the lease.

Saying goodbye to Heath was terrible, worse for me as the one left behind; it was always worse for the one left behind.

When Heath left, I held him but he was rigid, his face bore no emotion – it was just this mask of control and calmness. I kissed him with all the passion I could muster so he would feel it in his bones, but he pulled away first.

'Keep the doors locked at night, be careful driving to London,' he had said. I nodded, wanting him to say a lot more than that. And then he drove off in his convertible, music on, a determined look on his face. I came back in and closed the door to my empty home. I was tempted to get in the car and go straight to London, but I can do this. I wanted to experience standing on my own two feet, so just do it, Catherine, I coached myself.

After a night of updating and researching my potential

agents' list and binging on TV dramas, I went to bed. Heath and I messaged – I wanted to know he was there safely and he said he was.

He was there, and here was I, separated for the first time. Ever.

Chapter 7 – The storm without

Oh my God! A loud howl of wind rattled the window. My heart was hammering in my chest after that. I'd never heard these noises before because Heath was always here, and Hindley and Dad before him. Shadows of the tree branches were playing across the ceiling like a re-enactment from a fairy tale and not a good one – one with witches and evil that preys on girls who were lying in their bedroom alone. I know these trees intimately, I've climbed them all over the years, so they shouldn't be ganging up on me.

Come back to me, Heath. I'm pathetic.

No, harden up, princess, I scolded myself.

Heath, you're never far from my mind. It's cold tonight, what was your room like? Are you sleeping? Are you warm? Are you planning now to leave me or will you wait for me? Have I hardened your heart after years of making you softer?

I jumped with fright as the glass of the window banged against its frame; branches were scratching across the glass like skeletal fingers trying to get in. I shuddered at the thought.

I remembered when you first arrived here Heath, I remembered like it was yesterday. I was six years old, Hindley must have been 11, and he was already a bully and full of himself. Dad came home after a week away on business and bounded through the door with his usual gusto. He was like the moors himself – larger than life, blustery, full of energy and power. I couldn't wait for him to come home from his business trips, he put the energy back in the house. I could feel Mum relax too when he walked in the door as if we were all safe again. And he always came back bearing some quirky little gifts he had picked up for us; I adored him.

But this time he brought you home. I didn't see you at first, he closed the front door and there you were behind him. Ha, you were dark, thin and scraggly and everyone froze... it was the quietest I've ever heard Hindley.

I remember Mum asking Dad who you were with a look of surprise and shock. Hindley was an ass, calling you out for being dirty. But Heath you did look wild... your eyes were so dark and huge, your hair was wild and unkempt, and you looked like you'd be up for a fight with the slightest provocation. To be honest, you scared me a little bit but if Dad brought you into our home, I guess you had to be okay.

'Looks like a homeless kid from the gutter,' Hindley had said. He could have done with a year at charm school. But I guess from his perspective he was no longer the only boy; you threatened him and his position. Dad was so disappointed in Hindley's comments. He shook his head and said: 'Sometimes, son, I wonder where you come from. Charity begins at home, remember that.' Yeah, remember that, Hindley.

And then Dad introduced you as Heath, our new brother and told us to make you feel welcome and part of the family.

I can still see you studying us all and looking towards the front door like you'd bolt as soon as we all went to bed. Dad asked me to show you around but you wouldn't take my hand, so you followed behind me as I walked around each room. You said it was a mansion with disgust in your voice. You made me feel bad for living here. It's the only home I'd ever known.

Hindley was fighting with Dad about you staying and I was pleased when we got away from them. I asked you how old you were and you said eight, you were two years older than me. Another big brother for me, but I don't think you had that in mind even then. I asked where your parents were and you said you didn't have any. I'd never heard of someone not having parents and when I reached for your hand that time, you took mine. Remember? You smiled at me, and I loved you then, and I've loved you ever since.

When I turned thirteen and you were fifteen, you promised to marry me and that we'd be together forever. I still wanted that, I did. I just had to go it alone for a brief while, for the first time in my life. See if I liked myself, did that make sense? I wish I could explain it in a way that didn't hurt you.

The wind was howling again. Thank you, wind, I was getting lost in history. I closed my eyes to sleep but the wind got louder. Please, just give me a good night's rest.

Sleep … come to me.

More tapping on the window; ignore it.

The branches were scratching, the glass-like fingers rapping to get in. Go away. More tapping, more scratching. More knocking on the window.

For the love of God! I rose and pulled the window frame

up so I could snap them off… the ones that I could reach. The timber frame was so heavy, I edged it up and put it in its hinge. Cold air rushed in from the moors. I put my arm out and grabbed the small branches scraping against the window. The wind was whipping my hair into my eyes, the cold air was stinging and my eyes watered. I could barely feel my face and hands they were so numb from the cold.

That's when the hand seized my wrist. I screamed, it was dark, strong and icy cold, and the fingers gripped me tightly.

I screamed again and tried to pull away but the hand wouldn't release me. I was terrified, my heart was pounding, the branches were still shadow dancing around the room, and the wind was howling now, in my ears, in my room. Then I heard the voice.

'Let me in,' it said. 'Let me in, Catherine or I will die out here without you.'

'Let me go,' I screamed, terrified, pulling and twisting in terror. It was a male voice, but I didn't know it… it wasn't you, Heath, was it?

'It's me, let me in,' I heard it say again.

'Who are you? Go away, you're not my Heath. Who are you?' I was crying out in terror. My wrist was red and raw from rubbing against the timber window pane as I tried to pull away and pull my arm back in.

'It's me, Cathy, your Heath, let me in.'

'Heath, is it you? Is it really you? I can't see you, show yourself.'

I strained to see him but could see nothing in the dark and fog. The hand was freezing cold on my wrist and the wind was making it impossible to hear all his words.

'I'm lost,' I thought he said.

'But this is your home, Heath, I am your home,' I yelled back, and I pulled to release my wrist again. His fingers would not release me.

'I'm frightened. Please, Heath, let me go, you are home.'

'I'm lost on the moors,' the voice said, again. 'Help me, Cathy, come find me, find me.' And then the grasp on my wrist was released and I fell backwards. I heard the voice moan 'I'm lost'.

I rushed backwards, away from him, away from the window and rubbed my wrist.

Then I woke up gasping, I was crying and Heath wasn't there. The curtains were closed and I raced over to open them. Behind them, the window was closed as well. I pulled up the window and leant out and called: 'Heath! Come back, please.' I yelled as loud as I could but my voice was carried away by the wind, lost to the night, lost to the moors.

I've lost him. It's an omen. I sank to my knees and looked out. There was no one in the garden, no one on the long driveway and no one in the tree outside the window. There was a light on somewhere in one of the other apartments, I could see it glowing and reflecting on the small pool of water nearby. Eventually, I rose and closed the window, resting my forehead on the cold glass.

It was a dream. Oh, Heath, what if you were right? What if this was the beginning of our end?

Chapter 8 – My brilliant career

Four weeks later …

If I had learnt anything from Heath during our years together and my time doing our acting degree, it was the importance of immersion into the character. I'm a crack whore who would say anything to get my next supply – don't panic, I haven't become that … it was my part. I'd been called back for a second audition which was super brilliant. It had been an amazing four weeks and if you believed that fortune favoured the brave, then mine and Nelly's London risk might just have been worth it.

Except when it came to Heath. He'd barely had time to take my calls or talk with me. He said he was full-on with rehearsals and he was giving me the space to get on my feet. I'd seen his leading lady; I can't help but wonder how busy he really was and how much was my insecurity taking over. It nags away at me; it gnaws at me. In my happiest moments, there was this constant pain tugging at my heart—Heath— the pain of separation and missing him and worrying about him. I was still not sure I was doing the right thing, but I was doing it nevertheless.

On the bright side, everything was going to plan. Nelly

and I loved our place. On our first night living together, Nelly squealed, yes squealed, and she grabbed my hands.

'This is so exciting,' she said, her hazel eyes huge with enthusiasm.

'I know, so exciting,' I agreed, thinking that part of me should have been there but was missing. We danced around our new apartment for a few minutes thinking about how cool we were. It was called an art deco pad but that sounded cooler than the reality of our digs. It was old and had some interesting ceilings and a bit of stained glass in the windows. The bathroom and kitchen were updated in the nineties so weren't too bad, but the best part was that because it was an older apartment it was bigger than the new ones. We had a little balcony as well – lovely!

We were constantly cold calling, dropping in our CVs to agents, finding out the places to hang out so we could make the right networks, whatever it took. Heath sent me through a list of agents he had conned from an actor friend which was good of him. But the email was so formal it took the shine off the find. I rang him to thank him and didn't expect him to answer but he did. It was awkward.

'Hey, how are you?' I asked, surprised to hear his voice.

'Yeah, good, and you?' he said, in a rushed voice like I was holding him up from his life.

'Good, okay, well you know. I, um, rang to thank you for the agents' list, really appreciate it,' I said, sounding like it was a first date conversation. *What the ...?*

'Sure no problem,' he said, 'I'm sure you'll get picked up.'

'Thanks. God, I hope so.'

Silence. Fuck.

'All good with you?' I stumbled on.

'Yep, busy, you know how it is in the pre-production phase before opening. Anyway, I've got to go, so thanks for the call and take care there,' he said.

'And you,' I said, but the line was dead before I had finished. He was punishing me.

For a while, I fell into a deep dark hole of self-pity. Was it the end? Was he right, were we best just to call it off and see what pans out? Was I crazy and should I just rush back to him?

I did my best not to think about it all the time – that didn't work, and to 'stay up' for Nelly, and she did her best not to ask me too many questions about Heath. I was stalking Heath online but he had zilch social media presence. Thank God other members of the production company, especially Lockwood, posted photos and I got to see Heath at rehearsals.

Back at the kitchen table working on our laptops, Nelly and I had been tweaking our CVs to try and meet the jobs on the market. She sighed and stood to make us both a cup of tea.

'Believe it or not my CV is looking okay,' I told her.

'I'd believe that – star of stage and screen,' she teased me.

I laughed. 'If you don't look at it too closely, the lead in the *Wylde* commercial, along with roles in at least one dozen professional plays, several in the West End, and a solid selection of good reviews makes me look serious about my craft. By the time I finish putting some spin on it, I'm bound to get work, I've impressed the hell out of me!' I joked.

'You go girl. What's the footage from?' she asked over my shoulder.

'Me playing Joan of Arc and just a few grabs from other roles. It's not the best quality, but you get the picture,' I said with a shrug. 'B-grade movies here I come.'

But it worked; I had three agents who had agreed to meet with me – I just needed to convince one to take me on. In the meantime, Nelly and I had registered online with a platform connecting actors and producers and I secured a call-back for a small part in a film to be shot in London – the audition for the crack whore. Given the lack of sleep I was having at the moment worrying about Heath and our future, I didn't need a lot of eye make-up to look wasted! I was perfect for the part – sad but true.

I got a call back for 4pm; it was a long day thinking about it … I just wanted to get it over with. At my first audition, only the casting director and one of the producers were present, but when I got there this time, there were a few more people in the audience. There was this room at the back with darkened glass … you know like you see in the cop shows when they were interrogating someone and I think the director might have been in there.

I was watching from the side of the stage as the auditions were going on; the casting director kept subtly glancing up that way when she was impressed with someone's audition. Well, I was impressed with them, so I'm gathering that was what she was thinking too.

The casting for gang members was before my audition and I would have enjoyed watching them if I hadn't been so freaked out about my audition. Then they called for the whore and pimps. My life was so glamorous. They were re-auditioning three of us in each role and partnered us up together. My pimp was pretty hot actually – a slim, black guy with a hoodie and the cutest smile you've ever seen. He introduced himself as Kyle Hughes. It would be interesting watching him turn nasty. We were on next.

We waited in the wings and whispered our lines in a quick run-through. I didn't like watching anyone audition for the same part as me because I didn't want to pick up anything they were doing and subconsciously do it, if that makes sense. I was so nervous and excited. Heath always said this was the best time of our lives and one day we'd realise that but not now because we had our eyes on the prize. I wondered if I'd ever feel that way. I didn't want to be the one who didn't make it.

Then, we heard the casting agent thank the two on stage. We were up.

'Kyle, Catherine, next,' she called, and with a brief smile to each other, we took the stage.

Immerse yourself, immerse yourself, I coached.

The casting agent introduced herself as Tamara and gave us the same spiel she gave the first two, which was nice of her because she could have just said, 'What I said to them still stands.' She was probably mid-forties and pencil-thin. It was accentuated by her black pencil skirt and a crisp white top. She had on excruciatingly high heels so I suspect she was lucky to hit my shoulder height without them.

'So, Kyle, Catherine, this is a desperate scene, a pivotal scene for these two characters in the film,' she said, and we nodded our understanding. Tamara continued.

'Kyle, you've had a gutful. You want out of this life. You loved Catherine's character once and now you hate to see her wasted like this; you want to take her away from it all but she can't leave. She has a kid to support and a debt to pay back and an addiction to feed.'

Kyle nodded. 'Thanks, Tamara, got it. Angry, frustrated, desperate.'

She gave him a nod and a smile and then turned to me.

'Catherine, you love Kyle's character and you know this is your last chance to be with him, but you can't just run off with him. You feel like you have to stay for all the obligations you have to meet. To do that, you have to release him and watch him walk away. You also want that drug hit more than you want life itself at the moment.'

'Thank you, Tamara,' I nodded, and she squeezed my shoulder as she took the stairs carefully in her heels and went back to her seat.

I've got this. I am feeling this already, I just have to superimpose Heath's face on Kyle's and tell him I have to stay here, I have to do this and I'll nail the emotion.

'Ready?' Kyle asked.

I nodded. I was in the space; I didn't want to waste words.

Tamara called out, 'In your own time.'

Kyle began and spat his words at me, then he grabbed my hand and I pulled away. I began to shake and tell him he didn't understand. I told him I loved him but he could run away, I didn't have that freedom, I had to do this. I delivered the lines about him putting me under pressure and cried when his shoulders slumped with my wounding words.

When Tamara called cut, I stood up straight. For just the smallest moment I had forgotten she was there and that we were acting. I wiped my face and Kyle grinned and hugged me. 'You were great. We did alright I think,' I said, near his ear as we hugged.

'Fucking hope so,' he said, and grinned.

And then we heard slow applause and turned to see a tall man walking towards the stage clapping us. He was gorgeous, fair with short hair and clean-shaven. And so charismatic, I knew him – Edgar Linton!

'Bravo, we've found our whore and pimp, thank you to everyone else who came,' he said and dismissed the waiting actors, even those who hadn't auditioned yet.

Kyle beside me gave a whoop of delight.

My face lit up. 'Edgar!'

'Well, hello again, Catherine.' He looked around, put his hands in his pockets and rocked back on his heels. 'No fan club?'

I laughed; I knew he was referring to Heath. 'No, he's in Oxford rehearsing for a play.'

I could see Tamara looking surprised that we knew each other. Edgar offered his hand to Kyle, they shook, and Edgar told him it was good work. I think Kyle floated off-stage.

Edgar glanced at his watch and then at Tamara.

'I think I'm done here for the day,' he said, and Tamara nodded.

'I've got a few extras to cast and it's a wrap, Edgar,' she said. Everyone was on a first-name basis with him.

He looked back at me. 'It's after four, officially drinking hour. Care for one? I've earned it.'

'So have I,' I said, and wiped my face a little … unbelievably it was still wet from my tears. I grinned, 'So, you spied on my performance?'

He laughed. 'That I did, very raw and real. Grab your things and I'll see you here in ten?'

'Sure,' I said and departed as he headed off stage to catch up with Tamara.

I tried to look cool and calm, but I was thinking *Holy fuck! I've just got a part in Edgar Linton's new film. I didn't know it was HIS film and I don't know how big a part, but who cares! I've been auditioning in London for four weeks and I've just got a part, in his film.*

Edgar Linton.

And now he wants a drink. I'm going for a drink with Edgar Linton.

The universe was telling me I did the right thing going out on my own, standing on my own two feet.

My first thought went to Heath. I couldn't wait to tell him that I got the part –I'd wait for the paperwork first just in case.

I quickly put some powder on my face, especially around my dark eyes. My face was slightly flushed with excitement; a much better look than the face I had been carrying for the last fortnight. I applied a small bit of lipstick, ruffled my hair and gave up on that, and put the tiniest bit of perfume on so it wasn't obvious that I had raced backstage and groomed, which I had because after all, I was playing a crack whore.

Oh my God, people will see me with Edgar Linton. This was beyond cool. I wonder how long it would take to get the contract for the role. It should be easier to get an agent now that I've got a part, kind of reverse strategy but whatever.

I did one final check-over and declared myself ready. Edgar saw me appear on the edge of the stage and finished up with Tamara. He gave me his hand as I came down the stage stairs – such a gentleman - and we headed to the exit.

'Got a favourite place?' he asked.

'I've only really been to the places near the theatres where we would all gather after a performance. So no, no idea. You?' I asked.

'Several,' he said, and took charge. I love a man who takes charge.

I expected him to find a hidden away place where no one would bother him or see us but no, he went to a very cool bar where he knew the owner and we were shown to a great table with views of the street and nearby Thames River.

'Should we have champagne to celebrate your new film part?' he teased.

I had this stupid grin on my face.

'That would be brilliant, but I haven't got a contract yet. I'm a stickler for seeing it in print,' I said.

'Ah, and clearly you are trusting.'

I gave him a smirk.

'Fair enough. You've had your fingers burnt then?' he asked, and ordered a ridiculously priced bottle of champagne.

'I've only been burnt once, but once is enough.' I told him about a play part that I'd been offered Friday and found out on Monday it had been given to someone else. I had celebrated all weekend prior – it was a hell of a letdown.

'I can fix that,' he said and reached into his jacket for a pen. He flipped over a coaster on our table and scribbled. 'This is to confirm that Catherine Earnshaw has the part of Portia in the pending film, *Between Night and Day*.' He signed his name, wrote the date and handed me the coaster.

I held it to my heart. 'Thank you. You know I'm going to frame this coaster?'

Edgar laughed and then he narrowed his eyes at me. 'Same name as Heath. Are you married?'

'No,' I assured him, rather too fast. Why did I do that?

'He was adopted so he took my family name,' I explained.

'Ah,' Edgar said like that meant something. He webbed his fingers and leant forward, his elbows on the table as he studied me.

'That was very, very convincing this afternoon,' he said. 'I have to confess I didn't notice your performance that night on stage when I met Heath.'

'In Heath's shadow? Well, we were all in Heath's shadow,' I said, with pride. 'Plus, it was a tiny part.' I didn't tell Edgar that the strength of today's performance was again due in part to Heath because I had been channelling my pain for him.

'Thank you for the call-back, it meant a lot to me,' I said.

'That was all Tamara's doing and choosing. I wasn't around for the first auditions, so clearly you impressed her too,' he said.

I was relieved to hear this because the thought was running through my head that he had invited me for a drink to piss Heath off; he can't have liked being turned down on his film offer.

Our champagne arrived in an ice bucket with two beautiful flutes. After it was poured, we clinked glasses and I savoured its crisp, bubbly, dry flavour.

It was my turn to study the very enigmatic Edgar Linton. 'If you don't mind me asking, how come you are auditioning without using the usual agency channels?'

'A couple of reasons,' he said, and he had another mouthful of champagne before answering. 'When I made my first Indie film, I went to a lot of agents but my budget was piss poor.'

I smiled, knowing the feeling of trying to get a look in. Edgar continued. 'But Tamara took me on. She had a medium-sized agency but she said she never turned down a client large or small because every chance for her actors to work was a wonderful opportunity. I love and respect that attitude.'

'So right,' I agreed. 'And that film did okay?' I teased.

'It did well,' he shrugged, modestly.

I laughed again. 'It was a huge hit,' I corrected him.

'Yeah, well, I've had Tamara with me ever since and I won't use anyone else. Plus, I like her to find fresh talent, to put out the call on the acting sites not just through agents. I didn't have big names in my other films, and they did well.'

'And now they are big names,' I agreed.

'That's not to say I wouldn't welcome a few of the bigger names to work with,' he said, with ambition in his eyes.

'Well thank you, Edgar, I'm extremely excited to play this role … to be stretched and to get the opportunity.'

He nodded acknowledging my words. 'To beginnings,' he said and filled up our glasses again.

'To beginnings,' I echoed and tapped my glass to his. We held each other's gaze for a few seconds more than we should have, especially for a girl in love with someone else.

Chapter 9 – A star is born

Later that night I got myself settled in bed, propped up with my phone and a book. I did this every night intending to have a long talk with Heath about his day and mine, but in four weeks he had answered only a couple of my calls, claiming he was still at the theatre with late rehearsals or meetings. I could believe that some of the time. I took a deep breath and rang. Heath answered; I was frozen waiting for either his face to appear or his message bank to kick in and it was him. Live.

'Are you there?' he asked.

'Yes, yes, I didn't know you were real,' I said, and he laughed.

'Cathy, how are you?' he asked. Just the sound of his voice filled my eyes with tears – his baritone words resounding in my chest. He sounded a little happier. I wonder if he was warming to the idea of us being apart for work, or not missing me quite so much after our first month apart. The latter made my stomach tense; I always felt stress in my stomach.

'Hey, I'm free this weekend,' Heath said.

'Really!' I squealed better than Nelly. 'Oh my God, Heath,

that's only four days away. Four days and then I will see you! I feel like I haven't seen you for forever,' I gushed.

'I know, I've missed you,' he conceded.

This was sounding more like us, like the old Cathy and Heath, Heath and Cathy.

'Not as much as I've missed you,' I countered. 'Will we go to Wuthering Heights or do you want to come to London?'

'Let's go home and walk the moors, go to our favourite café, sleep in our bed,' he said.

'Yes,' I agreed and exhaled. 'Perfect.' I grinned at him like a Cheshire cat.

'So, what's new with you?' he asked.

'Heath, I got a part.' He gave a loud cheer which would have woken up half his residency block.

I told him about my crack whore audition and Kyle who played my pimp and had him smiling and sympathetic with my rendition of how my lack of sleep gave me the perfect make-up for the job. Then I told him about Edgar Linton appearing and signing both Kyle and me and that we didn't even know we were auditioning for one of his films. The smile disappeared from his face and then he put on a different face – a professional face.

'Cathy, that's brilliant, that is exactly what you wanted and you've done it in record time – four weeks and you've landed a part with a respected director,' he said. 'I told you that you were getting the parts on your own merit.'

'Well, I'm still not convinced about that, but thanks for saying so,' I conceded. 'Besides, you brought me to Edgar's attention, remember?'

'No, you pulled it off. I just told him that you were good and clearly, he's seen the light,' he said, with insistence.

'Thank you, my love,' I said.

'And four weeks,' he said again, 'you work fast. Any news on Nelly's career, has she got a role?' he asked.

'No, but now that I'm on the inside I can keep my ear to the ground.'

'When do you start rehearsals?' he asked me.

'Not for another month. Edgar said I should have a contract by next week and there's a meet the cast and crew cocktail party this Thursday night. That's exciting! Plus there'll be a few meetings in the coming weeks just to establish everything.' I was so excited that I was talking faster. 'I am so happy,' I said. 'I've got my first film role for my CV without resorting to a B-grade movie like '*The Day the Zucchinis Ate the World*'; I'm working with a respected director, and I've got a guy I love who is doing a great job at what he loves,' I said and sighed. 'Everything is perfect.'

Heath didn't look quite as convinced. And with those three words, I jinxed it.

*****

The next morning over breakfast I told Nelly everything. We already had our routine of tea and toast established and I delivered the news so quickly that I can't believe she kept up.

'This is bigger than all of us,' she exclaimed. I loved that Nelly wasn't prone to exaggeration. 'You should have woken me last night to tell me.'

'I was asleep when you came in,' I reminded her.

'Oh yeah,' she said. 'Cathy you have done it, done it big time!

I shrugged. 'It is only a minor part, I think … I haven't seen the script yet. For all I know, it might be five minutes on screen.'

'Who cares!' she exclaimed, waving a piece of toast at me. 'It's five minutes in an Edgar Linton film.'

'You're right,' I grinned. 'I'm going to allow myself to be thrilled and stop worrying,' I said with conviction. I placed a mug of tea in front of both of our places at the table and dropped into a chair.

'You go girl. Speaking of actors, it was good the actors' networking gig last night, you should come next time.'

'Okay, I will. You know, Tamara, Edgar's casting manager, still has some roles to fill. I don't know what, but you should email her or call her and tell her we just moved here together and you're keen to cut through. She'll love your theatre discipline and Edgar said he wants fresh talent,' I said.

'I will, thanks. You don't mind me dropping your name?'

I laughed. 'She'll probably have no idea who I am. But yeah, name drop away, I'm going to from now on. Act fast though, I don't know what she's got left.' I brightened with another good idea. 'Is your brother still coming to stay for the weekend?'

'He is. There's a big comic exhibition on,' she said and rolled her eyes.

I laughed. 'What a good sister you are. Anyway, he can get off the couch and crash in my room for the weekend – I'll change the sheets … I'm going home to have a hot weekend with my boyfriend!'

'Your lover,' she said, grinning. 'How's the handsome Heath?'

'Happy … and handsome.'

'You are so much happier,' she said, studying me. 'I'm relieved.'

'Aagh, was I that much of a drag? I'm sorry,' I said.

'No, just the opposite. You were trying so hard not to be a drag that you were like this unnatural hyper bunny,' she teased. 'So, what was Edgar like in the flesh? He's gorgeous.'

I agreed. 'Tall, powerful, dynamic, charming … he's got this sort of aura about him – I know that probably sounds stupid but I'm sucked into it completely when I'm with him. It's like people pivot to him when he enters the room. Know what I mean?'

She nodded. 'I get that. Do you think he might like you … you know, in that way?'

I scoffed. 'Hardly. Besides, he knows I'm with Heath. And seriously, look at him … he's probably got hot and cold running chicks at his disposal.'

Nelly laughed at my description. 'Maybe, but he hasn't got you and that's an attractive challenge.'

I narrowed my eyes at her.

'Be careful, Cathy, is all I'm saying,' she said. 'Don't break too many hearts, especially yours!'

Chapter 10 – The cast and crew cocktail party

There I was—me, Catherine Earnshaw—on the set at the studio for *Between Night and Day*'s cast and crew cocktail party. I was like a deer in the headlights, looking around, trying to take it all in because I'll never, ever, have this first again. The first time I have been on a film set for the first film that I have ever had a part in. Thank God Nelly was with me; it's always better to know someone in the room! One day, I'm going to be the big name in the room that people will be sneaking glances at! But for now, it was just me and Nelly being us.

Edgar wasn't there yet – you could tell because the room had strange nervous energy but no real presence. Everyone kept glancing at the door each time it opened, expecting him at any moment. Nelly and I took a glass of champagne from the waiter as he passed and thanked him with kindness. We've all been there and this time next year he might be a star. Or he could be a student studying medicine and paying off his degree, or he could be a professional waiter. I'm raving; I did that when I was nervous. I recognised a few actors from television roles and pointed them out to Nelly. How exciting.

Then I saw Travis Taylor, oh my God! He was in the latest sci-fi blockbuster and he was gorgeous. Edgar must have been teasing me when he said he wouldn't turn down a well-known actor ... he had one lined up for this film! I turned to Nelly.

'Travis Taylor at 2 o'clock!' I hissed. She followed my gaze and her jaw dropped.

'Gorgeous,' she muttered. 'He must have the lead. Oh wow, Cathy, this film is going to be big. I wonder who the leading lady is and if she'll be a name.'

We looked around but didn't recognise anyone equal to Travis' star quality, yet. I ran my hand down my dress again – Nelly and I rented our dresses for the evening. Crazy huh? But neither of us had anything decent for a studio cocktail party! I had on a fitted silver dress which the lady at the dress store said complimented my pale skin, blue eyes and auburn hair, thank you very much. Nelly with her brown honey skin, wavy dark hair and hazel eyes looked spectacular in a rose-gold, knee-length cocktail dress. Yep, for the price of a night's rental, we looked the part.

'Thank God we dressed up,' she said, reading my thoughts. We glanced around the room; the guys had dolled up as well. Everyone from the set dresser to the television actors that we recognised were dressed to kill. And then the door opened and he stepped through. Edgar Linton, with his sister, Isabella and casting director, Tamara, and—oh wow—one of the hottest Indie actresses out – Holly Bale. Following her were a few other people whom I'm guessing were the producers and the movie's investors. Everyone started to clap and cheer as we all got caught up in the excitement of the moment. Edgar grinned and gave a small nod. He stopped to grab a drink and handed the ladies one first. Clearly, he wasn't going to go straight into speech mode.

'The beautiful people are here,' Nelly whispered in my ear. 'I saw Holly Bale's last film.'

I turned slightly away so I didn't look like a voyeur studying them and gave Nelly my attention.

'And?'

She wrinkled her nose. Mm, a not-so-good film review from Nelly. I grinned and introduced myself to the girl next to me.

'Hi, I'm Danielle, but everyone calls me Danni,' she said. Her make-up was impeccable, and her eyebrows were amazing.

'Hi, Danni, what's your role?' I asked, after introducing Nelly too.

'Make-up artist,' she said. And there it was.

'I knew that,' I said, admiring her and she laughed. 'You have eyebrows to die for.'

We made small talk for a while, all the time I was secretly watching Edgar, Travis and Holly, like everyone else in the room. Nelly hadn't let Tamara the casting director out of her sight, she wanted in for this film and she was zeroing in on her!

About fifteen minutes after their grand entrance, we heard the sound of a glass being tapped to get everyone's attention and we turned to the front to find Edgar in the middle of a stage that was about a metre off the ground. A middle-aged woman stood next to him holding the microphone.

The room was hushed. I forgot to breathe for a moment but feeling Nelly beside me, I came back down to earth.

I'm okay, I'm here, I'm meant to be here, I'm fabulous! I reminded myself.

Edgar's gaze ran over the couple of hundred people present and landed on me. He smiled and raised his glass; I blushed and did the same. I felt eyes turning towards me. I loved it. Nelly nudged me.

'Uh oh,' she said under her breath and gave me a wicked smile.

Fuck more like it. This was trouble. I was kind of thrilled; it was a weird feeling this rush of excitement and flirting. I've never had that. I've only ever had the solid love of Heath – that has been my world and my strength. This was a buzz.

'Hi everyone,' the lady beside Edgar said, 'and thanks for being part of Mr Linton's next film.'

We all cheered again, after all, it was our pleasure.

She continued. 'My name is Naomi Thornbury and I'm the Executive Producer. Shortly, our production team is about to hand out scripts to everyone. These are for your eyes only so no releasing them to the outside world or putting them on social media. You know the price for doing that,' she warned. The room was quickly sobered. 'If you haven't got your contract yet, you will have it by the end of the week. It's never too early to learn your lines. I'd like to take this opportunity to thank Tamara Lang of T.L. Casting for all her hard work and for finding all of you.'

Again, we all cheered heartily. Lord knows I was happy to find Tamara and even more excited that she had found me!

Naomi, the Executive Producer continued. 'As you have probably noticed, we have many very talented performers with us tonight and two in particular that I would like to introduce to you. Meet our lead actors for *Between Night and Day* – Travis Taylor and Holly Bale.'

They stepped up on stage. Travis shook Edgar's hand and Holly kissed him on the cheek. Then they grabbed each other's hands, stepped forward and took a little bow, laughing the whole time. We all gave them a resounding round of applause and cheering.

'Want to say a few words?' Naomi asked, handing over the microphone.

Travis offered it to Holly first who said a few gushing words about Edgar, well I think she did because I was too busy trying to subtly watch Edgar, to listen closely to what Holly was saying. Travis followed after her and said he was coming around to collect everyone's autographs on his script during the night. What a sweetie – way to go, Travis, you've won my heart for being so down to earth.

Naomi thanked them both and then introduced Edgar.

'Ladies and gentlemen, the man who will bring out your best and bring this story to life on the screen – Edgar Linton.'

The roar and clapping were thunderous, and Edgar genuinely looked slightly abashed, or he acted well. He thanked Naomi and took the microphone

'Hello everyone, and I think you will bring out my best!' he generously said. He held the room in the palm of his hand; I subtly glanced around to watch everyone enamoured with him, including me, I have to confess.

'I look forward to the months ahead and making this

film, our film, with you.' And then he abruptly finished, insisting we socialise and enjoy ourselves. That was it ... not one for speeches. A jazz band started up in the corner and drink waiters appeared en masse with trays of drink and food. I had to eat something or I'd be under the table after one drink.

I was still subtly watching Edgar as he moved off the stage and everyone wanted a piece of him. For the first hour, all I could see was his back or the back of his head, as he shook hands, signed scripts and posed for photos. Everywhere I looked I could see Isabella posing with the cast or crew ... she was almost in as much demand as Edgar. She seemed to be very close with the leading actress, Holly – they were acting like best friends forever. I wondered how well they knew each other before Holly got the role. Oh God, I'll never be able to pull off that sort of smooching. I might have to be one of those 'aloof' stars with a tight inner circle. Sigh.

The party had got much louder and Nelly and I had done our share of dancing as well. The get-together was a brilliant idea; we'd all be so much more relaxed with each other when we officially began work on set. I intended to keep sober though ... the last thing I needed was to do something embarrassing and then have to live with it for the rest of the production – even though there would be a few stories like that, there always were.

Nelly and I took a break from the dance floor to get some ice water and Nelly pounced—well almost—on Tamara. I was about to offer my vote of support for Nelly when I felt a hand on my shoulder and wheeled around to find Edgar Linton looking gorgeous and holding two champagne glasses.

'Refill?' he asked like we had been talking all evening.

'Thank you,' I said, putting down my now empty water glass and accepting the flute. We clinked glasses in a toast and I saw flashes going off. That will be on someone's social media feed before I have my first sip. Yah!

We talked over the noise until he indicated we should step out onto the set apron, which was just a big flat area in front of the open doors. I followed behind him, waiting as he stopped for photos with the cast and crew, and shook hands. We finally made it outside; it was cooler and quieter with only a handful of actors nearby talking or having a smoke.

'Ah that's better,' he sighed, 'I'm not one for the party scene,' he confessed.

'Really?' I teased. 'I would have thought you would be partying every moment you weren't directing.'

He smiled. 'I like intimate gatherings … to have people over. People I like,' he emphasised. 'A small group that you can talk with over the music, chill with a few drinks, swim if you want to, sit down to really good food, you know that sort of thing.'

'No, I can't say that I do,' I said and smiled. 'My life of late has been acting, pushing my CV on agents, rehearsing, grabbing a kebab for a late dinner while driving home and when I'm free, heading home to spend spare time on the moors.'

Oh my God, I'm with Edgar Linton and I'm talking about kebabs. Shut up now.

'See you are like me … the need for space, especially green space.' He turned to study me. 'Speaking of which, after the

Cat on a Hot Tin Roof performance, Isabella said you lived at Wuthering Heights. Do you know our place is on the moors? I get out of London and go there between films.'

'I know,' I said, 'Thrushcross Grange.'

He smiled and looked surprised that I would know the name of his home.

'Don't panic, I'm not a stalker,' I assured him. 'We used to ride past your property all the time when we were kids – Heath and I.' I didn't let on that we would spy through the windows sometimes and laugh at the two of them.

'I'm surprised we never met you or Heath when we were younger,' he said.

'Yes, we were on the moors all the time.' I guess that said volumes. Edgar and Isabella probably never left the house to go into the 'wild' … they probably just admired the green view from the windows, while Heath and I were like wildlings.

'Wuthering Heights is the large grey mansion that was rezoned to townhomes about a decade ago, right?' he asked. 'You can't buy in or sell without every tenant's agreement. That the one?'

I nodded impressed. 'You know a lot about it.'

'I checked it out. We thought about doing the same to our place when Mum and Dad died,' he said, with a glance upwards to the skies, 'but we just couldn't bear subdividing our family home.'

I nodded my understanding. Edgar and Isabella were both wealthy enough that they didn't need to subdivide to maintain it. Thrushcross Grange was enormous, it sat within its own parkland and the front door was about three kilometres from the entry gate! I'd passed it a thousand times when driving and riding, it was only about six or seven kilometres away from Wuthering Heights.

'I love your place, so white and manicured,' I said, before realising how stupid that probably sounded but it suited the shiny Edgar and Isabella.

'Yes, that describes it well,' he laughed. 'So, wuthering … it means strong winds, stormy atmosphere, doesn't it?'

I nodded. 'It's well-named because where we are located faces north and we are exposed to all the stormy weather – Dad called it our tumultuous atmospheric station,' I said with a smile, reminiscing about him. 'The house is strong,' I assured Edgar.

'I imagine it would have to be.' He took another large mouthful of his champagne, almost emptying his flute. 'So, a kebab hey?'

I shrugged. 'Well, some nights I swap it for a sandwich.'

'Of course you do.' He grinned and then narrowed his eyes. 'You look like you could do with a good feed. Have you tried Aria? It's the best restaurant in London, I think – not that I've tried every restaurant,' he added.

I gave him a wry look.

'What?' he looked innocent.

'Edgar, you are funny. I'm a struggling actor. Aria would cost me more than my weekly rent.' I could have played along and said something sophisticated, but really, what's the point?

He had the good grace to look embarrassed.

'I'm an idiot,' he grinned. 'Then allow me to take you there for dinner, my shout. How about this time next week, Tuesday?' He saw my hesitation. 'I assure you, I'll be able to pay my rent afterwards.'

I laughed. 'Show off. I'd be delighted, thank you.'

He gave a small nod and smiled, and then we were invaded by Isabella and her posse. She was carrying the champagne bottle and had enjoyed quite a few glasses already, no doubt to make sure it was a good vintage. Unlike her brother, Isabella appeared to be a party girl – a little wild, too pretty for her own good and rich too. She insisted on filling my glass up and it overflowed. Everyone was laughing, we had another toast, more photos and selfies were taken and Edgar and I were separated by people wanting to be near him. As soon as I could, I gave Edgar a wave and slipped away, back inside with the pack I felt more comfortable in.

Good job me … I had fifteen exclusive minutes with Edgar Linton—the hottest director in town—and I spoke about his white house and my dietary habits. Oh well, at least that was probably the most down-to-earth conversation he'd get tonight.

More to the point, I had a dinner date with Edgar Linton. It was a date, wasn't it?

And I'm a girl with a boyfriend, who wanted this film role. I wanted to go to dinner too. Was that wrong? Of course it was, he didn't ask me just to make sure I was eating three vegetables a day!

This was getting complex.

*****

Entertainment Weekly

RUMOUR FILE: Pre-film party the place-to-be as Edgar Linton's new film fires up.

Will this be the cast and crew to deliver another round of accolades to director, Edgar Linton?

By Bonny Hawkins

Studio 12 was the place to be last night as a couple of hundred cast and crew members turned up to enjoy a meet and greet before shooting begins on Edgar Linton's new film, *Between Night and Day*.

It was a mixture of the who's-who, rising stars, new faces, and behind the scene gurus at the party hosted by the director himself. Amongst the crowd was his supermodel sister, Isabella, and her permanent clique, competing with film favourites and leads for Linton's new film, cast members Travis Taylor and Holly Bale.

Casting director Tamara Langer of TL Casting was there to overlook her choices and while media was not invited, our sources have supplied a selection of behind the scene photos from the pre-party. If the film turns out to be as hot as the party, Linton should be dusting off his tux now for the next awards ceremony.

Seen leaving the party with the hot director was *Wylde* girl, Catherine Earnshaw. No news on an official split from her stage star boyfriend, Heath Earnshaw (no relation) but one has to wonder. Also seen leaving together were Travis Taylor and model, Dew Warne, Isabella's best friend!

Rehearsals begin next week with filming scheduled to start in three weeks.

Chapter 11 – Heath, hearth and home

As I drove into the village, a feeling came over me. A feeling that I don't get anywhere else that I have ever been – it was hard to describe but it was like peace transcending on me. I loved the feeling. I loved that as I came around the bend just past the village, the moors opened up to me and my grey mansion—my share of it—came into sight. It was like I could breathe again and I'm where I should be. I was home.

I pulled into the driveway and Heath's car was there! He was home first and I was like a kid at Christmas … ridiculously excited! I parked next to him, grabbed my bag off the passenger seat and rushed up the stairs; I couldn't wait to see him. When I opened the door he was coming towards me and I rushed into his arms. Heath picked me up and whirled me around before planting me back down and studying me.

'Cathy, we're home,' he said, and I leant up to kiss him. We seemed to kiss for the longest time and all the city's pace and the month of activities and the separation washed off us, and it was just the two of us again.

I pulled away to look at him.

'You look gorgeous,' I said like I was mad at him for being so handsome.

'Okay, well that's good isn't it?' And then he laughed. 'Oh, I'm supposed to look thinner and darker and moodier because I've been pining for you!'

'Yes,' I insisted, with the hint of a smile.

He picked me up again to kiss me and looked into my eyes, he made my heart beat faster.

'Trust me, Cathy, when you are not with me, I have to remind myself to breathe – almost to remind my heart to beat!'

He put me down as tears welled in my eyes. I wrapped my arms around him and held him so tightly that I didn't want to let him go. After a while, Heath pulled me away.

'I'd like to carry you into that bedroom right now—'

I looked keen but Heath closed my desire down.

'—but there's still an hour or so of light left, so let's go out for a walk on our moors,' he suggested.

'Yes, I need the walk to leave the city behind,' I agreed. 'I'm sure I'll feel like my old self once I'm out there among the heather on the hills,' I proclaimed and breathed in, anticipating its freshness. 'Did Lockwood come back with you?'

'Yeah, he's at his place. He said he'd catch up with you over the weekend.' Heath held my coat for me as I slipped my arms into it. He pulled it around me and kissed me before releasing me. I led the way, keen to get outside and breathe in the fragrant air; so different from the London air.

It didn't take us long to be alone with the earth. I held Heath's hand and felt the chill from the moors seeping into my bones. The wind moaned in my ears as we walked along, close to each other.

'I've missed this,' I said.

'God, me too and it has only been a month or so,' Heath agreed. 'I didn't think you would miss it, Miss London,' he teased me.

I grinned and gave him a shrug. 'It's in my blood.'

Heath cleared his throat. 'I saw the pics on social media … from your cast party. You looked like you had a good time.'

'How did you see them? Don't tell me you've got an account at last?' I asked him. Heath hated social media and didn't have an account of any description.

'Don't be crazy. But I am surrounded by people who do nothing all day but take selfies of themselves at rehearsals and post them. Half of them follow you and the rest you follow!'

I smiled. 'You're going to have to come into the 21st century one day.'

'Yeah, I'll let you know when I arrive,' he said. 'Dan read me the piece in the *Entertainment Weekly* too,' he added, referring to one of the cast members.

My breath hitched. 'Well, you know that was crap about me going home with Edgar,' I said and scoffed. 'I went home with Nelly. I did have a drink with Edgar and a chat outside the studio, with all the smokers, but then he went back in to do the rounds and Nelly and I hit the dance floor. It was fun, but I felt like a fish out of water without you there … it took me a while to get used to standing alone,' I said to him, glancing at his face for a reaction.

I think I handled it okay – casual, cool, the truth, and only one small omission about the pending dinner date. Heath was known to have some green in those eyes—our high school dance comes to mind—another story, another time.

'Uh-huh, so, did you have fun? What's your part like?' he continued, taking me at my word.

'The part is good,' I said. 'I'm the girlfriend of the lead's brother and I'm on screen for about twenty minutes of the two hours.' I smiled as I told him, the excitement brimming in me. He pulled me into him and kissed me on the top of the head.

'You'll steal the show. I can't wait to see it.'

The remaining day and evening were wonderful. We cooked together, shared some wine, made love, talked and chilled.

But I blew it. I ended up hurting us both and Nelly was right, I was careless with his heart.

It happened the next morning after our perfect night. Heath had gone to the gym in the village – a creature of habit. Lockwood came over to have a cup of tea with me and we opened the windows and doors and sat out on the small balcony, in the crisp morning air.

He wrapped his hands around the mug of tea. I caught up on all his news and the set gossip, and what he was planning to do next.

'I can't believe you and Nelly secured roles so soon – you both rock!' he said.

I smiled and shook my head. 'I can't believe it either. It's not supposed to be like this. We're supposed to struggle and starve a bit first. Still …' I hesitated, 'one film does not make a career.'

Lockwood nodded. 'My friend says you are only as good as your *next* film.'

'Mm, I'll have to process that.'

'So what's up?' he asked.

I turned to face him. 'Nothing. Why?'

He raised his eyebrows at me. 'You're holding out. You're talking to me now ... we've spent hours in the car driving and talking, hours on set waiting in the wings, baring our souls, I know when you're holding back ... so what gives?'

I sighed. Was I that transparent?

'Everything gives,' I told him. 'I feel like everything is happening at once.'

He frowned. 'That's good though isn't it? Or is it something more? You seem troubled. You don't have to tell me,' he shrugged, 'but if you are worried about something, I can help, or listen, or maybe both.'

'Thank you, Lockwood,' I said and smiled. 'I just wish I were out of doors – a girl again, running around with nothing to worry about but what's for dinner and where we are going to play next,' I moaned.

And then I started and I couldn't stop. I told him everything. I blurted it all out because it was such a weight off my shoulders to share. I told him about Edgar and the flirting, and how I wanted Heath but I wanted to experience some life, and I asked Lockwood did any of that even make sense.

Lockwood nodded. 'I hear you. And the older we get the more complex relationships get because everyone comes with baggage and preconceived ideas of what they need and want,' he said, waving his hand around theatrically. 'But Cathy, you and Heath have something so amazing.'

'Do we? Because it is all I've ever known and I have nothing to compare it with. I need to live a little, love a little, so I can appreciate what I have.'

'I get that but most people spend years of their life looking for what you two have, and some people never find it, but you've got it right here. What if you begin with Edgar, lose Heath, and then realise you got it wrong and you've thrown away the best thing ever?'

I groaned and put my head in my hands.

'I wish I had met Edgar first and Heath now, later in life, or that Heath had gone away for a few years for whatever reason and come back to me, and swept me up. God, I sound pathetic, like I've watched too many soapies.'

Lockwood shook his head. 'No, I understand, I really do. I met a guy when I was eighteen and I knew it wouldn't last at that age when you are sorting out who you are and what you want to do. But if we had met later, even now … at twenty-six, maybe we'd have a chance. I've learned a few tricks now and had my heart broken. I know what a good relationship is.'

'Yes, exactly,' I said, appreciating that he did understand.

We stopped to watch two birds soar over the trees in front of Wuthering Heights until they disappeared from view.

'Does Heath have any idea about how you feel?' Lockwood asked, 'because I'm pretty sure he thinks you are in London for career reasons and that you'll be engaged soon.'

I shook my head in the negative. 'No, he doesn't know, because I'm not sure myself.'

'Wow,' Lockwood said. 'I've only known you guys for five or so years, but I can't imagine you not being together. At college, no one said your name without Heath's following or vice versa.'

I nodded, getting emotional. 'I know. If what you say is true and I make a bad decision and Heath leaves, God, what would I do? I could as soon forget Heath as forget my own existence! I am Heath, he is me! Whatever our souls are made of, his and mine are the same.'

Lockwood's hand went to his heart. 'I live for that, I wish I could find that,' he said. 'Think you could fall in love with Edgar?'

I tilted my head to the side while I thought. 'I could. But it would be different from my love for Heath, I think. It is too early to say but I'm guessing my feelings for Edgar would be like the seasons … you know, time changes them,' I shrugged. 'But my love for Heath, well it is solid as a rock … I need him.'

'But you want Edgar.'

'I want to *experience* Edgar,' I said and gave Lockwood the hint of a smile. 'That is so wrong isn't it?'

He grinned. 'I'd like to experience him too.'

I playfully hit him and we laughed.

I didn't know that Heath had forgotten his phone and had come back for it. I didn't hear the door open because all the windows were open and I was on the balcony, not far from the dining room table where Heath's phone sat. I didn't know that hearing his name he had stopped and heard the entire conversation. He heard me say I wanted to know what it was like to be kissed by Edgar and romanced by him.

I didn't know that I had just changed our destinies and broken us.

Chapter 12 – Heath leaves home

I heard the front door slam and I jumped up. Lockwood gasped.

'Was that Heath?' I asked, wide-eyed and panicked.

'He must have heard us. Go quick, catch him,' Lockwood said, and I rushed for the door hearing Lockwood's words as I retreated. I took the stairs at an incredible pace and met Heath at his car. I placed my hands on his chest to stop him and saw his eyes were damp.

'You're free Cathy. Let him romance you,' he said.

'No Heath,' I begged him, 'you don't understand.'

His gaze was as cold as ice; he looked at me without any of the love and warmth that those eyes showed me last night.

'I do now. I heard every word you said.'

'It was girls' talk, just ravings. Please don't go, Heath, come upstairs and let's talk. Please let me explain,' I clutched onto him, my hands still on his chest.

'I heard you say what you were feeling,' he said and turned to open the driver's side door.

I placed myself between him and the door. 'Heath, please … no! I don't know how to be without you. Don't go, please,' I pleaded.

He closed his eyes momentarily, then opened them, took a deep breath and looked up at the balcony where Lockwood was looking down upon us. He returned his attention to me.

'Cathy, tell me what it is about Edgar that you like or want? Is it because he has light hair and fair skin or does he dress better than me? Does he treat you better than I do? Do you find him more attractive than me?' He spat the words out. 'Or is it that in my current line of work I don't have a chance of being as rich or as successful as he is, nor do I have any interest in being so? Or are you just finished with me?'

Tears were streaming down my face and I was in panic mode trying to stop him from leaving. 'No, Heath, it was just talking, silly, childish stuff, a crush ... I was taken in by all he could offer me, the opportunities. I don't even know him, I don't know if I even like him so I can't say if I feel anything for him ... it's just new,' I babbled on; I tried to save us.

For just a moment he looked torn and then he took a deep breath and seemed to stand taller, finding the strength to leave me. He was dry-eyed now, distracted as if he was willing himself to forget my existence.

And then he laughed. It made me frightened of him. I dropped my hands from his chest and stepped back.

'I know it has only been a month, but I am such an idiot,' he shook his head. 'I pictured our reunion in my head all the way here on the drive; watching it unfold in slow motion, with you clutching me like you couldn't live without me, and me holding you so tight that it would fill me up for the next length of time we were apart. I would hold you until you pulled away first because I never would.'

I openly sobbed now and I struggled for some words to put it all right. I had nothing but pleading.

'Heath,' I said, and took a step closer to him. He blocked me and put his hands up in front of him.

'No really, Cathy, don't come any nearer.'

He would never admit to being so upset as to cry. In all the times Hindley beat him, he would never give Hindley the satisfaction of being broken and would never let me see his pained or tear-stained face, even as a young boy overpowered by my brute of a brother. And now, he blinked quickly not to show me tears or how his heart ached. This was not how it was supposed to go down – I don't know how it was supposed to go.

'I've missed you so—' I began.

'Not enough,' he cut me off, anger flaring in her eyes. 'You have not missed me enough in four weeks to keep me! You filled the void if there was any, with Edgar Linton.' He said Edgar's name like it was poison on his lips.

I stood to full height. Two could play at being angry and I had tried to reach him a hundred more times than he had tried to contact me. Who was thinking of who?

'I have been consumed by you from the moment I left here until this moment. Did you think I was calling all the time out of duty?'

He scoffed. 'Clearly. Everything I have done for the past month has been for you. I gave you your space.'

'I know, and I love you for it.'

Heath crossed his arms across his chest and glared at me. He felt like a stranger. I wanted to go to him but we weren't in that space.

I continued: 'I'm not looking for another guy, I just wanted to experience standing on my own two feet. You've done that since you were young. I've always had people to lean on and direct me.'

'And now you have a new man to help with that,' Heath said.

'No!'

'I would have preferred you were honest and had just called it off a month ago.' He stopped as his voice wavered and he took a deep breath. 'At least now I know what you want. You want him to romance you, so please take the opportunity without guilt or obligation. We're over Cathy, you are free.'

I made a desperate wailing sound that I didn't recognise came from me. My hand went straight to my heart, the source of pain.

'Please don't go, please don't say those things, Heath,' I struggled to breathe, 'you've broken my heart, Heath don't go,' I begged.

He jeered, his pain making him cruel. 'I have not broken your heart! This is all your doing – you have broken it; and in breaking it, you have broken mine, Cathy.'

He clutched the car door for support and I covered my face with my hands. What have I done?

'If you truly loved me, Cathy, what right have you to leave me for the feelings you say you feel for Edgar Linton … seasonal … an experiment at best? I hope he lives up to it.' He shook his head. 'I am such an idiot.' His eyes flared with anger. 'How long have you been with him?'

'I haven't been with him!'

'Have you slept with him, kissed him?'

'No, yes, no, I kissed him. It was nothing, like a kiss you'd give a friend.'

His jaw tightened, and his face masked all emotion.

I dropped my hands to look at him but he wasn't looking at me, he was looking at the moors.

'Goodbye Cathy, be careful—' he started to say, and then realised losing me meant he wasn't responsible for me anymore, '—forget it,' he finished.

I stepped back and he slipped into the driver's seat, closed the door, and within moments was driving away.

He didn't look back, not once.

PART 2

Chapter 13 – My new life

One month later

Week four and still no word from him; Heath had ghosted me and I looked the part. He ignored my calls and text messages, Lockwood said he refused to accept my letters and never asked for news of me. Heath was true to his word; he had set me completely free.

I never wanted to revisit those last few weeks … I never thought I could cry that much, survive on so little food and sleep. I knew what it meant to hit rock bottom. I didn't feel anything like myself and I struggled daily to find joy in the new experiences and little victories I was having.

I knew Heath was not in London but yet I was always searching for him, seeing a flash of his face in a crowd and hoping he had come back for me. I wrote copious messages to him, pouring out my heart:

I know you think I don't love you anymore, but I love you more than life itself.

I am broken, please call me Heath.

I know I don't deserve you or your love, but please Heath, forgive me, come back to me.

Meet me at Wuthering Heights this weekend? We can talk on our moors.

I flinched anytime I heard or read his name, but regardless I stalked everyone in Heath's cast and crew list for their social media feeds to catch a glimpse of him or some news of him, and occasionally I would. Self-inflicted wounds.

His production's opening night was a great success and he dominated the reviews, along with several of the minor players that had stepped up. I saw the photos of him on stage and ran my finger over his face on my screen. He looked the same. How was that even possible when we were part of each other and not together? I don't know why but Edgar Linton didn't look quite as desirable now. Maybe the element of 'can't have' made him more attractive before. That seemed so unfair.

I did my best not to mope around and ruin our London experience for Nelly, and luckily, we had visitors nearly every weekend so I didn't have to keep up a front all the time, but I was exhausted from the pain. I tried not to pump Lockwood for information every time I connected with him or when he stayed the weekend. He saw Heath every day and I desperately wanted to know more.

Thank God I could keep busy. Edgar must have scored my phone number from his casting director, Tamara, and he messaged me to reschedule our dinner – he had to go away for a week to direct some on-location scenes and as he put it, press the flesh with a few financiers. I was being punished for wanting him when I already had it all, now I had nothing.

But by the start of the third week, I had turned a corner. I was cried out, rehearsals were getting serious, I had an agent interview, and I felt a little stronger. I was still broken, but not shattered. I felt like the pieces of me had been fitted back together and were glued into place – all the cracks were still visible and the slightest tremor could shatter me, but I was holding it together.

It's going to be a brilliant day, I said to myself as I tied my hair back. We started shooting last week, that was exciting and most of my part was being filmed this week.

Today I'm going to be great on-screen; it's going to be a great day.

I smiled at myself, then rolled my eyes. I looked thin and exhausted. Thank God I'm playing a crack whore ... call it performance art that I'm getting into the part.

Whatever, get out there.

*****

Sometimes it was the weirdest things that triggered a memory. I was on the Tube heading to work at the studio—one day I'll have a driver—when I looked down at my arm and saw a massive bruise; I ran into one of the props on set yesterday. It took me straight back to our childhood and suddenly I felt a wave of missing Heath. My brother, Hindley, was so cruel to Heath, always beating him.

On weekends and school holidays, first thing in the morning as soon as we had done the expected chores, Heath and I disappeared out of the house and ran to our moors. They were our playground with so much space. We lost ourselves in the trees, creeks and caves. It was a kid's paradise. We had our favourite cave where we could see out across the moors and no one could see us. And we could see if anyone, especially Hindley and his friends, were coming.

We raced into our cave and Heath and I fell into each other as we sprawled on the floor; his breath hitched.

'What's up?' I asked him.

'Nothing,' he said, and shrugged, pulling his T-shirt up higher on his neck, and then I saw it. A string of bruises.

'Heath!'

'It's nothing,' he cut me off.

'It's not nothing, Hindley did that, didn't he? I'm telling Dad.'

Heath grabbed my hand. 'No Cathy, that only makes it worse. I can handle him.'

'Dad has to know, besides Hindley only does it when Dad's away on the road. He thinks he'll get away with it,' I said, anger boiling in me. Heath couldn't accept sympathy … I don't know why, maybe he never got any from his mum or dad, if he ever knew them. We didn't talk of it.

I reached out my hand to touch the bruising and he allowed me to lower his T-shirt a little and look. I gasped, the bruises were dark and yellow and ran across his shoulders.

'I can handle it,' he said and shrugged me off. 'I won't always be smaller than him,' Heath said, and then he smiled. I'll never forget that look. It was one of satisfaction, a promise.

Hindley died in a road accident when he got his first car. Heath never said a word about it … not even a word of condolence. He probably wished he had a chance to finish him off himself. I blinked away tears and came back to the now, hiding my face from other train passengers. I scurried through my handbag, found my phone, stuck my earphones in and hit play on my music list. I glanced up at the Tube map – six more stops. Stop thinking.

The following week …

Nelly looked at me and I gave her a subtle smile. We walked together towards the lift in our professional dress wear and waited until it came to the fourth floor. I stood aside to allow two men out and then Nelly and I filed in. She pressed the ground floor button and the doors closed. And then we turned to each other.

'We have an agent,' she screamed, and we hugged and laughed, and sang the words over again to make them seem real.

We have an agent … we have an agent … we have an agent!

Then the lift doors opened and we straightened up and walk out into the street crowd as though we were sensible, professional people.

Nelly took my hand and we hurried ahead to have champagne at our favourite pub to celebrate. It was nearing four p.m. and our work for the day was done!

'I can't believe it,' I squealed. 'Four months in London and we have a film shoot and an agent as well, I can't believe it.'

We stared at each other, grateful that we were there to share this new reality of our lives.

'If it hadn't been for Tamara – meeting her was the biggest break of our lives,' I said. Nelly nodded.

'She's so generous ... to recommend us to her agent friend, to hire us, she is making us,' Nelly said. 'When we accept our acting awards, she has to be the first person we thank every time.'

'Agreed,' I said. We entered our favourite haunt and found a table just inside the door. Not long after we were accepting a glass of sparkling wine from the waiter – it was cheaper than champagne and looked just as good.

'Celebrating ladies?' he asked, delivering our order. He was a mature man, handsome, and we were in our business suits.

'Indeed, work victories,' Nelly said, to him and gave him one of her charming smiles. It always reeled them in.

'Well congratulations,' he said, with a wink and headed off.

We clinked glasses.

'To our brilliant careers,' Nelly said, and I laughed.

'To us.' I sipped and sat back with a sigh. 'Haven't our lives changed so much in the last four or so months? I can't believe it.'

'I know. If you had said to me six months ago when we were on stage that we'd be working on an Edgar Linton film, living in London in an apartment together, and we would be signed to an agent, I would have asked you to share the glue you were sniffing,' Nelly said and grinned.

I laughed and shook my head. 'So bizarre, the whole

thing, and getting an agent couldn't come at a better time.' Then I sobered. 'I'm finished filming my part next week, so I don't have a job to go to – I'll be out there looking for the next best thing.' I sighed. 'Oh, the joys of acting.'

'Yeah, that's a reality check. I've got two weeks left,' Nelly said. 'It was so good of Tamara to give me a role as an extra.'

'I'm sorry it wasn't bigger but she had almost finished casting when she met you. Otherwise—'

'It is perfect,' Nelly said. 'I'm on set a lot and it allows me to study the director and director's assistant which you know interests me more. Weird isn't it when you think the film won't be out until next year … we will have forgotten what we did by then, we'll have to see the film to remind ourselves!'

'I hope Jo and James can get us work – I mean J&J, our agent,' I said, and laughed because it sounded so surreal. 'We're really doing this, Nelly.'

She nodded. 'We are. But I'm still trying to catch up with it all … you, Cathy, you're different now,' Nelly said, studying me.

I knew I was different; I was hardened. I felt older, a little burnt, but I didn't think it was obvious on the outside.

'How so?' I asked.

She shrugged. 'You'll hate me saying this but you are more mature and confident.'

'That's me,' I teased, 'mature and confident … I wish. Anyway, I don't mind you saying that at all,' I said, relieved that she didn't say I had become a hard-nosed bitch or a drag.

Nelly slipped her jacket off and put it over the back of

the chair. I knew from her silence what was coming next. I wish people wouldn't ask me about Heath but I guess it was inevitable for a while and Nelly was one of my closest friends.

'Have you heard from him at all or is it officially over?' she asked in a lowered voice.

'Heath?' I asked, as though I never gave him a thought. The truth was that I spent every waking moment trying not to think about him. 'No, it is well and truly over. I don't know what he's doing these days and I don't want to know.'

'Right,' she said. 'So what's he doing?'

I gave her a prize-winning smirk and then spilt everything.

'He's seeing Isabella Linton.'

Nelly nearly fell off her chair. 'What the fuck? Are you kidding me?'

I shook my head. 'She went to Oxford to see his play, and since then she appears to be going to Oxford quite a lot. There were pictures of the two of them all over her feeds – out to dinner, out at plays and events.'

'Holy crap, I didn't see that coming,' Nelly said. 'Well, that's too weird. If you married Edgar and he married Isabella, you two would be in-laws as well as step-siblings. Weird.'

I shook my head. 'That will never happen.'

'Why?' she asked. 'It could you know.'

I shook my head again. 'I know Heath, he's just doing this for effect. He couldn't stand someone as vacuous and party-focused as Isabella!' I continued, 'I know this was my doing, my fault, but I tried to right the situation and he didn't have one ounce of forgiveness in him.'

She gave me a sympathetic look but she loved Heath too. 'He was devastated, Cathy. It might take him a while to come around.'

I shrugged. 'People feel with their hearts, Nelly, and since he has destroyed mine, I don't feel for him at all.'

I can't believe I was saying that crap, who was I kidding?

She exhaled. 'Yeah, well I'd like to believe that but I think whether you want to or not, you still do feel very deeply for him. I think you always will.'

I looked away, getting my emotions in order.

'I know you've thought about this,' she said, hesitantly, 'but Heath's got no one but you in the world. You said he was adopted by your father, so I'm guessing he was abandoned as a child? He's probably got a few issues in that department and your leaving has probably brought all that to the surface.'

I nodded. I had thought about that, a lot. 'It was in my thoughts,' I said.

'To hell with the glasses, I think we need a bottle and something to eat.' She grabbed the menu and we ordered.

We observed the comings and goings in the courtyard of 'our' pub on Paradise Row and twenty minutes later and halfway through our shared cheese platter, Nelly declared, 'I'm in love' as though it was so not a big deal.

I looked at our cheese platter and shrugged.

'It's good, but the one we had last week in Hackney Road was better.'

Nelly looked confused and then laughed.

'Not with the cheese, you dill, with Travis Taylor,' she moaned, thinking about the lead in our film. 'He's so down to earth and gorgeous.'

'Yeah, glad you've set a realistic target,' I said. 'Not that you couldn't snare Travis, I'd go for you if I were him, but you've got a bit of competition – pretty much every female on set.'

'I couldn't bear to be his girlfriend. I'd be perpetually jealous,' Nelly said. She changed the subject for the worse. 'Edgar's back tomorrow,' she said, dropping a quiet bomb if there were any such thing. 'I heard Tamara telling the assistant director.'

'That so?' I played nonchalant as I smeared camembert on a cracker. I did know; the assistant director mentioned it on set.

'Have you heard from him?'

'Not since the text to say he had to go away to direct a couple of on-location scenes so he'd have to postpone our dinner,' I said, with a casual shrug. But truth be told, I was keen on him coming back. I needed the distraction and excitement of a date with Edgar Linton and I didn't care if everyone in the cast knew about it. My minor parts directed by his assistant were almost done. Next week were my big scenes which Edgar would be on set to direct, so who knows what might happen after that.

'Are you following him online?' she asked.

I wrinkled my nose. 'No way, I don't want to look like a fangirl. But I'm checking him out on the quiet.'

Nelly laughed. 'Yeah well, don't panic if you see women draped over him, his publicist runs the account, not him.' 'No way.'

'Way,' Nelly said, finishing off her glass of sparkling wine. We heard our names being called and looked up to see some of the guys from the cast heading toward us. Looks like it wasn't going to be an early night after all. Thank God. Every hour I'm distracted was an hour I'm not in my head. If I can go to bed completely wiped out, I might just sleep. I've banned listening to music – every single sad song was written for me.

Then my phone rang. Speak of the shiny devil, it was Edgar Linton.

Chapter 14 – Heath takes revenge

'You have to try this mushroom,' I said, offering Edgar a dainty piece of mushroom in the exquisite sauce.

He winced. 'I'm not a mushroom guy.'

'Get out of here,' I said, shocked. He pretended to rise and leave, and I laughed.

We were out to dinner at Aria. It had taken some coordination but I only had one week of filming left for my role and then Edgar and I were no longer connected.

'I'm more of a seafood guy,' he said.

'That so? Interesting,' I said, giving him my best analyst look. 'I knew there was something fishy about you,' I said, with a laugh and he groaned.

I got serious. 'You know I finish up next week? How wonderful this experience has been, thank you, Edgar.'

I think my sincerity caught him off guard.

'No, thank you, Catherine,' he said. He always called me by my full name. 'And I thank Tamara for finding and casting you. I appreciate all you have added to my film,' he said.

We stopped talking as the waiter filled our glasses. We

could lash out and have a few drinks as Edgar's driver picked us both up and was probably outside eating a burger waiting for us, while Edgar and I ate at one of the most expensive restaurants in London. I had more in common with our driver, I couldn't afford an entree let alone a meal here. I glanced around; it was all so tasteful … quiet, low conversations, subtle waiter service and beautifully presented dishes. It was a very sophisticated dining experience and worlds away from Nelly and my pub experience – but I am a down-to-earth girl at heart and love our local haunts. The waiter left us and Edgar cleared his throat, regaining my attention.

'I'm sorry I haven't had time to see you more during filming, but that is what it is like when I'm working,' he said.

'No apology necessary,' I said. 'I've worked on the stage; I know what it can be like – all or nothing.'

'I've only directed you for a couple of days now but how did you find the experience – the film? Tell me honestly,' he asked.

I thought about my answer before responding.

'Because it was my first film, I have no benchmark to compare it with. I was terrified the first few days but I kept going back to the basics of immersion – blocking out the noise of cameras, lights, and crew and just trying to focus on the actor opposite me and the moment, kind of like I did on stage,' I explained.

He nodded. 'I know when I'm directing I don't make allowances for levels of experience, but hopefully, I was encouraging and not terrifying,' he said, sipping from his glass.

I realised he wanted to hear what I thought about *him* more than my real experience, so I got to work boosting his ego, not that he needed it I suspect.

'You were amazing,' I said. 'Patient, thoughtful, encouraging. You gave positive feedback which I wasn't expecting and not once did you lose it, even when we were doing those 16-hour days. I thought you might then … we were all a bit wired.'

He smiled. 'I have a psychologist friend who always reminds me of the hard road back.'

'What's that?' I asked.

'Well if you get stuck into someone, it is like putting nails in a fence. You can apologise later but when you pull the nails out, the marks are still there.'

'Wow,' I said, 'quite an analogy.'

'You might be new to film but you are not new to acting; your stage work was a great discipline for what you did on screen. You were well ahead of many of the cast,' he said and thrilled me with his words.

'Wow, high praise, thank you,' I said and smiled delightedly. Heath always said the stage was a great training ground. *Don't think about Heath.*

I responded. 'The stage is a good discipline – you don't get a chance to fix what you get wrong so you have to work at one-takes!' I said. I finished my beautiful entrée and sipped my wine.

'Speaking of the stage, I understand you are no longer with Heath,' Edgar said.

I snapped to look at him, then tried to save my dramatic

reaction by trying to look casual and shrug. Forget it, I wasn't going to pull that off. So, I nodded.

'That's right, we broke up a few months ago now, three or four…' I let my voice trail off.

'I see,' he said.

'How did you hear?'

'Isabella caught up with him,' Edgar said and thrust a knife into my heart with his five words. Oblivious, he kept talking.

'She's more a theatre fan than I am, so she took a group of friends to Oxford and saw his play. They caught up afterwards.'

'Right,' I said.

Please stop talking or I will die. Isabella was not into theatre, she told me that Edgar was into it, not her. She's gone there for one reason, and one reason only. To hitch up with Heath. Had she told Edgar that she was actually dating Heath or was he just being kind or discreet not breaking that to me?

I took the lead. 'I understood they were seeing each other,' I said.

'Oh right.' He looked surprised and didn't confirm or deny he knew that. Maybe he didn't, he sure as hell didn't look thrilled.

I lost my appetite and did what I've been doing for the last few months – I moved into an acting role. To watch me, you would have thought I was having the best night of my life.

Chapter 15 – Edgar's abode

I couldn't get the image out of my head of beautiful, glamorous Isabella in bed with my tall, brooding, striking Heath. I only had myself to blame; this was all my own doing.

We ventured out of the restaurant into the cool of the night and Edgar's driver opened the door for me; I thanked him and slipped into the back seat. Edgar whipped around to the other side and slid in beside me before his driver could open the door. A few people on the sidewalk were taking photos. I don't know if they knew who Edgar was or if they were just taking photos of someone getting into a chauffeur-driven car so they could work it out later. They wouldn't know who I was, yet. One day, that would be different.

Edgar reached for my hand. If I wasn't so torn, I'd truly appreciate how exciting this moment was and how gorgeous he was in his dark suit.

'I could try a few corny lines,' he said, 'like inviting you to come up and see my etchings, or I could just invite you up or I can drop you home,' Edgar said, turning side on to face me. He gave me a smile that would melt three-quarters of the female population. The other quarter would be lesbians or dead.

'I'd like to see your etchings,' I said, and he laughed.

Fuck you, Isabella and Heath, two can play at this game. You will never have Heath, Isabella, he was revenging me and now I too was playing with fire.

I wished I could wind back time, but the wheels were in motion and I was hurtling into life without Heath.

I did this.

I was going up in the elevator to Edgar's penthouse when the thought struck me … I wonder how many people Edgar had bedded. Heath was the only person that had ever touched me. I lost my virginity to him on my seventeenth birthday. He said it was special, and that it must be intimate or at least a gift given to lovers, and we did it at our special place on the moors. He was two years older than me, and I didn't ask if I was his first; I didn't expect it to be even though we had always loved each other and promised ourselves to each other. He had been away at college studying drama for the year while I was finishing my last year of school and I think he had lovers but had not fallen in love. Sure, it's a double standard but I guess I wanted him to know what he was doing.

We always said once I turned 17, we would officially date and make love and we did. I've played that scene in my head so many times. Heath was so intense.

'I just need to know…' he said, leaning on one elbow and looking into my eyes as we lay inside our rock shelter, hidden from the world, '… that you are definitely ready for me to take your virginity,' he asked, looking so sincere.

'Just take me,' I teased him, 'how hard can it be?'

'Oh, it's hard,' he assured me, with a grin, and I laughed. 'No, seriously, Cathy, answer me.'

I touched his face. 'I have been waiting forever, and you are the first and only man I want inside me.'

'I love you,' he said, gazing down at me.

'I love you,' I whispered the words to him. I'd only ever loved him.

When Heath had begun to undress me, my breath hitched. Occasionally he would glance at me to make sure I was still okay with it all, and I begged him to continue.

'You are the most beautiful woman I have ever laid eyes on,' he said. 'The only person I have truly ever wanted.'

We had been the main person in each other's lives for the longest time, he was my everything.

He paused again. 'If you don't like anything, just say so. We can keep practising until we've tried everything and then start again,' he said, with a bad boy smile, and I tried to smile and look comfortable but I was completely naked and he wasn't.

Then he slipped off his jeans and boxer briefs and my eyes widened at the size of *it,* erect. That had to do some damage. He slipped on a condom, and then distracted me with kisses and with his fingers.

We didn't talk but now and then he would remind me to breathe or to relax and then he made me come and I felt like I lost all control and was embarrassed. He used my wetness to enter me. I was aching for him. There was pain and there was pleasure; I get it now. My body braced as he entered and he paused again.

'I promise, I want you in,' I assured him, and he chuckled.

'It's okay, you are supposed to be tight, it's a good thing,' he assured me.

My fingers dug into his back as he pushed a little more, then edged in and out. I gritted my teeth and closed my eyes as he entered a little more each time but I wanted him.

'Don't go hard and fast, will you?' I asked him, a little concerned. I had heard of guys doing that, and tearing the skin.

'I won't do that,' he assured me. 'Look at me.'

I opened my eyes to gaze at him.

'I won't do that. Slow, nice and easy, just relax, yes?'

I nodded. 'Yes.'

And he was gentle, and loving and then he was completely in me. He looked down on me and I smiled, and I cried a bit, because I'm pathetic like that, but he kissed me and let me be emotional.

'Okay?' he asked.

'Amazing, we are one,' I said. 'I can feel you everywhere.'

'I can feel you all around me.'

Heath closed his eyes, breathed, and then asked me if I was ready. Holding his weight above me, he moved a little faster and faster until he exploded and I had already come but I loved the feel of him coming in me. I loved the power I felt being able to make him lose control.

He opened his eyes and really looked at me. We held each tightly, listening to the wind outside on the moors and feeling like we had been reborn here and now.

*****

The elevator's robotic female voice announced the floor in a very sexy voice.

'The penthouse, goodnight Mr Linton.'

I raised my eyebrows at Edgar. 'Did you choose that voice?' I asked.

'Maybe,' he said, and smiled at me. I shook my head.

'Come on, are you telling me you wouldn't have picked a sexy male voice to greet you every time you left or came home? What voice did you choose for your car's navigator?'

'No comment,' I said, not wanting to incriminate myself, and he laughed.

The doors opened and Edgar owned the entire top floor. He turned the lock in the elevator panel ensuring that no one else could travel up to his level and sent it back down below. Here we were. I followed him in and he told me to make myself at home. Sure. Mine and Nelly's place would fit into his loungeroom. While he turned on a few lamps I wandered to the window and let the view blow me away. I could see all of London sprawled below. He joined me.

'It's something isn't it?'

'It sure is.'

When I turned to look at him, he made a move. His hand found my back, his lips found mine, and his hand found my waist. He didn't waste time offering me a drink or showing me the view from his balcony. He led me straight to his bedroom. It was scary and exciting and grown-up. It was different from any experience I had ever had with Heath.

I helped him remove my clothes and he was stripped in seconds. It wasn't slow or passionate; it was needy and exciting and sexy.

Chalk and cheese. Dark and light. We came quickly.

'First round,' he grinned, and left his hand on my breast. 'Drink between rounds?'

'I need it,' I said, and he rose and walked naked to his kitchen. I hoped the windows were well tinted because any voyeur with a camera could sell those shots of a naked Edgar in a heartbeat.

'Champagne?' he called.

'Perfect, thank you,' I responded. He was something – tight butt, lean, sophisticated, tall, muscly and not an ounce of fat on him. Super sexy.

I studied what I could see of him from the bed, and hoped I was the only one doing so. Reading my thoughts, he entered with a cold bottle of champagne, two glasses and an explanation.

'One-way glass,' he said. 'Walk around naked as much as you like.'

'Ah, good to know, I'll do just that,' I said, drawing the sheet to cover myself and propping up against a pillow. I took the glasses from him as he popped the cork.

'I can't stay late,' I said.

'What? Why?' he looked shocked. 'It's Saturday night!'

'I have my final scene on this film I'm working on first thing Monday morning,' I teased. 'Even though I'm a wasted crack whore, I'd like to not be too wasted tomorrow so I can practice my lines and get the scene just right in my head.'

He filled our glasses and clinked his against mine in a toast.

'I respect that, thank you,' he said.

I nodded and sipped. Dry, delicious and bubbly. I gave

an appreciative groan and then after some small talk and champagne appreciation, he teased my mouth with his delicious cold, champagne-flavoured tongue and it began again.

Chapter 16 – The last scene

I finished in make-up, thanked the girls for the last time and gave them both a hug. I looked like shit; they did a great job. It was my last scene today in Edgar's movie and my most difficult scene. It had very few words and lots of pain and emotion. I was telling my lover—played by Kyle Hughes who I met at the audition and who had a few minor supporting actor film roles under his belt—that I couldn't meet his expectations; I couldn't just walk away and run off with him. I needed my supply, I needed to look after my sick mother, I needed to be here now even if I was only half here … and he was going to say goodbye and leave me. It was an elaboration of the scene we did for the audition.

I felt very, very raw this morning and Nelly read me just right. She was coming in early with me – she had a couple of scenes mid-morning. We didn't have breakfast, it was too early and my call sheet had me in from 6am, and Nelly from 7.30am. We sat on the Tube and she reached for my hand.

'So, are you worried about the scene, or sad because it is your last day, or just not a morning person, or none or all of the above?' she asked.

I smiled and looked at her. 'I appreciate the multi-choice at this hour of the morning.' I glanced at the window which only reflected my image. 'Honestly?'

'Honestly,' she insisted.

'I did it with Edgar on Saturday night.'

She gasped.

'It was good, actually, it was great,' I told her. 'But now I'm really emotionally into him and today I leave the set and if he doesn't call, I won't see him again. Plus, I'm doing a scene today which is so close to home for me that I know I'm going to hit a wall after it, and I'm unemployed from tomorrow. Yep, cheery day, sorry to be a drag.'

'And, the real issue?' she asked because she knew me so well.

I grinned. 'What, that wasn't enough drama at this hour?'

She smiled. 'Spill it.'

I breathed out. 'Saturday night with Edgar was like saying a final goodbye to Heath.'

Nelly nodded and gripped my hand tighter. 'Tonight then, let's lash out and go to our pub, have a drink for your last scene, stay out and not think about anything heavy.'

I gave her a grateful look.

'Brilliant, I'd love that, thanks.'

'Sure, and you'll have to do the same for me on my last day. As for Edgar, I've no doubt you'll be seeing him regularly. He's launched your film career, *Wylde* girl, he's not going to let you go without taking full credit,' she said and nudged me.

I smiled. 'Yeah, we'll see. But thanks for saying the perfect thing.'

Our stop came into view and we rose and headed to the door.

My last scene. Another last scene.

Chapter 17 – It's a wrap

I took a deep breath, blocked out the fact that Edgar stood behind the cameras, fully dressed, and that this was my last time on set with him – for this film anyway. I could tell Kyle was pumped too. He gave me an encouraging nod, and it began.

'And action,' Edgar called.

I was snorting cocaine off the table when I heard the door open. It was too late to hide it and I knew Connor (Kyle's character) hated it. I stood and tried to block him at the door. He looked over my shoulder.

'For fuck's sake, Portia,' he hissed, using my character's name.

I wiped the powder from under my nose and started to make excuses.

'Forget it,' he said. 'We have to talk.'

I nodded and followed him as he turned and moved towards the kitchen. He indicated a seat but I shook my head and stood behind the kitchen chair. I was nervy, wired, and bad energy was running through me. I played the role with twitches, lots of small movements and glances around.

"Sit down for chrissake," he hissed.

I sat down and ran a hand through my stringy hair. He studied me and seated himself, taking a deep breath. You could hear a pin drop in the studio.

'I'm leaving,' his voice softened, 'I want you to come with me.'

I made a small snickering sound as if it were impossible, and I looked down at my hands.

He said it louder. 'I want you to come with me. Get clean, be what we once were,' he reached for my hands. 'We can do it, Portia,' he said, hopeful.

I shook my head and fidgeted.

'Why the fuck not?' he demanded, his voice getting louder. 'It's not like this is the dream life!'

'I can't leave now, there's Mum, she's sick,' I said with a small shrug, and wiped my nose again.

'Oh, the mother who has done fuck all for you all your life? That mother?' he snarled.

I nodded and rose, and he rose too, coming around to me and pushing me against the wall. I cried out. My body was frail, thin and sore and I was frightened of him.

'I don't want to go. You go, I'll come later … I promise,' I said, in this whining, wheedling voice.

He laughed. 'You'll never come. You'll stay here and steal, beg and borrow until you get what you need and then it will show you an early grave.'

I pushed him off and moved around the table.

'Just go,' I hissed. 'I've got enough shit going on, I don't need your drama.'

He laughed again. 'Drama? Honey, I'm the least of your dramas.'

I started to chew on my nail.

He softened and took a breath. 'Remember when we met? We had all these plans, babe. All these things we were going to do together? Fuck, it's not too late.'

I glanced at the door.

'Where's that girl?' he asked. 'That girl who was fun and free and sexy.'

I pushed my hair back behind both of my ears and smirked.

'She fucked off a long time ago. I suggest you do the same,' I said and held my chin up.

He slapped his hand on the table and startled me.

'Last chance, honey,' he said and held out his hand.

I folded my arms across my chest. His eyes narrowed and then he stormed out. I flinched at the sound of the door slamming and then I started shaking, and crying and eventually, I sunk to the ground. I held the position.

'Cut,' Edgar Linton called. 'Nice work, let's do another take.' He walked over to where I huddled on set, giving Connor, or rather actor Kyle, an encouraging pat on the back as he passed. He offered me his hand, I accepted and he pulled me up off the floor.

'Nice one,' he said, and gave me a wink. I smiled my thanks and reached for a tissue to wipe my face. One of the make-up girls ran on set to touch me up again. Edgar moved away and paced around the set for a moment adjusting a few things that weren't to his satisfaction while the set manager rushed in to assist, a worried look on his face. I had a feeling that Edgar might be a bit of a perfectionist but too early to call that after just one film and a minor role at that. I hadn't been able to watch or study the leads in action which was a real shame, because Edgar liked to clear the set; if you were not in a scene, he didn't want you there. Sure, I could have called in a favour but I didn't want to play the advantage card.

For the first time, I knew exactly what Heath had meant about doing scenes over and over again. I was so invested in that scene that for a moment I forgot I was acting. It emotionally drained me. Now I had to find that emotion and do it all over again. And again. *Crap.* In the theatre it would be one take a night that you would build up to delivering.

Ten minutes later, Kyle and I were back in position, I took a deep breath and we took it from the top again bringing out our Cooper and Portia. I think it was as intense, it was hard to tell. I don't know if it was the same for everyone else, but every time I did a repeat scene, I lost something – the spontaneity, the genuine emotion, hard to call.

We did the scene again – three takes and then it was over. Done. I had completed my first feature film role and if I didn't hit the cutting room floor during editing—which was highly unlikely as my character was so entwined with half a dozen other characters—then I would be attending a preview later this year. Unless Edgar gave me a heads-up down the track, I would have to wait about eight months to see which of the takes he finally used. How exciting!

Lunch was called and Edgar came over to congratulate Kyle and me. We were done.

When we were alone on set, he placed his hand on my back.

'That was really powerful,' he said.

I felt my face light up. High praise indeed. 'Thank you,' I said, 'it means a lot that you said that. I have to confess, I felt it.'

'It showed.' He gave me a teasing smile and said, 'You haven't been a crack whore in real life, have you?'

I laughed. 'Ah, exposed, bummer! I have to tell you, seeing my face after make-up, I almost convinced myself.'

We walked towards the canteen. I didn't worry about washing my make-up off yet, there were all types of looks, characters and costumes in the canteen on set, and no one cared or blinked an eye.

'I thought I might go home to Thrushcross Grange for the weekend,' Edgar said. 'Head off Friday evening and back late Sunday. I was hoping you might come with me.'

I clapped my hands together like a kid at Christmas. 'I'd love to, thank you. I'd love to see your home, and I can drop into mine down the road and check it is okay too. Thanks!'

'Done,' he said and gave me one of his sexy smiles. 'I wasn't going to invite anyone else,' he clarified. 'I thought we could just chill out after this huge week, have a few drinks, walk in the gardens, I'll show you the bedroom,' he teased.

'More etchings?'

'Oh plenty,' he assured me.

'It's a date,' I agreed. 'I look forward to it.'

He nodded, opened the canteen door for me and he left me there to mingle with a promise to talk before Friday.

How exciting, I was on top of the world, what a fantastic finish when I thought I was going to hit a wall today.

I stopped. *This might be real this relationship.*

*****

On Wednesday my agent—I'll never tire of saying 'my agent'—called me with an audition opportunity. Thank God. It had only been one day since I finished Edgar's film but it felt like a hundred while I sat around searching online for opportunities. The audition was for a small film role but that was great, after all, my latest movie offering wasn't released until next year so I didn't have any runs on the board other than theatre reviews and getting the role in Edgar's film. Although, now that I've been outed dating him occasionally, that's lost a bit of cred too.

Wow, what a week, what mood swings. I'm on a high and this weekend I was going to stay at beautiful Thrushcross Grange. How many times had Heath and I passed that sprawling white mansion with its manicured gardens and I had yearned to go in but returned to my sprawling dark and wild Wuthering Heights; that was before Dad had it subdivided and we moved into a wing.

Thank God Lockwood was working at the same production company as Heath, so I could check with him if Heath was going to be on stage this weekend and not at home at Wuthering Heights. I know eventually Heath and I had to discuss selling or buying each other out but I wasn't giving up my home and I suspect he felt the same.

Besides, I wasn't ready yet to cut him out of my life. I'm not sure I would ever be – my stepbrother, my lover, my heart and soul, my ex.

Chapter 18 – The review

Entertainment Weekly

REVIEW: Heath Earnshaw and Ursula Medina in Shakespeare's Measure for Measure, directed by Eric Dixon, at the Royal Exchange Theatre, Manchester.

A solid cast can't save this dour and bleak production of Measure for Measure.

By Marc Ferguson

As bankable and versatile as the cast of this production is, no one can save this dour delivery of Shakespeare's *Measure for Measure*. Leads Illuka Davidson (playing Angelo) and Edward Carlin (in the role of the Duke), plough through the power and politics with very light relief.

In its attempt to make a contemporary statement, director Eric Dixon's *Measure for Measure* was just too glum and that's a great shame given the dark comedy elements it presents.

Not even Heath Earnshaw (Claudio)—despite a solid performance—could raise the level of this production. At times it appeared that Earnshaw – a natural in every role I've seen him in – must have wondered how he got involved.

There's always room for an updated and contemporary re-telling of Shakespeare in any format or forum. I have had the pleasure of seeing some magnificent adaptations of this very Shakespeare classic including a wonderful gender-swap version, but unfortunately, Dixon's wasn't one of them. He buried himself in tension, fragmented societies, world-weariness and bleakness.

For my money, it was a waste of Earnshaw's talent. Dixon had his character wound so tightly that Earnshaw barely got to scratch the surface of his layered character, Claudio. Ursula Medina (in the role of Isabella) is a star in the making but Dixon was not able to bring out her best. I would love to have seen Davidson, Carlin, Earnshaw and Medina in their roles with another director at the helm.

There is humour in this play, the master wrote the lines as such, but don't come expecting to leave laughing or even entertained, it is dull and drawn out. Save your money for another re-telling or go along just to see the performers doing their best with the interpretation they've been given.

Measure for Measure is at the Royal Exchange Theatre, for a three-week season.

*****

Lockwood was spending a few nights crashing on our couch and trying to get work in London before he was due to get back to the production company that both he and Heath were in. He kept me up to date on Heath—bless him—

and mentioned that it was opening week for Shakespeare's *Measure for Measure* and that Heath was playing Claudio. Heath told the company that he could only commit to a small part. He had something up his sleeve.

I read the review while holding my breath. Even if I wasn't with Heath, I always felt his pain and victories and I knew how this would affect him. He'd be angry, frustrated, and worried about his choice of productions. I wanted to call him but I couldn't … he wouldn't answer me anyway.

And then another small article on my screen caught my eye and I inhaled sharply:

Entertainment Weekly

RUMOUR FILE: Stage actor to take to the big screen?

Rumour has it that celebrated stage performer, Heath Earnshaw, requested a smaller role in Eric Dixon's production of *Measure for Measure* at the Royal Exchange Theatre, Manchester, because of another commitment. Insider sources believe it may also be because he has little faith in the production. But the most bankable rumour is that Earnshaw has signed on the dotted line of a film contract and the ink is just dry on his first leading role on the big screen. Watch this space.

*****

You have to be kidding me! I had been so caught up in Edgar's praise of my work and the thought of going to

Thrushcross Grange for the weekend with him, that for just a moment I forgot to think about Heath constantly.

Suddenly, that changed.

The anger boiled inside me – I can't believe that Heath might have signed up to do a film. He hated the film medium; he wouldn't accept Edgar's offer when it was put on a platter for him and now he's doing a film! And what part has Isabella Linton played in this or was it all about revenge?

First Isabella, now the film! If this was your way of getting back at me, Heath, it worked.

Chapter 19 – Dizzy days

My agent had two pieces of good news for me this week. First, she had locked in a date for the film audition which I was offered – a small part but it was to be in the morning before heading off that afternoon with Edgar to Thrushcross Grange for the weekend.

The second bit of good news – because of the increased following I had been getting thanks to winning a part in Edgar's film, being outed with Heath earlier with the 'star-crossed lovers of the stage romance'—*whatever*—and being photographed with Isabella Linton (sigh), the perfume company wanted to do an updated version of the *Wylde* girl commercial. However, this time I was being paid quite a lot more since I wasn't an unknown university student like the first time and their perfume was also more established. There was a God. The contract and shooting dates were yet to come.

I was out to dinner with Nelly and Lockwood celebrating Lockwood's last night with us in London until his next crash on our couch, whenever that would be, and we all agreed our eating-out lifestyle could not continue until we were big stars or at least one of us was, and they could shout. Nelly was particularly excited about the *Wylde* girl commercial because she knew only too well from doing the production budgets, that commercials were a nice little stream of income.

'It will be your shout after you get paid for that,' she said. 'Do they want a sidekick for you? I could be *Tame* girl,' she suggested.

We all laughed.

'Yeah, there's not much that's tame about you,' I said, 'that would be acting.'

'Are you thinking about staying with the acting stuff or are you going to try for production shit?' Lockwood so eloquently asked Nelly.

She shrugged. 'I'm worried if I just direct or produce that I'll lose my nerve and skills to act, but I'd like to direct more than anything.'

Lockwood's eyes widened. 'Wouldn't it be the coolest thing in the world ever if we were all in a film together and Cathy was the star, Nelly you were the director and I was the production manager?' he sighed.

'Let's just make that happen,' I said. 'Oh, I sounded like one of those inspirational gift cards then.'

Nelly put her hand down flat on the table with a bang. 'You are right, Cathy. Let's make it happen,' she said.

I put my hand on top of hers and then Lockwood did the same and we all raised them and high-fived.

'That is bound to happen now,' I teased. 'Maybe one day we'll have our own production company and then we can pick and choose roles and productions,' I suggested.

'Now you are talking,' Nelly said.

'And we've only had two drinks,' Lockwood grinned. 'Imagine what we could come up with after four!'

*****

My audition was at 9.45am in a hired studio near Oxford Circus Station – I hoped it wasn't an omen that my audition was going to be a circus. In a clinical hallway that looked a bit like a doctor's waiting room was a row of chairs where three or four people sat waiting. To the side of them were a desk and a girl with a very stylish haircut accentuating her heart-shaped face. She could have been a model or a star herself. She gave me a practised smile that didn't look happy at all, ticked my name off the list, and gave me a two-page script.

'Your part is the female,' she said, with a smile bordering on a smirk.

I thanked 'Happy' and sat down with the other actors to get up to speed. An Indian guy and an older woman caught my eye and we exchanged brief nods and smiles. Another girl about my age didn't look up or acknowledge me. Clearly, we weren't all going for the same role.

Then a woman who was about my age and height burst through the door of the room in front of us. She was all smiles which she dropped pretty quickly once the door closed. Must have been part of her performance. She scanned the waiting actors, her eyes reaching mine and she sussed me out with a less-than-excited look. The competition. Then, Happy got up, walked to the front, stuck her head in the room and moments later told the Indian guy he was on. He caught my eye and I gave him a look of encouragement and he smiled.

I went through the two pages in front of me. I knew from the brief my agent gave me that it was a Romcom—a romantic comedy—and my role was the dizzy sister of the lead actor. He was unlucky in love and needed help. I was determined to have him married if it was the last thing I did on this earth. Sounds like Jane Austen's *Emma* meets *Bridget Jones's Diary*. It wasn't going to be award-winning stuff, but if it was as big a hit as *Bridget Jones's Diary*, who's complaining?

Righto, dizzy, huh, I can do that. A giggle, a hair toss, a look of determination at my brother, some arm folding and 'tsking', let's do this. My phone vibrated and I looked to see a message from Edgar wishing me luck. My heartbeat hastened and my adrenaline spiked at seeing his name. He was filming this morning but still he remembered and sent me the message. I replied with a heart and kiss. I smiled like a love-sick teenager – ooh, I must channel that for my audition.

And then I waited. Fifteen minutes, thirty minutes, forty minutes … I was losing my shine and energy, but eventually, the three people in front of me came and went, and by that time there were four behind me. My call-up came.

I fired up and entered the room. On the stage was a guy sitting on one of two stools, who I guessed was going to read the lines to me. Three people sat in the front row with folders on their laps, making notes.

'Hi Catherine,' the guy in the middle seat of the front row said. He rattled off their three names and I nodded to each of them and then introduced myself to the fellow actor next to me. He seemed to appreciate that.

'Hey, the name's Callum,' he said, introducing himself and extending his hand to shake. 'Hope you get it,' and he gave me a wink.

I sat next to him and jokingly eyed him suspiciously. 'Thanks. How many people have you said that to today?' I asked.

He laughed. 'Only twenty, honest.'

I grinned at him, and then waited for the cue. There was a method in my madness – I wanted to make him like me and I wanted to feel comfortable with him so that we'd come across as natural. Let's hope that worked. There were a couple of coffee cups on a small round table between us and that was the total props for improvisation.

'In your own time, thanks Catherine,' came the call, and I began.

I took a deep breath and began acting with Callum. I cocked my head to the side, studied him and crossed my arms.

'You know what you need?' I asked.

'God, yes,' Callum said.

'No, seriously, as your sister, it is my duty to say this…'

He groaned. 'I feel a lecture coming on.'

I gave him a sympathetic look. 'I'll make it a short lecture.'

I took a deliberate deep breath. 'You need to be more spontaneous in love. There, I've said it.' I smiled, and looked surprised, 'I feel much better.'

I saw my three 'judges' smile a little. That's good, it meant the delivery was fresh.

Callum took a sip of his imaginary coffee and then frowned at me.

'What does that mean exactly?'

I waved my hands around and stood up. 'You know, don't analyse everything to death.' Then I did a little jump and smiled. 'Be a little more of a man in the moment.'

He looked confused and I rolled my eyes and put my hands on my hip.

'Just fall in love for the sake of it. I mean you're always so intense. You enter relationships because they look like they would make for a good partnership.'

'I'm a lawyer!'

'I'm just saying, it's not working for you.' I checked my notes, which I was allowed to do because we weren't expected to learn all the lines.

'When I met my guy,' I sighed at the happy memory, 'I was totally absorbed by him. I couldn't relax until he called and I heard his voice. I couldn't sleep for thinking of him. I ached to be with him. I was a wreck. And he was the same.'

Callum grimaced. 'Sounds awful.'

'It does sound like a medical condition,' I agreed, and the three 'judges' laughed.

I don't know why I did it because it was risky, but I adlibbed that line. I just didn't want to break the momentum of the moment by referring to my lines. I hoped it would work in my favour and I didn't come across as being unable to follow a script.

'Thank you, Catherine, we'll be in touch with your agent,' one of them said, and I thanked them for the opportunity, shook hands with Callum and made my stage exit.

Fingers crossed, I guess. But now I had something else to look forward to – a weekend away with one of the country's most sought-after directors, and bachelors for that matter! And, a weekend on my moors. That afternoon, I read the validation I needed to enjoy my time with Edgar... confirmation that Heath's treachery was in full swing.

*****

Entertainment Weekly

Stage actor signs to new Ramirez film

By Bonny Hawkins

Award-winning director, Nadim Ramirez (*Life Lessons, Cease to Exist, A Mirror Image*) has signed up some of the country's most exciting talent for his new drama, *The Meaning of Nothing,* including a surprise newcomer to the screen but not to acting – Heath Earnshaw.

You heard the rumours here first and we are happy to take the credit – awarded stage actor Heath Earnshaw will play the lead.

Ramirez has a reputation for creating edgy films and giving his actors plenty of rope – this should suit Earnshaw and bring out the best in the young actor.

Speaking with Earnshaw earlier today he told *Entertainment Weekly*: 'Nadim has forged a new direction in filmmaking with works that are unprecedented in style and delivery. In terms of discipline, we are on the same page. I love his vision and I think we are a good fit. I'm excited to take on this project.'

Earnshaw previously turned down a film offer from director Edgar Linton preferring to remain on the stage.

Nadim Ramirez was recently listed in the top five of the most important film directors of the decade, his storytelling style is quickly becoming a template for filmmakers.

The Meaning of Nothing is shrouded in secrecy as insiders tell us the script is unique.

We can't wait for this piece of cinematic vision. Rehearsals start next month. Stay tuned for behind-the-scenes updates.

Chapter 20 – Visiting Thrushcross Grange

It was glamorous and exciting to be sitting next to Edgar in his silver Mercedes convertible as we sped towards Thrushcross Grange in the early afternoon before the weekend began – he had given himself a Friday early mark. I could smell his cologne; I watched as he drove with confidence – his hand on the wheel adorned by his Armani designer dress watch costing more than I earned in a few years. Not to mention how good his 'casual look' actually looked on him – white linen shirt, cream pants and tanned boat shoes. Gorgeous, sophisticated and bed-worthy. I was pleased to be going 'home' for the weekend too. It was only four hours drive from London, but impossible for a daily commute.

I tried not to keep track of Heath's movements but I still found myself searching for every bit of information I could find on him. While on my searches, I found nothing overtly sleazy about Edgar – phew! Sure, he had the usual bevvy of A-lister women hanging off him in photos, but only a few 'official' past relationships and no overt displays of sex. It made him even more attractive. And I liked the rumour mill about us, it was a buzz.

There were two ways into our village, one that passed by Wuthering Heights and another that came past the golf course and Thrushcross Grange. Edgar took the gold course route which was a little disappointing because I was dying to see home. I wondered if it was habit or tactical on Edgar's behalf.

'I'm going to drop home tomorrow and check on my place,' I told him.

'Sure. Did you want to go there now?' he offered, prepared to spin the car around.

'No, tomorrow is good. I'm sure you've got a few things you need to do without me around.'

He smiled. 'I love that you're not the clingy type.'

Note to self; don't be the clingy type!

'Do you still own that place with Heath?' he asked. I suspected he knew the answer.

'Yes. It's our family home. But Lockwood tells me he's away this weekend because the stand-in is filling his shoes. He's gone to Brighton,' I said.

'Yeah, Isabella told me,' he added.

I turned to look at him. *He's in Brighton with Isabella. For fuck's sake.*

Edgar saw my expression. 'Isabella has a modelling gig there and I think she invited him for the weekend.'

'Good,' I said, trying to sound super nonchalant. 'I didn't want to run into him at home.'

Aagh, the knife in my heart just twisted. I was wondering why he was going to Brighton and if it had something to do with his so-called film, but no, it had something to do with his love life! Why would he do this? Why would he be with her when she was so not his type? Why would he agree to do a film now when he wouldn't do one when I encouraged him to consider it? I hate you, Heath. I love you too.

Edgar slowed the car down and put the right indicator on. I couldn't see anything but a row of trees and then, as we turned, Thrushcross Grange came into view.

'And ... we ... are ... home,' Edgar said, drawing out his sentence as he hit a remote, opened the gates and we drove slowly up the driveway towards the house. 'We've got the place to ourselves this weekend,' he said, and gave me an inviting smile.

'Oh, I thought it was just you and Isabella that still lived here anyway, on and off,' I said.

'We do. But there's our property managers—Mr and Mrs Cartwright—they live at the cottage on the adjoining estate. They are both oldies now but they've been with the family for a hundred years.'

'Wow, that long,' I teased.

He laughed. 'They are officially retired but I want them to use the cottage because they've earned it.'

'You big softie,' I said, giving him an adoring look. 'I'm so glad you look after them.'

'They're like family,' he said. 'Besides their standards are old world and second to none – so, they do a great job of managing the cleaners and gardeners, and any contractors we need since Isabella and I aren't here much. It's good to have someone present. You know what I mean?'

Oh sure, I've given my staff the weekend off too!

I nodded. I do understand. Mum and Dad had a very good team when we owned the estate, especially in the stables, but as Dad got older and Mum passed away—I still can't say the 'D' word—we had to let them all go and then the estate was transformed into the exclusive townhomes. We weren't the first to do it in the district, we were one of the last, but it feels right now. The pressure of running an estate like Thrushcross Grange would be too much.

I tuned back into what Edgar was saying about being alone this weekend.

'Given our visit, Mr and Mrs Cartwright took the opportunity to visit their grandkids. Mrs Cartwright showed me the photos once, Lord save me.'

'From kids or the photos?' I asked. He laughed but didn't answer.

The driveway went on forever, seriously.

'Do you always call them that?' I asked, 'not by their first names.'

'No way,' he said. 'They were here before I was born and they're ancient, I wouldn't dream of it.'

'That's lovely,' I said, respecting him even more. 'And what do they call you, just out of curiosity?'

He laughed and looked embarrassed. 'Um, young master.'

I laughed out loud. 'No?'

He grinned and shrugged.

Oh, that will stick,' I teased him, and he cringed.

Edgar pulled into the garage and turned off the ignition. He leant over and took my hand and then kissed it. 'The young master is at your service,' he said. So gallant. 'So, let me show you around.'

'And show me to my room,' I teased. I was expecting we might share a room, but I would be happy to have my own space just for dressing, bathing, and time out – you get the picture.

He laughed. 'Yeah, I think your room might also be mine,' he said, and I gave him a smile that said it better be.

I opened the door and met him at the back of the car where he gallantly grabbed both bags, slinging his own over his shoulders.

I turned to follow him in and stopped in my tracks. I had forgotten just how dramatic Thrushcross Grange was. It reminded me of a time when Heath and I snuck here to peek inside. How bizarre to think that the young Edgar and his sister, who we watched through the windows and we both thought were so insipid, would one day be in our lives to the degree they were now, and not because we were neighbours.

I hate you, Heath, get out of my head and heart.

I glanced at the large bay window frame and remembered the time when Heath dropped below the windowsill and pulled me down beside him.

I couldn't help but giggle, and he smiled but held a finger to his lips in warning.

'They look so pasty,' I whispered.

'They match the house,' he said, and I giggled again.

I raised myself about the windowsill enough to peer into the huge room where the Linton family sat. It was like something from a postcard. The two children about our age sat in front of the fire with their books and their parents sat side-by-side with a small glass of red liquid looking at the fire.

'It's amazing,' I said. 'Look at those massive rugs, and that Christmas tree is huge.'

Heath shrugged. He was never impressed by that sort of stuff.

I studied Isabella and she looked like a doll. Fair and slight, tall, and all dressed in white.

'They look too clean,' Heath said and made me giggle again.

We watched them in silence, they were oblivious to us peeking in from the outside.

'The room is so beautiful,' I said, 'I wish we had those sorts of lights that drop from the ceiling. They're like drops of glass hanging from silver chains. I hate our modern stuff, it's so ugly, but Mum loves it,' I sighed.

Heath must have read my mood, and found me all of a sudden disgruntled with my life.

'You and I would die in there,' he said, with a nod to the postcard picture in front of us. 'You wouldn't be able to escape and explore the moors with me. And you wouldn't be able to ride your horse. You would have to stay inside and keep clean in your pretty dress,' he teased. 'I love our place.'

I recall at the time I smiled thinking he was teasing me, but on seeing his eyes I realised it was more than that. He was worried that I wanted that life. That I suddenly found the Lintons' world more attractive. Even as a teenager I could recognise his disquiet.

And he was right. I wouldn't fit in at Thrushcross Grange without changing who I was … I could do that. But I was only twelve and Heath was fourteen and we soon forgot the Lintons and Thrushcross Grange and scampered across the moors to Wuthering Heights again and onto our next adventure.

Chapter 21 – The skinny dip

I was still admiring the vista when Edgar nudged me.

'I don't like to rush you,' he teased, 'but the weekend is nearly over.'

I rolled my eyes at him for his masterful exaggeration and followed him inside. Thrushcross Grange was only a five-minute drive from my home, literally, but it may as well have been in a foreign country it was so different. Unlike Wuthering Heights, Thrushcross Grange was down in a valley where the weather wasn't so harsh. It featured huge windows and all the curtains were open; even from the outside I could see how light and welcoming it was. Around me were beautifully manicured gardens that I couldn't wait to explore, but for now, I raced to catch up with Edgar who had started the tour and I was lagging.

Inside was enormous and tastefully decorated; there were several fireplaces that I imagined would be very cosy to snuggle near at night.

The living areas featured a gold and navy printed carpet with burgundy-covered chairs, mahogany timber tables, and a pure white ceiling bordered by gold. Chandeliers hung from the ceiling – enormous crystal drops, shimmering with little soft lights.

Edgar waited for me and smiled when he saw my reaction.

'I guess I forget how special it is when it is all I've ever known,' he said, with a shrug. 'Wasn't Wuthering Heights like this once?'

I shook my head and gave a small laugh. 'No, far from it. It was big but dark and moody, and Dad and Mum had filled it with contemporary art and modern pieces. Not like your nod to the classics.'

Then I saw the pool through the glass doors. It featured a fountain and statues at each end.

'Wow.'

'Yeah, I thought we might take a bottle of champagne out there and go unwind. Don't worry if you haven't got your swimmers with you,' he teased. 'I thought we could skinny dip and get back to nature.'

'Our birthday suits?'

'Exactly,' he agreed and took the stairs two at a time to the upper level. I followed in hot pursuit, trying not to stop to admire everything around me.

Edgar did lead me to a separate room and bathroom.

'I'm happy to share my bed, but just in case you want some privacy, this is your room and bathroom,' he said. That was a relief.

'Thank you, I would like that,' I said. It was amazing. I had a panoramic view of the gardens and a distant view of the moors from the bedroom window. Wuthering Heights was on the other side of his mansion, which was a little disappointing. I was hoping I could see my home.

'So,' he said, 'why don't you get changed and meet me downstairs for a drink and a dip.'

I nodded. 'On my way.'

He turned to me just before he left and pulled me closer, and then touching my face and with one hand on my back, Edgar gave me a long and sensuous kiss. For a moment I had to remind myself to remain standing.

He pulled away. 'I'm a little serious about you, Ms Earnshaw,' he said, looking into my eyes.

My heart forgot to beat for a few seconds as I stood mesmerised by him. He didn't wait for an answer, pulling away and departing by gently closing the bedroom door. I was always a little shocked by Edgar's rare show of affection, they were so few and far between. I never really knew how he felt about me, while Heath was so open in his love for me. Edgar's words just now caught me by surprise. I felt a rush of excitement. I guess until now I hadn't really believed he was thinking long-term with me. I thought he might be getting back at Heath by dating me or I might just be a distraction; I wasn't sure he didn't have a new girl every film. But I thought back over the things he had said today and the way he had looked at me and held my hand. I think this was real.

I stood still, recovering from that kiss and then I looked around, exhaled and took in the huge room. It was all white and gold with the most enormous bed.

Imagine being a permanent part of Edgar Linton's life.

Imagine if I was a famous actor and he was an awarded director.

Imagine us!

Move, I told myself, before I lost myself in my daydreams.

I opened my bag, pulled out my swimsuit and an almost

see-through wrap dress that I brought to go over the top of it, and got changed.

This was going to be the most amazing weekend ever. Weirdly, it felt like Wuthering Heights was another world away, not in the same village.

*****

I arrived at the pool deck and looked for Edgar. The outdoor entertainment area was to die for – the hedges were groomed to within an inch of their life, the bronze statues of female figures draped in long robes holding lanterns were so beautiful – I couldn't wait to see them lit tonight, and the pool was enormous and so inviting. Then I felt a splash and Edgar pulled himself up to the edge of the pool, and gave me a grin as he splashed me again! He looked golden and gorgeous like the statues; his hair was wet and slicked back and his eyes were as bright and blue as the water he was immersed in.

'Are you wearing anything in there?' I asked casually, not getting too close.

'Let's just say I have a lot less on than you,' he teased.

I gasped. 'Are you naked?' I feigned shock.

'I am so naked. Strip and get in,' he said, running his hand through his wet hair.

I looked around and he laughed.

'Trust me, there is no one around for miles.'

I slowly removed my shoes and then my almost see-through wrap dress and hesitated again. I was wearing a two-piece swimsuit that was very respectable by his standards I imagine.

He grinned. 'Ah, you've never skinny-dipped, have you?'

I could have lied and pretended I was cool, but I'd never got my gear off in a pool or on the beach before, not even my top.

I shook my head. 'I don't like to alarm families and small children,' I answered, and he laughed.

'There's nothing like being natural and moving freely. We were born that way after all,' he said. 'C'mon beautiful, get your gear off and join me.'

I saw the two towels he had placed on the deck chairs at the end of the pool so at least they were within reach if I had to exit the pool in a hurry. I was about to expose my entire body for the second time to Edgar Linton.

Edgar moved and I turned expecting to see him coming for me but by the side of the pool was an expensive-looking silver ice bucket with a bottle of French champagne resting in it, immersed in ice. I knew it was French because I recognised the label from our dinner the other night. I had said I loved its crisp bubbly flavour and here it was again. *Thoughtful.*

'I'll help loosen you up,' he said, and while he was pouring, I stripped at super speed and dived in behind him, splashing him and beating him to the free strip show.

I surfaced and laughed and he splashed me.

'Well that wasn't fair, I'll have to punish you for that later.'

'Oh? What did you have in mind?' I asked, intrigued and a little too enthusiastically.

'Never you mind. I'll find something in my bondage room,' he said, and I laughed. At least I think he was joking; it was hard to tell with Edgar – I knew so little about him

142

and I knew every fibre of Heath. I guess that was what this weekend was all about.

He put the champagne glasses down on the edge of the pool and swam toward me. It felt amazing to be naked, just swimming in the cool water and now with his arms reaching for me. He ran his hands down my back and pulled me against his chest and then we kissed like we were the only two people left on the earth at this moment, right here, right now.

Chapter 22 – The invasion

I had my legs wrapped around Edgar as we held each other and kissed in his beautiful blue oasis. The afternoon dusk was warm and scented and the statue lights had come on even though it was only early twilight. Then I heard it. *Fuck!* Isabella's laugh.

I looked up in a state of panic and Edgar almost dropped me. Standing poolside was Isabella looking ethereal in a Boho white dress and bronze sandals, her blonde hair falling around her and loosely tied at the back of her neck. She looked like her brother – golden. And then I saw him, in a state of half undress, near the chair where my dress was draped – Heath.

'Oh my God, you didn't tell me you were coming here this weekend,' Isabella said and giggled. Yes, giggled. Like it was the most wonderful surprise ever.

Edgar smirked at her. 'You're supposed to be in Brighton, not cramping my style.'

They were laughing and talking like this was the most natural thing in the world.

'You are both naked!' she said, covering her eyes and laughing.

I dropped my legs from around Edgar's waist and stood in the water that only came to my shoulders. I moved behind him and pressed my chest against him so that Isabella couldn't see my naked body! And Heath in his jeans, no shirt, muscly and strong stood mouth agape, glaring at me.

I dropped out of Edgar and Isabella's banter. It was like our childhood all over again. The golden Lintons in their white house, and the invading savages – Heath and I. We were staring at each other. I was naked in a pool with Edgar, he was standing there half-undressed with this other woman as if they had been discarding clothes as they entered.

Heath and Cathy, Cathy and Heath.

The pain of seeing Heath with her was so acute, and knowing how seeing me with Edgar would cut him, I thought I was going to hyperventilate. But it wasn't pain written on Heath's face, it wasn't even jealousy. It was pure unadulterated anger. We glared at each other and then Edgar seemed to realise; he went into gentleman mode and pushed me a little further behind him, I held his shoulders and pressed against his back. Isabella made a show of stealing our towels, but Edgar sidled us to the pool's edge, hoisted himself out in one swift move and she turned her face with a show of dramatics and dangled the towels.

He grabbed one and wrapped it around his waist. Remembering his manners, he extended his hand to Heath.

'Hi, good to see you again, Heath, and welcome. Cathy tells me you've been passing this place for years on your adventures as our neighbours.'

Heath shook his hand briefly and responded with something short and less charming.

'We passed it a few times while horse riding,' he grunted. 'We'll give you your privacy and stay the night at Wuthering Heights,' he said, his eyes returning to me. I couldn't get out of the pool, I was naked!

Isabella pouted. 'I was so looking forward to staying home. Can't we crash the party?'

Edgar rolled his eyes at her. 'You heard what the man said, get out of here.'

'Fine,' she said, with a flick of her hair. 'But lets at least have a drink together. It's cocktail hour,' she proclaimed. She had no idea of the oppressive tension in the air, or if she did, she was enjoying it.

'Heath, will you have a beer if I grab a few?' Edgar asked. I cleared my throat.

'Ah-hem, towel please!' I said. Edgar turned to me and laughed.

'Sorry babe, I forgot.'

Babe. Oh, that will please Heath.

'I've got this,' Isabella said, 'you boys go and get drinks and snacks for the ladies.'

Heath, who never did what he was told, slipped on his white T-shirt and with an invitation from Edgar to help with the drinks, followed him in. Isabella brought a towel to the edge of the pool and dangled it.

'Thanks,' I said, grabbing it. I turned my back to her and walked up the pool steps, covering myself as I surfaced.

'Well,' she said, and laughed, 'this is cosy, and Heath was just telling me that he never saw you anymore and had no interest in doing so. Reunion time!'

I was taken aback by her comments; I think my mouth

fell open. Why would she say that? Isabella and I had hardly spoken to each other and when we had it was at least polite.

She continued. 'I probably should tell you, we're moving in together, so you two should sort out who owns what soon.'

'That so?' I said, and smiled, and didn't bite. Must have been disappointing for her.

She shifted uncomfortably, twirling a strand of blonde hair in her fingers and turning away from me. Then for all her beauty, I realised she was threatened by me. I had her brother and her lover, and her strength was her beauty, but it wasn't working for her probably for the first time in her whole adored life.

The truth was that I might be dating her brother but I didn't care if Isabella liked me or not. I did feel a bit sorry for her; it wasn't fair if Heath was just playing her for career purposes or to get back at me. I'm sure he enjoyed having the beautiful Isabella in his bed, but I know him, her lifestyle would never hold his interest. It was revenge. Cold, pure and simple.

I sighed. 'Be careful, Isabella,' I warned, 'Heath has a dark side.'

She laughed. 'I know, that's one of his most attractive features.'

She didn't get it. Heath was intense and focused. He hated the social spotlight and he wasn't one for crowds or parties. Isabella and Heath were polar opposites so if she really knew him, it wouldn't take much to work out that he had a motive or that this 'fling' was just for sport.

'He has a lot of interesting traits,' she said, in a sexual way and laughed.

Really? I lost patience.

'You can't seriously believe he is into you, Isabella. He's just doing his best to put the knife in me. Your company is superfluous.'

She physically stepped back as if I had hit her, her eyes widened and then she laughed, reasserting that she was the one in charge of this scenario – her house, her guy.

'Wow, Cathy,' she proclaimed. 'Look at me and look at you, which do you think he'd prefer?'

Ouch. I nodded. 'I deserve that,' I said, and she looked a little taken aback and embarrassed by her comment. I needed to rise above this; I was, after all, dating her brother. 'You think I'm speaking from selfishness, and I'm sorry it probably came out the wrong way.' I reached for my wrap and placed it over the towel. It was see-through so the towel had to stay on. I sighed. 'It's just that I know him, Isabella. I know him – he's my stepbrother.'

'You don't know him as I do,' she said and gave a smile that implied something was going on between them that I didn't know about.

Heath and Edgar entered as she spoke the words and she moved towards him and draped herself over him, accepting the glass of champagne he held for her.

'Can I share our news, Heath darling?' she asked, and didn't wait for his answer. 'We're engaged!'

Chapter 23 – Confrontation

That was the quickest cocktail hour in history, more like fifteen minutes. You could have heard a pin drop at Isabella's announcement. Heath looked uncomfortable as he watched me for my reaction, I looked like I needed one of those defibrillation machines to start my heart again, and Edgar looked less than impressed with his potential new brother-in-law. He snapped out of it and congratulated them both. I didn't say anything. I should have but I couldn't. Forming words, let alone breathing, was out of my control.

Heath drank half his beer, placed it on the table and got Isabella's attention.

'Best we head off,' he said. He thanked Edgar for the drink, nodded at both of us and was walking away before she had time to debate the subject.

I cleared my throat and called to him. 'I want to come by home tomorrow, preferably in the morning, to grab a few things. What time will you be out?' Let's put it out there that I have no desire to see either of them.

His eyes narrowed. 'We'll be going for breakfast in the village at our—' he almost said favourite café but it wasn't their favourite café, it was mine and Heaths, '—at one of the cafes, so from 9.30am for a few hours.'

I nodded. 'That will work,' I said.

'Bye then, Cathy,' Isabella said, and Heath turned away from me.

'Bye Isabella, and congratulations,' I managed to say. Better late than never.

Edgar saw them out.

When they were out of sight, I leant over like a boxer punched in the stomach. The air rushed out of me; the pain was as if I had taken a direct hit.

I. Hated. Him.

How could he do this to me? Such pain. Let me just crawl into my bed, bury myself and cry my heart out. Heath knew how to wound me. Our sufferings were entwined but this, this was too much. Treachery!

Then Edgar came back in. 'Well that was awkward,' he said and grabbed his beer. 'Are you sure you want to risk going over there tomorrow?'

I straightened up and nodded, trying for my best 'normal' face even though I had just been hit with one of the biggest shocks in my life while standing.

'It'll be fine, I just want to check everything is okay and grab a few things. I'll make sure they are both out. The walk will do me good after months in the city.'

'You're going to walk?' he said like the idea was so foreign.

'I am. Do you want to meet me in the village for lunch and we can drive home together?' I asked.

He smiled. 'That would work perfectly for me. I've got half a dozen calls to make in the morning and stacks of emails to return.' I think he was relieved he didn't have to entertain me all morning. He moved closer. 'Let's go to bed and eat later,' he said, with a very sexy smile.

'Well,' I said, 'now that you've suggested that, who could eat?' God knows I can hardly breathe with the pain and shock but I'm an actress … be here now, I told myself.

He put his drink down, grabbed my hand and I followed him to his bedroom up a flight of stairs that looked like we were on a movie set. Surreal, the whole night was nothing short of surreal.

*****

Entertainment Weekly

RUMOUR FILE: Edgar Linton and the *Wylde* girl get out of town

Our sources tell us that hot director, Edgar Linton, and his supporting actress (in more ways than one) Catherine Earnshaw, headed out of town Friday afternoon in his silver Merc for a romantic weekend away.

The two have been getting hot and heavy since casting director, Tamara Langer of TL Casting, signed Catherine to play Portia in Linton's soon-to-be-released film, *Between Night and Day*.

The two lovebirds met a few months earlier when Linton caught Earnshaw on stage with her then partner Heath Earnshaw in *Cat on a Hot Tin Roof*.

But while Linton offered Heath Earnshaw a film contract,

he's clearly offered Catherine Earnshaw a piece of his heart or maybe, soon the whole thing.

Watch this space.

*****

The next morning the weather was dark and gloomy, a storm was building outside, a storm was building inside of me as well. I was wrathful when I should have been beyond excited and in love. I was struggling with heartbreak and trying to keep it together in front of Edgar. They say the easiest way to get over pain was to fall in love again … whoever said it was right.

Thank God Edgar was in my life and made me feel wanted or I'd be at rock bottom, even though Edgar was the catalyst for all my self-inflicted dramas. The highs and lows of my life these last six months had been like a rollercoaster.

I stood at the large windows looking at the bleak day and Edgar came up behind me and held me.

'You'd better drive,' he said.

'No, I'm dying for a walk. I'll be fine, I know the moors like the back of my hand and I've been caught in storms out there hundreds of times.'

I turned in his arms to face him and smiled.

'What?' he asked, his eyes narrowing with suspicion.

'Thank you for last night, it was wonderful.'

'I aim to please,' he said.

'Oh that you do, young master, or maybe that should be the *Master* now,' I teased him, and he grinned. I pulled away. 'I'm going in case it gets worse out there. I'll message you when I've started walking to the village, but work on meeting me about midday, okay?'

'Perfect,' he said.

I stood on tiptoes to give him a kiss which went on for too long and we were dangerously close to returning to bed when I used my extraordinary powers of self-control to pull away … it helped that his phone rang.

I ran my hand down his front, feeling his hardness and he groaned.

'Enjoy that call,' I said, and following in Isabella's steps, gave him a flick of my auburn hair, a backward glance and an attempt at a sexy look. What the heck?

'I'll add that to your punishment list,' he called, adjusting himself and looking uncomfortable.

In the hallway, I put on my runners, grabbed my waterproof jacket and backpack, and ventured out onto my moors.

*****

Oh God, it was so good to be back in nature, to have nothing around me but green space and empty moors, the wind moaning in my ears – I've missed it. It would take me just short of an hour to walk to Wuthering Heights and I needed that hour of roaming. The walk to the village later would be longer, but that was fine too. Great actually.

The sky was darkening, and the wind was whipping my hair across my face. I stopped to tie it back. I didn't bother with a hat; it wasn't sunny and I wanted to feel the fresh air on my face. I didn't realise how unfit I had got during the months in the city; walking wasn't easy on the moors. You had to watch where you placed your feet – there were rocks and soft mounds, and little brooks and waterfalls. I was home.

I don't know where that hour went, I was so lost in thought, lost in my head, that it sped by and then the large dark façade of Wuthering Heights came into sight. It looked even darker and wilder having just left Thrushcross Grange. Of the townhomes I could see, I noted that some of my neighbours were home. Mrs Johnson's garden continued to thrive despite the wind, I guess she was on the right side of the building. Lockwood's car wasn't in his parking bay, I knew he was visiting Nelly in London and … nope, Heath's car wasn't in the garage, nor was his fiancée's BMW either. The garage was empty. Good.

I headed up the stairs to my home. I wish we still owned the whole estate, but I knew it would be impossible to maintain. And it would be impossible to leave. I unlocked and opened the front door and the memories rushed out at me and escaped down the hallway. I took a deep breath and entered. It was so weird being here alone and having it all look so normal. It should have been different somehow.

I went to my room; it looked like the room of a girl I once knew. I stood in the doorway studying it. Then I made my way down the hallway and saw Heath's bedroom door was closed. I walked along further and glanced in at the main bedroom that we once shared – it was pristine as if it was waiting for its inhabitants to return.

I stared at the bed knowing that Heath and Isabella would

have slept in that bed last night, where we used to be. God, it all seemed so wrong.

I went back up the hallway and slowly opened Heath's bedroom door. I almost expected to see him lying on the bed, his headphones on, like when we were teenagers, but the room was empty. Clean and empty. Then a high wind blustered around the house, and rattled Heath's windows, scaring the hell out of me. It was the motivation I needed; I closed his bedroom door again and moved into action. I grabbed a few things that I wanted from my room, packed them in my backpack, and standing at the door ready to leave I tried to picture everyone I loved as they once were – Mum, Dad, Hindley and Heath. How we were when we lived here as a family.

Closing the door behind me, I departed. I didn't know when I would next be home, but I knew it would not be with Heath. Everyone I was ever connected with and loved at Wuthering Heights had gone.

Chapter 24 – Wild encounter

It was only mid-morning but outside it was dark and the wind was blustery, yet it wasn't cold. I was grateful that I was meeting Edgar in the village at noon – it would be a much-needed distraction. I should start thinking of my time with him as a wonderful new start. The walk to the village would take me over an hour, so I had plenty of time. I stopped at the gated entrance to the Wuthering Heights estate and looked back, I blew it a kiss – corny but she was my love, my rock, my base. I wasn't sure when I would be back. And then I turned and continued my walk along the moors to the village.

I rarely ran into anyone walking, except very early in the morning or at the end of the day when you get the occasional walker with their dog. In this weather, I could be assured of having the moors to myself. My favourite place was ahead – a little brook where the water was always icy cold and fresh, and you could sit beside it and listen to its gentle song. Today, the brook was full to the brim and rushing by, and despite the gloomy skies, the birds were in fine voice.

I opened my eyes and sat down to trail my hand in the cold water, tasting it on my fingers; delicious and fresh. I glanced at my watch and then to the skies and could hear my father telling me not to ramble out on the moors all day. I had a place to be so I rose and skipped across the brook to the dry side and continued up a small rise.

At the top, I saw him. *No!*

My heart stuttered and my breathing quickened. Heath was walking across the moors towards me. Dressed in his jeans, black boots, a black T-shirt and black jacket, he was barely visible against the backdrop of the sky. He was by himself.

I glanced around. There was nowhere to hide – no tree, no rock, no dip to rush to and slip behind out of his sight. Then he saw me and stopped still. He looked like he always belonged there; it was as if this meeting was destined. I put my shoulders back and kept walking, Heath did the same. There was no avoiding each other and we were the only idiots in the world who would be out walking the moors in weather like this.

I would just greet him and move on, I told myself, and then we were but metres from each other and I couldn't take my eyes off him and his step became purposeful. We stopped and stared, neither of us spoke.

I turned away from him and looked out across the moors. They were cold, dark and hostile, just like us.

'Are you cold?' he asked.

Those three words caused me so much pain. He didn't accuse me of anything or ignore me; his first words were concern. If I had said yes, he would have given me his coat.

I shook my head. 'Thank you, I'm fine,' I said. 'It's not cold.'

'No,' he agreed.

It was the strangest feeling, like I was in one of those dreams where you see in the distance where you have to be but can't get there no matter how hard you try.

'Cathy,' he whispered my name, and I looked up at him and made eye contact. His eyes were warm and loving and he was there in front of me – the Heath I've always known.

I straightened and swallowed. I'm full of pain and he will know about it.

'Where is your *fiancée*?' I asked, with the words sounding bitter as they came off my tongue.

'I wanted to walk home, she wanted to drop into Thrushcross Grange for a while … she doesn't like the walk.' He had the good grace to look embarrassed as he said it.

I laughed. 'The boy who lives for being on the moors is going to marry a girl who doesn't like to take a walk – a match made in heaven, good luck with that.' What a cow I was, but I couldn't help myself.

His eyes narrowed with anger; I knew they would.

'That was quite a surprise last night,' I said, referring to their engagement. 'I guess I should offer my best wishes to the happy couple.'

The wind howled right on cue as if it could not believe the words coming out of my mouth – that Heath was getting married and not to me.

He stiffened in front of me and drew in a breath before speaking.

'You, Cathy, were all I could see as I came out on that terrace last night. The love of my life, the only woman in the whole goddamn world that I want to spend forever with, there naked in the pool and wrapped around Edgar Linton. If looks could kill, he'd be dead.'

I stored the words away to think back on them later but shot back a barb hoping to share the pain he caused me with his engagement notice.

'But why would you even care if I was naked and pressed against Edgar, you were there with your fiancée. You've found the one, after all.'

'So have you by the looks of it.'

'I really care for Edgar,' I agreed.

'Care!' he laughed.

I retorted: 'Well maybe one day soon I'll feel the love that you feel for Isabella for him too – that depth of love when you know you are going to be together forever.'

His jaw locked and I knew he felt nothing for her. He wanted to hit back at me, for me to feel the pain I caused him, and he had succeeded. We stood back in our corners; a stillness fell around us momentarily while thunder rumbled in the sky above us. I hated what I was saying. I hated the person I was now with him.

He shook his head, looked away momentarily and then returned his gaze to me. His eyes bored into me.

Everything had shifted – we were no longer looking at the same sky or standing on the same earth. And then I realised this was pointless. We hated each other and wanted to wound each other to remind us of our love. How hopeless.

I took off as fast as I could, taking Heath by surprise. A huge bolt of lightning terrified me but I kept going.

Heath called my name and I turned to see him following. I don't know why. What remaining insults did we have to fire at each other? If he was worried I was going to be felled by the storm, well, right now that would have been a relief.

I sped up, walking as fast as I could and he caught up beside me and grabbed my hand, I pulled away.

'Leave me,' I hissed at him.

I kept walking but when we reached some huge rocks, 'our rocks' that were our childhood caves, he reached out and grabbed my hand again.

'Just stop, Cathy, for the love of God, stop for a moment!'

I wheeled around on him, pulling my hand out of his grip and we glared at each other. We were both so angry that we'd probably implode before we got a word out. The wind was howling around us but we stood in the middle creating our own storm.

We both breathed heavily and then Heath spoke, his words hitting me like weapons. He spoke with more emotion than I had ever heard him express.

'Cathy, why would you do that to us? Do you know what hell you have put me through?' he asked, anger rising in his voice. 'Every waking moment I thought about you. I looked out for you at every performance, hoping that you had changed your mind and come back to me.'

I butted in. 'I asked you to meet me at home, I called and messaged but you ignored me.'

'You were calling me while you were seeing him,' Heath answered. 'If you were serious about saving us, you would have come to me. Instead, I'm working my butt off trying to stay busy and distracted, all the time wondering if you were with him or who you were out with, who you were kissing.'

I returned to my pain. 'Why Isabella? Do you love her?' I asked, not wanting to know but needing to hear the answer.

'The shiny Lintons,' he scoffed. 'She asked me out over

and over again, she's a distraction. You told me films would raise my profile, well she's doing that with her million sycophant followers excited by every photo she puts up of the two of us. She's an accessory.'

'You're going to marry her. Of all the ways you could have caused me pain ...' my voice broke and Heath looked away. He could never stand it when I was teary and this time he couldn't hold me and fix it.

'Cathy ...' he moved towards me and I stepped back. I wanted him so badly I almost weakened and ran to hold him, but I was still seething with anger and I hadn't worked through that yet, and that's partly because he hadn't said what I needed to hear. I wanted him to say he'd call it off with her in a heartbeat if I came back to him now, but he didn't say the words. I just needed to be us again and that was gone.

I needed to know he wanted me because I'm different now too. I've lost the carefree side of me, and it took so long to get that back after Mum and Dad's death. I am older, maybe even harder. Nothing about us was the same.

'You put these wheels in motion, Cathy, this is the freedom you wanted,' he reminded me. 'Look what you have done to us. I am in anguish.'

I laughed cruelly. 'I'm not wishing you to feel any greater torment than me, Heath. After all, misery loves company ... what a fine couple we could be.'

Even then he didn't take my prompt; he didn't say we could be a couple again or that he would drop his accessory, Isabella. Perhaps he wanted her more than he was prepared to admit. She was fun and sexy and rich, all the descriptions you wouldn't put on me.

We had run out of words and now it was just us, the moors, the storm around us, and our hearts beating fast.

He let out a ragged breath and I ached for making him so anxious – that same ache I've been feeling for the past months.

'I have to go, Heath,' I said. 'Edgar will be waiting for me.'

'Yes, I know how much you *care* about him, best you run to him then,' he said.

I turned and walked away, across our moors to my new life.

*****

Entertainment Weekly

RUMOUR FILE: Filming begins and tension abounds

Filming has begun on director, Nadim Ramirez's drama, *The Meaning of Nothing* and our industry spies tell us that the set is a hotbed of tension and dare we say, passion.

Lead actor Heath Earnshaw—fresh from a successful stage career in the West End and applauded for his portrayal earlier this year of Brick in *Cat on a Hot Tin Roof*—is adjusting to life on a film set.

It's fair to say the numerous takes are taking their toll on Earnshaw and the waiting around apparently hasn't done much for his sense of humour either. Production assistants have been sent to track him down and bring him back when he was required on set – rumour has it he has been found in the gym, at his apartment, and on one occasion watching an amateur theatre stage production! Homesick to tread the boards? Our sources tell us Earnshaw has not endeared himself to the hair and make-up team either with his lack of interest in touch-ups. A friendly 'talking-to' from the director has him staying put on set but running laps around the studio to keep awake and keep him on his game. Oh, dear!

Regardless, Earnshaw turns heads and rumour has it he has won many a heart—male and female—on set. It won't surprise you then to know that Earnshaw's current flame, Isabella Linton—model and sister of awarded director, Edgar Linton—has been visiting the set and giving anyone who gets a little too friendly with her leading man a look best described as daggers.

Speaking of insecurity, lead actress, Trinity Bailey, is said to be counting lines to ensure she has enough screen time. Insider sources say Bailey's insecurity reared its head when director, Ramirez—known for allowing his actors plenty of freedom—had been heavily instructing her on the tension he wanted for his early scenes. Our sources say the tension between director and star is not transferring to film.

Add to this, a dramatic soliloquy written for Bailey was reworked by Ramirez and given to Earnshaw, who Ramirez was heard to say would carry it better. We hear from our insiders that the writer and Trinity Bailey were less than impressed, but let's not forget it is Ramirez's film.

The film is based on the true story of an artist who loses interest in his muse and believes killing her will release his creative juices again. His muse goes missing but his last painting captures her death and is considered his best work ever. But is it enough to charge him with murder or is the subject of his painting from his imagination?

Let's just hope they all get through the filming process alive and art doesn't imitate life!

PART 3

Chapter 25 – The red carpet

Six months later...

The church was filled with friends and family, the groom looked gorgeous and I cried as you would expect. My co-star, aka 'movie brother', walked down the aisle with his beautiful bride on his arm and we threw confetti and cheered. I had managed to marry my 'brother' off and in the final scene of the movie, at his wedding reception, my cousin revealed he couldn't find the right woman. The camera zoomed in on my expression – *challenge accepted*!

'Cut and that's a wrap,' the director yelled.

The last day of filming was always a mix of feelings. The excitement that it was done after all the lines learnt, the early starts, the victories and tantrums (there are usually a few) and a sadness that this cast and crew who had been together day in and day out for months would now disband, and even if you worked with them again on another film or stage play, it would never be the same dynamic.

It was great getting the Romcom and a terrific contrast to the drama of the crack whore, not to mention fun to play something lighter. It would show versatility on my acting resume. Besides, my 'brother' in the movie played by Skip Bryant was the hottest of the hot. If everyone who followed him on social media saw the film, we'd have a hit on our hands!

The last six months were so full-on that I was getting addicted to change. Nelly had scored one of the director's assistant roles on a large action film being shot here in London, Lockwood had a one-year production contract with a London-based theatre company, Edgar and I were going strong and he was about to start shooting his next film … and Heath—*I know, why am I thinking about Heath?*— had finished shooting his film, *The Meaning of Nothing*, and was back on stage where he belonged.

He and his fiancée had moved in together in some trendy pad that she posted photos of all over her social media accounts. When she wasn't strutting down the catwalk, she was taking selfies of herself in beautiful poses or draped over her fiancé. *Whatever.* They deserved each other; I know I sounded like a bitter and twisted ex … I was!

Nelly, Lockwood and I had moved into a bigger place together which was fantastic and even though we were all working, we managed to see each other in our comings and goings, and have at least one dinner a week and a few drinks or ten at our favourite pub. We were all in relationships – Nelly and Lockwood both had gorgeous guys and I had my gorgeous guy, Edgar. We never socialised together though … Edgar wouldn't fit in with their guys – he was only three or four years older, but he was in a different headspace. We were 25 going on 20, he was 28 going on 38!

I saw Edgar in bed more than anywhere else – late at night and very early in the morning when I had sleepovers and before our schedules intervened. To say Edgar was pissed with Heath's promising advance reviews for a movie that wasn't his, was an understatement. He was still smarting that he was the first to offer Heath a role, and then Heath had taken up the opportunity with some other director. Suffice to say his name gets mentioned very little at our place; even Isabella has learnt not to update her brother on her fiancé's activities.

Edgar was talking about moving in together since we'd been going out for nearly a year now, but I liked living with Nelly and Lockwood and they were good company for the many nights Edgar or I were working and couldn't see each other.

As for me, my life was what every student at acting school dreamt of achieving, I guess. I just finished making my second film, I had an agent, and I was in an amazing relationship. For the first time just a week ago, I turned as a photographer called my name and snapped some pics of me walking back to the Tube station after filming. My first paparazzi – all one of them! It was exciting and a little scary too. Plus—wait for it—my agent sent me scripts to consider. I still had to audition but some producers wanted me without the audition process – OMG. Sure, they were probably parts you wouldn't take but it was still flattering.

Edgar was absorbed in his next project and we had had the 'talk'. We agreed it wouldn't be good for either of us to do another film together so soon … just a credibility thing. I needed to be seen to be in demand by other producers and directors, and he needed to be unbiased and cast the best person for the role and not automatically put his fabulous girlfriend into a part – ha!

To make the cut-offs for the annual film awards, Edgar's film, and mine too, *Between Night and Day,* was right at the start of the date range, and I noticed that the production company making Heath's film had listed it for release in the last week of the cut-off. So *Between Night and Day* and *The Meaning of Nothing* were going to be competing in the same categories for the best drama, best screenplay, best actor and actresses, best-supporting actors, best lighting and so on. Imagine if Edgar, Heath and I were all nominated for awards. Freak me out!

But first, we had the opening night red carpet launch for *Between Night and Day* and Nelly and I couldn't wait!

*****

Entertainment Weekly

RED CARPET FILM PREMIERE: Premiere release for *Between Night and Day*, directed by Edgar Linton, executive producer Naomi Thornbury.

By Bonny Hawkins

It's the hottest movie ticket in London and impossible to get—we know, we tried—but fans of director Edgar Linton and actors Holly Bale and Travis Taylor can still see the stars and the who's who on the red carpet for the world film premiere of Linton's *Between Night and Day* this Saturday from 7pm in Leicester Square, London.

The director's sister, model and socialite Isabella Linton, has told *Entertainment Weekly* that she will be on the red carpet to support her brother. She was not able to confirm if her fiancé, actor Heath Earnshaw, would be attending due to clashes with his stage schedule.

Linton's drama which is set in contemporary London and Dublin is already creating award buzz with notable performances including that of stage regular but a newcomer to the screen, Catherine Earnshaw.

The public entry gates for access to the red carpet will open at 5pm and close when filled. Press pens will open from 5.15pm. The stars will arrive at 6.15pm, the film will screen at 7.15pm.

Our Entertainment Editor, Marc Ferguson's review will be online after the preview.

Between Night and Day will be released in cinemas nationally from Sunday.

*****

It was so exciting! I was no stranger to opening nights, Nelly, Heath, Lockwood and I had experienced these on stage over a dozen times. They were exciting and the media photocalls beforehand created a buzz of interest as well, but for a film release, it was completely different – a much bigger and glamorous event with fans coming out to see the actors and director and a real red carpet! Having met some of the production, marketing and publicity teams, I learnt how much work went into these opening nights. I was relieved I just had to get glamorous and frock up!

Unfortunately, I didn't get that girl shopping chromosome and after an hour of shopping and a coffee, I was glazed over. Nelly was truly disappointed in me.

'It's your birthright. How can you not enjoy shopping?' she asked, as we sipped our cappuccinos.

I sighed. 'It's so boring and after a while, like ten minutes, everything looks the same. It's torture.'

'Next, you'll be telling me you hate going to the hairdresser,' she said, pushing a strand of her dark hair behind her shoulder.

I didn't answer.

'No, Cathy, no. Really?'

I grimaced. 'I don't like the small talk you have to make. And I've never walked out of a salon and thought, wow, I look great.'

Nelly shook her head. 'I'm at a loss. I am a professional shopper and I love going to the hairdresser. Being spoilt, having my hair washed, leaving with styled hair better than I could ever do it – it's dreamy,' she sighed.

We both took a forkful of the Hummingbird Cake we were sharing.

'At least you've got a dress and it looks gorgeous,' I said.

'Yes, but I'm in the gallery, you're in the VIP seats with Edgar. You have to look good; you'll be walking in on his arm and people will want autographs and the press will be taking photos ...'

I cut her off because she was stressing me out. 'It's not the BAFTAs, it's only our film premiere! I'll find something,' I assured her.

She looked at me suspiciously.

'In the next hour,' I assured her, 'you watch.'

Nelly nodded. 'You've got that right. I'm taking charge,' she said.

I smiled. 'Good.'

'You planned that, didn't you?' she asked, her eyes narrowing.

'Me, never,' I said, innocently, 'but a blue dress would be nice.'

Chapter 26 – The Premiere

I must have been holding Edgar's hand too tightly as we sat in the back of the chauffeur-driven car on the way to the premiere because he kissed my hand and then groaned.

'Ouch! I may need that hand again to sign contracts,' he said and smiled at me. 'Nervons?'

I gave a small, unconvincing laugh and loosened my grip a little. 'No, yes, you bet.'

'You'll be fine, just walk down the red carpet, wave, smile, stand where the photographers tell you to stand, smile, nod, and look your natural, beautiful self.'

'Got it,' I said. 'What if I get asked a question?'

'Just go for the cliché stuff – it was a great experience, a great cast, a fantastic director,' he joked. 'You'll do fine,' he assured me. 'Did I tell you that you look stunning?'

'No!' I said, most indignantly and gave him a sly smile.

Edgar laughed. 'Gee, I thought I said it four times, my mistake.' He kissed my hand again. 'You look beautiful. I love your hair out and that pale blue dress is stunning. Very Hollywood.'

I smiled, thanked him, and was secretly thrilled. Thank

you, Nelly … she could have a fallback career dressing the cast if she got bored directing actors. Speaking of beautiful, Edgar looked gorgeous. I inhaled his scent and admired his dark suit and white tie look. So handsome against his blonde features.

I cleared my throat. 'I'm not nervous about the crowd, I'm used to crowds, especially in live theatre,' I said. 'I'm nervous about the reviews after the screening.'

I then realised what I said and quickly corrected myself.

'Your film will be brilliant but what if I ruin it? What if they say '*Earnshaw was the weakest link*' and that I dragged your film down?' I took a deep breath and noticed Edgar was completely calm.

'Trust me, no one will say that. I've seen the final cut; I've seen your work.' He took my jaw in his hand and looked me in the eye. 'Cathy, it was very, very good.'

I nodded and breathed out. 'Thank you.'

He leant in and gave me a very smudge-free kiss, and then he shrugged. 'But you know at the end of the day, it's just a film. Films will come and go, it's not the end of the world.'

I looked at him shocked, how could he of all people say that?

'Yeah, well I know we're not curing cancer here,' I said, 'but crap reviews might mean I never get offered another good role, and it might mean less funding for future films for you.'

He shrugged again. 'It'll be fine. I anticipate a few highs and lows along the way. You know *Psycho* never won an award.'

'Get out, no way,' I dismissed the idea.

'True story,' he said. 'Neither did *The Shining, Shawshank Redemption, Rear Window* … the list goes on. And, believe it or not, Orson Welles won awards but never for directing.'

'No!'

'True story,' Edgar said.

'Well that's perspective,' I agreed and smiled. Edgar squeezed my hand gently, and then our driver pulled over, and we were there.

I stopped him before he got out.

'I just want to say good luck tonight, and thank you.'

He smiled.

'No Edgar, I really mean it,' I said, taking his face in my hands and making him look me in the eyes this time. 'Thank you. Thank you for the role, for your love, and for making me feel beautiful and strong and talented. No matter what happens going forward, please know that you saved me, thank you.'

He swallowed, struggled to find words, and then embraced me. I hugged him and then pulled away. Blinking back tears, I took a deep breath and shivered with excitement.

'Look at that,' I said and pointed. I could see the stages set up and the fans, plus the press with their cameras. There were so many flashes and people – so exciting. The driver opened Edgar's car door first and Edgar exited and came around to my side. He took my hand and helped me from the car. Luckily my dress was quite fitted so I didn't have a train to trip over. Like I needed that stress.

The press had seen his arrival and the flashes were going off like crazy. Fans were calling out to both of us, and I put my hand through his offered crooked arm and we made our way to the red carpet. Ahead of us were the lead actors Holly and Travis, both with their partners. Nelly would already be inside; the crew walked the carpet before us. I glanced around and couldn't see Isabella, but there were several big names in the game including models and stars from Edgar's other film that were here for the film's launch as guests and were posing for pictures on the red carpet or signing autographs.

There was a special 'pose area' set aside for the media to get individual star photos. I dreaded heading over there, but I knew I would have to – I don't mind photos of me walking down the red carpet, but I'm not great at posing. I keep hearing Mum telling me to put my shoulders back, Nelly telling me to suck it in and Dad telling me to smile and not pout because I'm a very lucky young woman … aagh!

'Catherine, over here, please,' a voice called, and I recognised Marc from *Entertainment Weekly*. Edgar released me while he went and did an interview with *The Breakfast Show* entertainment editor.

Fans were calling my name – how cool was that? I waved and vowed to get over there shortly to bomb their selfies, which made them laugh.

'Hi Marc,' I said, 'I hope you like the film.'

'I saw an advanced preview at the media screening and I thought it was great Catherine,' he gushed.

I put my hand on my heart and breathed out. 'Thank goodness.'

He laughed. 'For your film debut, you have made an impact. It's a gutsy role and you looked like you felt it.'

I nodded. I had to be careful what I said, this wasn't a chat between us, this was being reported.

'I loved the role from the moment I read for it, largely because it wasn't a pretty role. It was dark and dirty, painful and frustrating. I wanted to get my character and give her a good shake sometimes. I wanted to tell her to run off with the man she loved, but I understood her obligations.'

'Is it fair to say there is a bit of life imitating art for you in that role?' he asked.

'Well, I've never been a crack whore … yet,' I said, and he laughed, 'but there wouldn't be one adult on the planet that couldn't relate to love, loss or sacrifice.' *Phew, I think I circumnavigated that one.*

He nodded and glanced around as Edgar approached.

'Thank you, enjoy the screening and the reviews,' he said, and we shook hands. He turned to grab Edgar as he came near, and I smiled at Edgar and headed over to the 'fans' to get pics with them as promised.

They were lovely and it felt surreal. I hope I never take it for granted or get tarnished by it. I remember meeting my singing idol when I was thirteen and I still remember the thrill. I wanted to be gracious because most of them weren't there for me of course, they were there for Travis, Holly and Edgar. But maybe in my next film or the one after, I'll have the lead.

Then Isabella arrived. And she was not alone.

*****

It was like I was moving in slow motion or through water. I only knew Isabella had arrived because a young girl in the fan area called her name and began waving frantically.

I was terrified to turn around and look to see if Heath was on her arm, but I had my question answered by the number of cameras that swung to me for my reaction. He was with her for sure.

Thank God for the publicist, Astrid, who saved me. She pulled me away from the fans and from whoever was coming up the rear and directed me back towards the red carpet 'pose area'. I was so uncomfortable with having to stand against a backdrop and move left, right, back, and front, while the photographers snapped away. God, what if Heath was watching me? He'd die laughing at my awkwardness – picture a baby giraffe trying to find her feet. I'm an actress, not a model. Why did I have to do that? But I didn't want to appear precious or difficult so I did what I was told and gave thanks that I didn't have to focus on Isabella's arrival.

Edgar was not far behind me and he joined me for some photos and then I was moved on most graciously so that the photographers could get some shots of him on his own. I went to the edge of the fan area while I waited for him and signed autographs.

It sounds bizarre to say but I felt Heath; his powerful presence behind me and I could smell his cologne. I loved his fragrance and it was his signature scent. I finished signing the autographs and, conscious that we were being observed and filmed, I turned and there he was, an arm's length from me.

'Hello Cathy, you look beautiful,' he said, his hands in his suit pocket, as he rocked on his heels. My heart stopped, and the pain came back from nowhere … as if it had been stored next to my heart and was released on seeing him.

He looked amazing. Fuck him.

I cleared my throat. 'Thank you, you look great too,' I said, taking in his dark suit, his short hair and how it accentuated his jawline. I glanced around for Edgar who caught my eye and nodded. He was on his way.

'Enjoy your night, I'm sure you will be brilliant,' Heath said, and turned back to the red carpet, hooking his arm for Isabella to link into as she made her way towards us.

Weirdly I didn't want Edgar, I wanted Nelly; I wanted to be inside with her, seated, talking about who was wearing what, gossiping and sharing our fears before the screening. I knew all the cameras were pointed at us. Edgar reached me and kissed his sister on the cheek. She reciprocated to me. God what hypocrites we were, pretending we were all such good friends.

I couldn't leave too soon without creating rumours so I glanced again at Astrid, the publicist, who read me. I love her, I owe her. A few moments later she came and moved us on, sending Isabella and Heath inside to find their seats, and pushing Edgar towards another reporter.

I left Edgar to finish his interview and indicated I was going in. I just hoped Heath and Isabella weren't seated near us. The cinema was small enough without having to share breathing space with them. Why couldn't they stay away and just let us enjoy our opening night? Surely Edgar doesn't need Isabella's support at every opening – he has me now.

I took a deep breath. I was about to see my film debut and Heath would be watching my first ever screen role at the same time. Agony.

Chapter 27 – The film was out there

Edgar slipped into the seat beside me; the cinema was packed with special guests, VIPs, cast, crew and media, and then the cinema was darkened. I couldn't hold my breath for two hours, so I would just have to get immersed in the film and get over myself and all my fears! Isabella and Heath were across the aisle with the guest VIPs, thank the Lord for that. And then, the film began. I felt queasy. Edgar must have read me and pulled me close for a kiss. I saw a flash – really? We can't even sneak a kiss in the dark of the cinema, sigh.

'I'd say good luck but it's a little late now,' I whispered to him.

He agreed. 'I'm proud of this film, and I'm thrilled with your work and everyone's, just wait and see.'

We sat back to watch – me for the first time seeing it all come together with a good edit, music and effects. I was immersed and it was so weird seeing my friends—the cast—on the screen. Wow, I'd have to get used to that.

Then my breath hitched; it was me, larger than life. Edgar squeezed my hand. Oh my God, I barely recognised myself. I looked dark and wasted – fantastic, the perfect victim cum crack whore. I got a bit upset seeing myself there, it was weird. I don't think it was because I could relate to my character, but it was as if all the emotion on my face was a storybook for me … reminding me of the break-up with Heath. How pained I looked; how raw it was then. Wow, it felt like a million years ago, but it was all there on display, and then the scene moved on. Would Heath recognise my anguish?

I had another six or so scenes and they didn't impact me as much as the first, and then it was over and the credits ran, and the audience got to their feet and applauded. We all joined in and I turned to applaud Edgar who gave me a grateful nod and then a kiss … it felt incredible to be his plus one on his star night. The crowd cheered and I was thrilled but I know they were also caught up in the red-carpet moment and having all the actors and crew there in the cinema. But I'm not complaining, the clapping was deafening, so I'm guessing they did like it! The reviews and box office attendance would be telling.

The editing, music, lighting, camera angles, acting, costumes, directing, producing, sets – every aspect was amazing and I needed to see it a few more times again to study it all and how it came together. Some scenes I had completely forgotten – it had been a while. I wanted to see what effects were used and when; I wanted to watch the other actors and how they presented their characters; I needed to see it with Nelly and have her interpret her work and share her thoughts on the outcome.

But now, drinks and celebration at the after-party; tomorrow the reality check of reviews would kick in.

*****

Critics' reviews – *Between Night and Day*

Edgar Linton has done it again – a masterpiece. Sterling performances by leads Travis Taylor and Holly Bale and a supporting cast second to none. I pitched from light to dark and back again, wishing it would never finish. Neil Chatters, Entertainment Tonight.

Edgar Linton can get his mantle ready for the top award; magnificent. 'Between Night and Day' is the film of the year. Des Jones, The Courier.

Disturbing, oppressive and brilliant. Watch out for Catherine Earnshaw with a performance so vivid that she made a world that is hard to understand at the best of times, make perfect sense. Sarah Palat, E-News Now!

'Between Night and Day' is compelling … a painful journey that has to be seen to understand the underbelly of life. Travis Taylor, Catherine Earnshaw and Kyle Hughes are faces to remember. James Ambrose-Clarke, The Guardian.

The film is dark and disturbing but all hail the ladies, Holly Bale and Catherine Earnshaw – shining lights. Jose Asay, Hits FM.

Dangerously close to being too much, but restrained and outstanding performances by Travis Taylor and Catherine Earnshaw save this film. Earnshaw is ready for that leading role. Ann Symonns, The Post.

Travis Taylor owns the lead role with piercing intensity. Director, Edgar Linton, has the gift of delivering stories off the screen and into the heart and mind. Notable mention to stage actress, Catherine Earnshaw, in her film debut. She played the addicted prostitute with great conviction. Young actor Kyle Hughes is on his way. Mindi Maron, Daily Mail.

Hands down the most compelling and powerful film I have seen this year. Mark my words – Travis Taylor for best actor, Edgar Linton for best director and two supporting cast members for best-supporting actors – Catherine Earnshaw and Kyle Hughes. P.J. Lane, FilmMatters.

I couldn't take my eyes off the screen no matter how desperate it got at times. This is the blueprint for the genre. Robert Cominos, SilverScreen.

Edgar Linton delivers again. Travis Taylor and Holly Bale are painfully believable and Catherine Earnshaw is in no one's shadow. Marc Ferguson, Entertainment Weekly.

Chapter 28 – Heath the tormentor

'He's a brute, I hate him.' I heard the words and knew immediately who the speaker was – Isabella.

Edgar and I had gone home to Thrushcross Grange for the weekend after the film premiere. I used the term 'home' like it was my residence but I'd spent more time at Edgar's mansion, Thrushcross Grange, in the time we had been together than I had spent at Wuthering Heights. I was going to drop into Wuthering Heights sometime over the weekend, but this afternoon, my soul needed to have a walk on *my* moors. Heading up the long driveway on my return to Thrushcross Grange, I saw Isabella's sporty little silver BMW parked out the front. Heath wouldn't be with her because he was rehearsing. Lockwood told me earlier in the week that he too was working on set this weekend. So, she had come alone … it was as I predicted, she was in pain and the cause was Heath.

I should have walked away and tip-toed upstairs and had a shower but I had to listen. I warned her but she thought my words were just from bitterness. Ha, she's learning fast now. I moved closer to make out what they were saying and glanced through the door frame to try and see them. Edgar was mixing himself a drink and Isabella had moved in front of the window. Bizarre that someone so beautiful with her pale skin, golden hair and green eyes, not to mention the model body, could be so insecure. Edgar returned to her side and passed her a drink.

'Leave him,' he said, with a sigh as though it was the easiest decision in the world. 'Cathy told you he was hard work.'

Isabella scoffed. 'She had her motives.'

'Really?' Edgar asked, and whirled the ice in his glass. 'What would those be? To keep Heath for herself?'

Isabella frowned and then softened. 'I know you don't want to think she still cares for him, brother, but this affects us both. Besides, if I leave him, he's single again,' she said as if it was a threat.

'Why would Cathy go back to him? We've been together for over a year now, she could have played that card anytime,' he snapped. 'Or do you think she'd only be able to get him back if you were off the scene?'

'I didn't mean that,' she said. 'This isn't about you or Cathy, okay?'

I saw Edgar shrug like he didn't care. He obviously felt secure in my love. He had a healthy ego fuelled by a childhood of entitlement, and now success and accolades.

'Cut to the chase, Izzy, what is the problem with him? Make it work or dump him.'

She laughed. 'You make it sound so easy. I love him, Edgar. I love him and I want him but he gives so little back emotionally. I barely know how he feels about me except that he always makes love to me when we're together, and he is so ardent … he does it as if he wants me – slow, attentive, passionate. It makes me think he does love me but he just can't verbally express it.'

Ah, God that hurt.

Edgar winced at the detailed description as well. Isabella slumped against the window frame as if the words had taken too much energy to say.

'Is he cheating on you?' Edgar asked.

'No. At least I don't think so. He's just caught up in his craft, as he calls it.' She rolled her eyes and then moved away from the window and collapsed into a seat. 'I feel like I'm dangling. He gives me just enough to love him and not leave him, but never enough to make me secure in that love. I can never get enough of anything when I'm with him.' I saw her blink away tears. 'Where's Cathy?' she asked, remembering me for the first time.

'Gone for a walk,' Edgar answered. He sat opposite Isabella and studied her. 'You know, you don't look well. You've lost weight. Maybe you should come home for a while.'

They sat in silence for a few moments.

'I can't,' she said,' I need to be near him.'

I understood Isabella's despair and felt very sorry for her despite not particularly liking her. That pain was familiar, although I was never insecure with Heath, but I knew that awful feeling of wondering and waiting. The irony was that Edgar was a little like that. Sure, he told me he loved me, but he directed actors with the same passion. He had never shown me any great depth of love. But the difference was, I didn't feel it either. Maybe we were both shallow. Maybe I had just taken a safe course, a safe ship in the harbour—no fighting, no drama, no commitment or intensity—we just co-existed and that met our needs for now. Poor Isabella looked wretched.

'Don't let this guy make you sick, Izzy,' Edgar said again, 'he's not worth it. He's the type who would seize and devour you without a second thought.'

She grimaced. 'You barely know him; how can you even say that? Has Cathy told you something about him?'

He shook his head. 'I know his type.'

That comment made me angry; Edgar had never bothered to ask about or get to know Heath. Once Heath spurned his film offer, neither Heath nor Edgar cared to know anything about each other.

Isabella rose and I pulled back a little further so I couldn't be seen.

'Can't you offer him another movie role?' she asked.

I nearly cried out aloud, but I needn't have worried, that was Edgar's reaction too.

'What the fuck for? I don't need him and he's already thrown one offer back in my face,' he said. 'He's not that fucking good.' He rose, harnessing his anger, and returned his glass to the bar. 'Hell will freeze over before that happens, even for you.'

I was worried Edgar would storm out and catch me listening as there was nowhere quick to run and hide, but he walked over to her and placed a hand on her shoulders, looking at her intensely. 'Izzy, if the relationship needs me to secure him for you through obligation, you know it is not going to work. I'm sorry,' he said.

Seeing them together like that was oddly ghoulish. It took me back to the time Heath and I peaked in through the windows of Thrushcross Grange. They were like waxen creatives. Back then, Isabella was having her hair brushed and Edgar was patting a small lap dog. I had to restrain myself from laughing out loud at the memory.

'So, are you and Cathy going strong?' I heard Isabella ask. Oh, this will be good. I leant in so I didn't miss a word.

'We're solid,' Edgar answered. 'But I have to admit, if I knew she was having any kind of communication with your boyfriend, I'd kill him. Is she coming between you?'

My blood boiled. Isn't that a question he should be asking me, so much for trust?

'No, he never mentions her,' Isabella said.

Aagh, that hurt as well. They were all hateful today, the lot of them. I suddenly yearned to return to Wuthering Heights and have a night alone there. Isabella interrupted my thoughts with a direct question to her brother.

'Will you marry her?'

I held my breath.

'I think that is inevitable,' he answered.

Oh. My. God.

Wow. Imagine my future as Mrs Catherine Linton or Ms Catherine Earnshaw-Linton. Wow, that sounds good.

'I best go find Cathy, the weather is setting in and she's out there in it,' Edgar said, his voice laced with frustration like he had to look for a pesky child. I raced on tiptoe back to the door, opened and closed it with a reasonable bang, and walked towards the living room.

'Ah, good timing, I was getting worried about you,' Edgar

said, and came to me, placing his hand on the back of my head. He pulled me in for a kiss. 'You're all flushed.'

'I was getting windblown out there,' I said, exhaling for effect. I turned to notice Isabella allegedly for the first time.

'Isabella, what a nice surprise. Are you alone?' I asked, looking around knowing full well she was.

'Yes, Heath's rehearsing this weekend and couldn't get away. Final rehearsal I believe.'

'Right,' I said, nonchalantly. 'Are you staying?'

'I was hoping to stay for the night if Edgar has no objections,' she said, almost smartly and reminding me that this was their home and not mine.

'None at all,' he said.

Well, bully for you two. Thanks for considering me, I thought. And then I decided to grow a spine.

'Well that works out perfectly,' I said, 'because I wanted to have a night by myself at Wuthering Height and return all the calls and messages from friends about my reviews and catch up with their news. I feel like I've neglected everyone,' I said. 'You two can have a sibling night together like old times.' I gave a small laugh like it was the most perfect idea. Edgar looked less than impressed. I offered a consolation prize. 'Let's meet for breakfast in the village, shall we?' I asked him and got a sulky reply. 'You too, of course, Isabella, if you would like to join us.'

'Thanks,' she said, with a smile that bordered on a smirk.

Not long after I was driving down the road to Wuthering Heights in Edgar's Merc, feeling wonderful. Was I outgrowing Edgar? Was I finally doing what I set out to achieve … be completely independent for the first time in my life? The thought scared me a little and momentarily I wanted to rush back. God, I'm so weak.

Then I thought about Isabella's question. Edgar plans to marry me – I have to confess that I was a little swept away with the romance and excitement of that thought. So sweet.

But will Heath go through with his marriage to Isabella?

Chapter 29 – Put a ring on it

It was dark outside, moody and warm. I opened the curtains and windows that faced the moors. My windows were high enough that no one could climb in or see-through. It was weird being here alone, sitting around in my singlet and matching brief, drinking wine like I had nothing in the world to worry about. The last time I stayed here alone, Heath had just left me after hearing my words to Lockwood. It felt like a hundred years ago, and my mindset was so different tonight. I played my song list, messaged friends and indulgently read my reviews again. They were fuel for confidence going forward. To say I was thrilled was a major understatement.

The buzzer startled me; someone was downstairs. *What the …?* I had accounted for everyone I knew who could drop in – some of my local friends didn't know I was home, and the few who did were meeting me for coffee tomorrow afternoon in the village. I bolted to the camera buzzer; Edgar was standing there. I pressed the button.

'Hey you, come up.'

He must have sprinted the stairs, he was there in seconds.

Was he checking up on me? Making sure I didn't have time to hurry anyone into the cupboard or out the window? I opened the door and he looked at me, his eyebrows raised.

'Is this how you dress when you are home alone?' he asked, with a smile.

'Every time.'

'I am dropping in unannounced more often,' he said, with appreciation.

'Where's Isabella?' I asked, looking behind him

'Not back there,' he joked and came inside. I closed the door behind him and he pulled me to him.

'This looks very sexy, I like the minimalist look.' He held me close and he felt so very good.

'I missed you,' he said in a rare show of vulnerability for Edgar.

'I missed you,' I told him. And I did. If I was being honest, a glass of wine had me melancholy and I kept thinking of Edgar not far away and that he loved me enough to tell his sister he would marry me. My mother would call that being in love with love, but it did soften my heart and make me feel secure.

He put his hands under my butt and picked me up with a glance to the bedroom down the hall. Edgar had only been here a few times, we normally stayed at Thrushcross Grange where he can work in his home office, but he remembered the way.

'You can pour me one of those later,' he said, nodding to my wine glass on the table, as we disappeared down the hall.

He placed me down on the bed and he stripped off. That's when the speed stopped; we made slow, satisfying love. It was a release and relief for both of us. After all, at face value things were good in our world… his film was a success, I had done my part, and we were strong even if his sister and my ex weren't.

Later, sated and naked, we turned side on and lay looking at each other. He was a beautiful man. Outside the wind was rising in tone, occasionally it rattled my windows and I felt right at home. He touched my face, pushing a strand of my hair back and then he took my hand, kissed and held it.

'I'm glad you came over,' I whispered.

'So am I.'

'Is Isabella okay?' I didn't care if she was or not, but it was his sister after all and I thought I should make an effort.

'She will be. I got her to drive me here and told her to seek out a few of her local friends – you know she loves a night out. Let her be a hit at the local pub with her gal pals. So … you are stuck with me here for the rest of the night.'

'Excellent,' I said.

It was quiet – as quiet as my tempest-prone home could be. We lay comfortable in the silence studying each other. It was one of the first times I felt complete with Edgar. Maybe because I was home in my safe world and not in his environment. Oddly, I felt like he was feeling the same – we were in our territory, not in the bustle of London. We had no demands on us, no immediate deadlines. For this moment, now, it was just about us and it was so powerful.

'Catherine Earnshaw …' he said my name.

'Edgar Linton,' I said his and smiled teasingly.

'Will you do me the honour of being my wife?'

Chapter 30 – The happiest girl

I am engaged.

Meet my fiancé, Edgar Linton … *ha* … how grown-up that sounded. Being engaged was the most amazing feeling – it was hard to describe. It was like this excitement of knowing you had someone to travel your life with, and someone who loved you so much that they wanted to commit to you in a serious way. And just thinking of all the plans you would make and things you would do together now that you were committed to sharing your future was so exciting. I was just floating.

But Edgar put me in an impossible situation. I knew everyone was going to ask me how he proposed and I would have to say that he did the deed when we were naked in bed, after sex. Really! I thought we should orchestrate a much better story … he was a director after all. We could come up with some brilliant scenes. But in all honesty, it was perfect at that moment.

Speaking of dilemmas, I wanted to tell Heath before he heard about it elsewhere; it was one of the first thoughts that crossed my mind when I came down off my high. But I was still angry and hurt that I heard about his engagement from Isabella blurting it out. No, it runs deeper than that. I know I started this, that I wanted some space to be sure about what I wanted. Yes, I kissed Edgar, but never, ever, did I want to shun Heath forever and the last thing in the world I wanted was a future without him. To get engaged to Isabella killed something inside me. It said that he wasn't waiting for me, that he didn't care, that if I wanted to find myself I could do so without him. So fuck him, he could hear about Edgar and my engagement the same way I heard about his – through Isabella.

Edgar didn't want to walk to the village café because he had calls to return and wanted to get home quicker after breakfast, so we drove down in his car and I was going to walk back to my future home, Thrushcross Grange, after breakfast. I needed the walks on the moors, they restored my soul. It was a warm and sunny morning, but that might not last; the weather could turn quickly on the moors. We picked a café which wasn't Heath and my favourite and selected a hidden away table where we could have some privacy. After ordering, Edgar reached across the table and took my hand.

'We have some big decisions to make,' he said, looking at me seriously.

I sipped my orange juice and nodded. 'I know, but I'll work the dress out, promise.'

He chuckled and rolled his eyes.

'Lighten up, fiancé,' I teased him. 'What big decisions?'

'Well, where shall we go to get you a ring?' he asked. 'I was going to pick one out and present it but I thought it would be more fun to do it together.'

'Absolutely,' I said, my eyes lit with excitement. 'I think we should get it at *Dream Come True*.'

He stopped mid-sip of his juice and looked at me. 'Really, from Mr Hurley in the village? You don't want to go to Tiffany's or somewhere with maybe a little wider range?' he asked, being most diplomatic.

'No.'

He shrugged. 'Okay. Mum used to get some gifts at *Dream Come True* occasionally.'

I was surprised. I thought his mother would go to the city for jewellery buying.

I explained. 'It's our village and he knows us, and he has been running that family jewellery store since we were kids. Besides I stay in touch with Camilla.'

'Is that the eldest daughter?' Edgar asked.

I shook my head. 'No, Camilla's one of the twins; they were in my class. It could be good publicity for them too if they wanted to promote it.'

He smiled. 'I love that you would do that. We could go after breakfast if they are open.'

'Really? How exciting,' I gushed like a kid and he laughed again. 'Next big decision?' I asked.

'Do we get our agents to officially announce it or shall we? I have to tell Isabella first or she'll explode,' he said.

'I think we should tell whoever we need to first, like Isabella and Nelly. We could call them straight after breakfast and swear them to secrecy for a few hours. Then, we could do a post online with the ring … or if we have to have one made, a pic inside the jewellery store and we announce it then. What do you think?'

He nodded. 'Brilliant.'

Our breakfasts arrived and we thanked the waiter who looked about sixteen and a little star-struck. He asked if we would autograph the serviette for him, which we did, and then ordered two coffees from him before he left us.

Edgar started on his bacon and eggs while I moved my food around on my plate to divide it between what I would eat and what I wouldn't. Two poached eggs were one too many and I didn't need the huge wedges of toast that came with the meal. Edgar looked on hungrily, intending to finish mine too.

'The wedding?' I asked, 'is that another decision?'

He nodded. 'But no pressure, we don't have to rush into it. Girls like a big affair don't they, so we can do that if you like?'

'You'd prefer a more intimate gathering?' I asked. It was so much fun thinking of all that was to come.

'Definitely, but we're only going to do it once so I'm easily swayed.' He looked at me so sincerely. 'I want what you want, so it is a day you will never forget.'

It made me love him even more. But I had lost Mum and Dad, and now Heath too, so my 'family' were a smattering of school friends, cousins who didn't live anywhere nearby, Nelly and Lockwood. If we had a big wedding most of the guests wouldn't be special to me.

'I'd rather something intimate, just immediate family and friends.' I could see that made him happy. I saw our coffees coming; the same waiter, we thanked him again and I paused to sip and inhale the caffeine.

'Depending on your next role and my next film, we'll have to schedule the wedding carefully,' he continued. 'The sooner the better … but enough time for you to get your dress sorted out.'

I nodded. 'Okay, that works for me.' I smiled with anticipation. So exciting.

'And then we have to decide what to do with Wuthering Heights,' he said.

I snapped to look at him. 'What do you mean?'

'Well we're both going to have a London base and when we come home, we'll stay at Thrushcross Grange, so do you need to keep Wuthering Heights?' he asked, taking another large bite of his egg and toast. He sat back and mumbled, 'Sell your half to Heath.'

I stared at him.

He frowned a little seeing my reaction and swallowed before speaking. 'Well, you don't have to decide right now.'

'No,' I said, 'I can never sell Wuthering Heights. It's part of me.'

'It's crazy to have it sitting there empty. I suppose we could rent it out.'

I shook my head. 'It's mine to worry about. I need it.'

'Why?' he asked, his eyes narrowing.

'Because it is all I have left of Mum and Dad, and my family.'

He sat back and studied me. 'Heath, you mean?'

'My two brothers, Hindley and Heath.'

There was a cooling between us. I lost my appetite and put my cutlery down, returning to my coffee. Edgar softened and reached for my hand.

'We've got our whole life ahead of us to sort out those things.'

He was right. I took a deep breath, nodded and gave him a weak smile.

Leave it for now.

'The only thing we need to do today is look at engagement rings,' he continued.

'I hope your credit will be good there,' I teased. 'I'm planning on something noticeably large.'

He laughed. 'Got a credit card on you just in case?'

I gave him a smirk and everything was back to normal between us.

Nothing on this earth will make me part with Wuthering Heights.

Chapter 31 – The offer

'You're not going to believe this,' Lockwood said, lowering his voice as we knocked back some drinks at our favourite pub. It was just the three of us sans partners; Edgar was away casting a film.

'Believe what?' Nelly said, between bites of our shared ploughman's lunch.

'I can't get over how enormous that rock is,' Lockwood said distracted, taking my hand in his and studying my engagement ring. 'That's probably the entire profit made on your film, *Between Night and Day*!'

'*Our* film!' Nelly teased him.

'It was our film,' I agreed and reclaimed my hand. 'I picked a humbler ring but Edgar insisted I have this one. I love it, I really wanted a square diamond.'

Nelly took my hand. 'I love a princess cut. Gorgeous. That must be three carats at least,' she said.

I took my hand back again and shrugged. 'How do you even know that stuff?'

'Because I have my ring designed in my head, I've just got to find someone to propose and then buy it for me.'

'Anyway, be quiet you two I've got news, it's about Isabella,' Lockwood said, holding the floor. He had the knack of delivering news like it was a soap opera.

I looked around to make sure no one could hear us; we were in the outdoor area but you can't be too careful.

Lockwood lowered his voice. 'Anyway, my friend said that when Isabella got Edgar's news that you two got engaged, she told Heath that she wanted to be married first, it was only fair since they got engaged first, and if he didn't set a date, she was walking down that catwalk instead of the aisle and walking off.'

'Wow, great line,' I said, and laughed. 'I've never given Heath an ultimatum. How'd that go down?'

Lockwood hesitated as though deciding whether to tell me or not. 'Well from what I hear there was a negotiation. He supposedly told her that since he was going to be away for a few weeks on the film's publicity tour, they should go home to the moors for a weekend soon and discuss dates. That seemed to work, I hear.'

Ah, stick a knife in my heart. Why do I ask when I really don't want to know?

'Apparently, the ultimatum went well then,' Nelly said, looking as surprised as I was.

I rolled my eyes. 'I guess it will be all over her Instagram feed when they go there, so we'll know all about their romp around her family estate! Let's change the subject,' I said.

Nelly squeezed my arm. 'I know you still love him.'

'He's my family. Our souls are made of the same thing, but Edgar's soul is as different as—' I struggled for a comparison.

'A moonbeam from lightning?' Nelly suggested.

'Yes, exactly, thank you, Nelly, how poetic of you. I knew you would get it.' I placed my hand over hers.

Lockwood sighed. 'Oh, Cathy, he's miserable without you.'

I laughed again, surprised. 'Ha, I doubt it. I wish,' I said, selfishly. 'Anyway, how do you know that?'

He touched his nose as though he had insider information.

Nelly hit him on the arm. 'Don't tell her that. She's just got engaged. Cathy doesn't need to feel guilty about Heath or any guy.'

'I don't think I will ever be able to lose him from my heart,' I said. I had got a bit intense but a glass of wine on a shared ploughman's lunch will do that to you. 'Please don't repeat that to anyone,' I said, alarmed.

They both shook their heads, and then we changed the subject before I became more maudlin.

*****

Nelly and I went to see our agent, J&J or Jaz and James; it was usually just Jaz though as James looked after the models and Jaz looked after the actors. It felt so cool to go into their offices. Our appointments were one after the other, but I didn't mind if we sat in together, neither did Nelly, and Jaz agreed that was just fine.

After Jaz's assistant had taken our orders for a latte, bless her, we sat around Jaz's boardroom table. She amazed me – she was a former catwalk model and commercial actor, and she still did some modelling when 'talent' over forty years of age was required. She was tall, very glamorous and very kind … she knew and got the industry and all of its ups and downs.

'We need to be very careful now, Cathy,' she said to me. 'Naturally, it is your choice and I'll present you with all offers, but you've just done a role that is getting critical acclaim, and your Romcom will come out not long after. So, your next move should cement how you want to be seen and what roles you want to be considered for going forward if that makes sense?'

I nodded. 'Thanks, Jaz, it makes a lot of sense.'

'God, those two films were so different,' Nelly agreed.

'Drama, romance and comedy, and let's not forget the *Wylde* girl commercial shoot coming soon,' I said. 'What do you think I should be doing Jaz?'

She smiled. 'My answer is self-serving … keep working!'

I laughed. 'Well, I'd like to do that.'

She pushed an envelope towards me. 'There's a couple of roles that would suit you. Have a read of the scripts and let me know if you would like to audition.' She picked up a sheet of paper from her in-tray. 'Speaking of the *Wylde* girl campaign, I finally got the contract. The advertising agency has kicked into gear and wants to do the shoot as soon as possible before you begin your next film project ideally. I reaffirmed to them that naturally with your high profile engagement you were more recognisable now, so the rate had gone up again, and they accepted it.'

She showed me the contract and I nearly fell off my chair.

'Wow, that's a lot of perfume sales to make that back,' I said, wide-eyed.

Jaz grinned. 'That's all about branding and exposure. Simon Nolan, the agency director, said he saw your interview in *Life and Love* last month and how you talked about the moors and being home. The good news—I think—is that they want to shoot it there,' she said, watching for my reaction.

'That would be brilliant,' I said.

She took the contract back from me and flicked through the pages, stopping on the page with the proposed shoot dates.

'There's more,' she continued. 'They would like to shoot it the following weekend.'

'Wow, that soon,' I said, and shrugged. 'Well, I'm available if they are, why not? Who are they thinking of casting as *Wylde* girl's bad boy? A different guy from last time?'

'*Wylde* girl the slut,' Nelly joked, and we both laughed.

Jaz hesitated and cleared her throat. Uh oh, I had a gut feeling this was not going to be good news. Of all the actors, in all the world …

'They'd like to cast Heath Earnshaw,' she said.

There it was. I laughed, and then I read her face. 'Oh, you're serious.'

Nelly's eyes were as wide as mine. 'I could chaperone.'

I laughed again, but it had a hysterical edge to it.

'Would Edgar be okay with that?' Nelly asked.

I looked from Jaz to Nelly. 'I don't know, but Isabella won't be.' I turned back to Jaz. Then it occurred to me, was this the weekend that Heath was going to go home for a supposed romantic weekend with Isabella? Did he already know then that he was going home to shoot the commercial before he began his publicity tour? Had he already signed on the contract line? Surely he wouldn't consider doing a commercial.

I asked Jaz: 'Can I say no to that and request another actor?'

'Of course, you can ask for whatever you like and then they'll come back with their counteroffer or not. But that rate they have offered you is on the condition he is in the commercial with you. You'll see the clause on page four.'

'I'm happy to earn less,' I said.

Jaz nodded, disappointed. It affected her payment too.

She continued. 'Well, if you decide to do the commercial with Heath you can request to see the script first, and put in clauses like no kissing or intimacy. Why don't you think about it first, and have a chat with Edgar? Heath hasn't signed on yet either but he has the contract and is free on those dates – it's just before his publicity tour I believe and he can get away. After that, he's committed for three months.'

'Ah, so that's why the agency is rushing – his next season on stage including weekend performances won't allow him to do it.' I nodded, understanding now.

'Sleep on it,' Jaz said. 'Then if you do want to go ahead, come back to me and we'll work through your terms and conditions and see if the agency finds them acceptable. But don't delay too long, the production house needs to book a crew.'

'Okay, thanks Jaz,' I said, not wanting to appear ungrateful. 'Heath will probably think it is beneath him to do a fragrance commercial anyway,' I said, 'although if he is getting paid similar, that would allow him to stay on the stage for a while.'

Jaz nodded. 'Most of the big names do fragrance commercials, there's a prestige to it. I'm not Heath's agent so I don't know what their offer is but given his profile, the film buzz about his soon-to-be-released film, and Isabella Linton's promotion of him, I suspect it would be similar.'

Jaz slipped the contract into an envelope and passed it across the table to me. Then she pulled out a folder and began on projects and offers for Nelly.

I tuned out. Heath and I in a commercial together. It would only be a couple of days of filming. Could we do it without killing each other?

*****

Edgar laughed with a sinister edge. 'You've got to be kidding! Of course Heath will sign up for the commercial, it was probably his idea. Isabella will have a fit.'

I sat on the edge of Edgar's desk in his London apartment and told him about my meeting with my agent, Jaz. He looked very handsome in his casual wear ... Edgar always looked like he had just stepped out of a commercial – he does tailored well.

Then I realised if Heath turned down the commercial, how hurtful that would be. God, it was a no-win situation.

What if they cast someone else as the *Wylde* girl and still made the commercial with Heath?

What if they cast Isabella?

She'd have Heath and my commercial. Now my insecurities were showing. I'm so sick of it all, the mess, the tangle, the connections. Maybe I should just walk away from it and let them fill my shoes. Make sure I put it out there that I'm saying goodbye to the *Wylde* girl, but that would be crazy reckless given the amount they were willing to pay. I stared out the windows of Edgar's home office as the thoughts ran through my head and he ran through the contract.

Edgar got to the last page. 'Holy crap, is that what they are offering? They must expect the tension between the two of you to sell some serious perfume,' he said.

'That's what I said to Jaz, more or less,' I agreed.

He put the contract down, moved to put his legs around me as he sat in his chair, and shook his head. 'You'd be an idiot to turn this down … it's only a two-day shoot, can you get through it?'

Clearly, money came before Edgar's insecurities and jealousy; I was just a little pissed off but a bit impressed too that he was so focused and secure. I secretly and stupidly hoped he'd be outraged and wouldn't want me to take the job. So much for that.

'So, are you saying that I should do it?' I asked.

He tightened his grip on my legs.

'It's easy money, isn't it? How do you feel about it?' he asked.

I took a deep breath. 'I could do without the tension, but if it is similar to the last time, we shot the campaign, we'll be constantly surrounded by the crew—make-up, dresser, cameraman, lighting, and the director—so we'll have little time alone. I could manage that.'

'Where will you stay?'

'At Wuthering— ah, at Thrushcross Grange.'

He smiled. 'Good, because I imagine he'll be staying at Wuthering Heights. I guess it comes down to whether you want to do another one of their commercials for them?'

I smiled at the thought. 'Having been on the journey since day one, I like being the *Wylde* girl.'

He grinned. 'I like it too,' and then he began to undress me in his office. It seemed like my relationship of late with Edgar was about eighty per cent sex. I quickly glanced to the windows where the blinds were open and he leant over, pressed a button and the shades went down. He continued his good work.

Chapter 32 – Wylde girl again

Two weeks later … the commercial shoot

We were lucky; the moors were being kind to us. It was cool, the light was soft, the vista was green and the wind was yet to reach its full force – the benefit of starting early; 7am early! The sun was just rising when I came in for hair and make-up, so we had a good long day to shoot.

I hadn't spoken to Heath about the commercial and he hadn't contacted me, but we both signed up for it and showed up as expected at the time on our call sheet. My start was earlier as I had hair and make-up; Heath would take less work. Edgar stayed in London; he was still working with Tamara on casting another film and Isabella informed me via Edgar that she and Heath would be staying at Thrushcross Grange the weekend prior and during the shoot. That was just perfect as far I was concerned. I much preferred to stay at my place, Wuthering Heights – I felt safer and at home, even if I was staying there by myself. Edgar didn't object; he just wanted me to stay wherever Heath wasn't staying.

I arrived the night before ready for work in the morning. I suspected Isabella would show up sometime during the shoot … although 7am might be too early even for the insecure! I was in the hair and make-up marquee looking particularly glamourous with hair rollers in and a huge bib around my collar when Heath entered. My breath hitched. I knew everyone would be watching us and expecting a reaction.

'Morning everyone,' he said, in his lovely baritone voice. He smiled my way. 'Looking particularly lovely this morning as always, Catherine,' he said, winked, and made everyone laugh including me. It was a good way to start. I could be a good sport and take a ribbing, and then I turned my eyes back to the mirror and focused on the work being done on me.

I had read and approved the script – there were a lot of separate scenes with us both staring off into space, a scene where we encounter each other like prey and I guess you could interpret the last scene of the commercial as Heath conquering *Wylde* girl as she gets on the back of his motorbike and they leave the moors behind. No kissing. Sure, let's just do this.

It took all my self-control not to make eye contact with him as his make-up was being done while my hair set. I could feel him watching me, but not once did I weaken. *Hard work.* He was finished in no time, declared himself a natural beauty and got another round of laughs. He left to start shooting his solo parts pretty much straight away. An hour later when I was ready, I was sent with a cameraman and director to do the same. The wind had got up now and the sun dipped between clouds now and then. The mood added to the shoot. They were amazing shots. I stood on the edge of a small waterfall where the sound of the water falling reminded me of bells. I had to lift my dress and wade with just my feet in the water … it was freezing but the water was so clean and clear. In the next shot, the wind whipped around me as I walked along a small stone wall in the most amazing full-on silver ballgown, my auburn hair floating around my head like a witch.

I was directed to look this way and that way, to look determined, sad, relaxed, one with nature … I think I just looked constipated but let's not go there. It was a long day posing but I was on my moors and very happy to be. During the day I changed three times – from a fitted leather pantsuit to two huge ball gowns; it was good fun wearing those amazing, expensive outfits.

Sunday was done – for our first day, we did all our solo shots. Tomorrow, we were scheduled to do our joint shots. The director said we did well and at 4.30pm he called it a day. I had help removing the dress but I left the make-up on … who wouldn't when you've had professional make-up done?

We all went for a drink in the village at one of the local pubs. I was amazed Heath came for drinks, he usually hated that social element but he got over it and came along; he knew a couple of the local guys in the pub and invited them to join us. I was keen for him to leave first and he did after Isabella rang him – I don't know why she didn't come to the pub; she loved an audience and being admired. I don't know if she came to his shoot today because I hadn't seen much of him all day except occasionally from a distance. Anyway, after an hour of socialising, he excused himself and I stayed longer so it didn't look like I was sneaking out to catch up with him – the things we do.

I remained another 20 minutes or so and then rose to say my goodbyes. I wanted to walk home to Wuthering Heights while there was still about forty-five minutes of light left. The moors would be beautiful in the dusk light and I could go through the day in my head and release it all on my walk. A couple of the crew also got up to return to their accommodation. Will, our director, told us that once he had found somewhere to go for a group dinner, he would text us if we wanted to join in – plan on a 7.30pm meet. I thanked everyone and vowed to see them at dinner or in the morning bright and early.

I was right; the smell of the earth and green was calming and the dusk was crisp with soft light. I felt exhausted … the strain of being in my old territory with Heath so nearby, being on guard with him. I increased my pace for the exercise. I was wearing jeans and a pullover and had a small backpack on, so I broke into a jog now and then. I was home in good time and ran up the stairs to my townhome at Wuthering Heights.

Heath was sitting on the top stair, waiting for me.

I came to a sudden halt. I couldn't breathe, I couldn't move.

'Hi Cathy,' he said like it was the most natural thing in the world for us to run into each other.

'Heath!' His presence unsettled me. I felt my heartbeat racing.

I didn't want to invite him in but I didn't have to, technically it was our place. He rose, moved aside and took a deep breath.

'Did you forget something?' I asked, fishing around in my backpack for my keys.

'No, I have my key. I was waiting for you,' he said, softly. 'I didn't want to wait inside in case I startled you, or you didn't come home and stayed on drinking. I thought I'd give you forty minutes or so before I headed off.'

I moved past him and unlocked the door. I was conscious of him beside me, the energy coming off him. He looked so brooding and commanding and I couldn't believe the pull I felt toward him. The entranceway wasn't big enough for both of us and I blocked the doorway. I turned to face him.

'Cathy, I live here too, I don't need to be invited in,' he said.

'Oh, that's right, this is your family home too, from when we were family,' I said, smartly. I hated myself sometimes. I stood aside and we both entered, staying put not far inside the doorway.

He grabbed my hand. 'Cathy, don't do this.'

'Do what?' I asked, conscious of his skin on mine.

'Don't end us,' he said the words slowly.

I looked at his hand holding mine, it seemed such a foreign thing now. Isabella's words to Edgar returned to haunt me: *"When we're together, he is so ardent ... he does it as if he wants me – slow, attentive, passionate."*

I tried to pull my hand away but he wouldn't release me. I glared at him. His eyes were dark and deep and he was here, the Heath I've always known. I tried to find my voice but I was reeling. I succeeded in snatching my hand away from him; he had no right to touch me anymore.

'I don't think this is a good idea … you coming in, us both being here. Don't you need to get back to Isabella?' I asked.

'Yes. I have to talk with you first. Just a few minutes … for a lifetime of memories.'

His words brought tears to my eyes. I blinked them back and straightened.

'Don't dream it's over, Cathy,' he said in a low whisper. I stepped away, closing the door completely and he followed me into the living area. I put my backpack down on the couch and turned to face him.

'Don't marry him,' he said. 'Don't marry, Edgar.'

'Heath,' I said his name in a rush. 'You're marrying Isabella.'

I leant against the back of the couch. He remained nearer to the door. His phone rang, and he grabbed it and looked at the screen. He swore under his breath, held his hand up to me imploring for one minute and quickly answered.

'I'm on my way. I'll be there in about twenty minutes.' He listened for a few moments and then said goodbye and hung up.

'It's us, Cathy, and they are the Lintons. What are we doing?'

I couldn't help but smile, I guess our situation was a bit 'out there' considering what we used to think about the strange, pale kids across the moors.

'Bit late now isn't it?' I asked. 'This ship has sailed … your ship has sailed.'

'Not for us, it's never too late. We're family, Cathy.'

'I've lost my family,' I said. 'I lost Mum and Dad, Hindley, and you – you who were my rock. Now, Edgar is my family and my future.' I knew those words would cut him and I delivered them with a cruelty that I later regretted when I thought back on my words.

His eyes narrowed as my weapons hit him – anger, jealousy, despair. 'I heard what you said to Lockwood, that you wondered what else was out there and if I was good enough for—'

'—I never said that,' I cut him off. 'I never said you weren't good enough, you misheard.'

'You may as well have. You wanted to get away from me and see who else might be out there … see if you could do better. So I gave you that chance,' he snapped back at me. His voice hitched, but he refused to give in to real emotion, he wouldn't let me see him be that vulnerable.

We waited in silence for a few moments. Then I cut to the chase of the wound that most cut me. 'Why would you get engaged to her?' I asked. It was my fixation; it had changed everything.

'I did it for us, for you so you could see how you feel … bring it to a head. You could confront your feelings and—'

'Really, you did it for us?' I stepped forward and around him, reaching for the door handle. 'Do you know what you did to me when you did that? You killed something inside of me Heath because up until then, you were the only person in the world who knew me, and I guess could really hurt me,' I said, my eyes blazing. 'I thought you would support my need to spread my wings, but no, you just clipped them.'

Heath stood taking the blows, his eyes dark and troubled, his jaw locked.

I continued. 'Next time you're thinking of doing something for me, please don't bother.'

I was so close to him as I opened the door for him to make his exit that he grabbed me and for just a moment pulled me closer. I sobbed against his chest and then I realised I couldn't do this; I knew where it would lead. I shoved him away with such unexpected force that I fell back a step. He grabbed and righted me.

'Get away from me Heath,' I cried. 'Go home to her. We're not Heath and Cathy anymore, it's now Heath and his model, Isabella, such a cool couple … we're nothing. Just leave.' As if I had commanded the weather, the house raged with me, windows and door frames rattled and the wind roared outside.

'Just go, please,' I said, 'please Heath.'

'You're really going to do this to us, Cathy?' he asked. 'Marry that stuck-up—'

'—You're engaged to his sister!' I said, cutting him off.

'I would drop her in a heartbeat to have one more day with you,' he said.

I couldn't believe the words coming out of his mouth. I wanted him to say that to me months ago before I accepted Edgar's proposal. Did he accept this commercial contract just to be sure to see me, just so we could have *this* conversation?

I took a deep breath and straightened. It was all too late.

'Edgar's amazing. Talented, gorgeous, sincere…' I couldn't stop. 'And we're going to be married,' I said in a slow and controlled voice. 'Go home to your fiancée.'

He glared at me and then turned, and took to the stairs. I stood frozen, listening until I could no longer hear his footsteps.

My past was walking away from me. I could have stopped him, but I didn't and hoped one day I wouldn't regret it.

Chapter 33 – Last day on the moors

I was not looking forward to my shoot with Heath today despite the glorious October weather and the chance to be on *my* moors. Last night after Heath left, I decided to meet everyone for dinner and get out of my head for a while. I rang Edgar before I left and told him that Heath and I had spoken after the shoot, but we had been shooting separately all day; he didn't seem too fazed but it was hard to tell with Edgar. He had his own grudge against Heath and I don't know how much jealousy weighed in on it.

I also don't know what Heath and Isabella did last night and I don't care, I'm just glad they didn't join our group dinner. I happily stayed in my territory and they stayed in the mansion. When Edgar rang later that night after dinner—probably to check I was home alone—I made sure he knew I was as I spoke face-to-face with him from my lounge room couch.

'Are you wearing that lilac underwear and drinking wine again?' he asked.

'As a matter of fact, I'm wearing my scarlet underwear

and drinking diet cola,' I teased and moved the camera so he could see.

'I'm getting a helicopter and I'll be right there,' he said, and I laughed. Sometimes, it was so easy with Edgar.

'Or we could just ... you know, do it by screen,' I suggested.

Edgar wasn't the most adventurous lover despite hinting that he had a punishment room, which I never discovered, so I suspect it never existed.

'Tempted but I'd rather pine and have you in the flesh on Tuesday,' he sighed.

'It's a date,' I told him. I signed off after a few more minutes and then talked with Nelly and a few friends online. It was lights out at 11pm in my Wuthering Heights pad. I couldn't get away with looking like a crack whore tomorrow; *Wylde* girl was all about glowing skin, bright eyes and a passion for life!

*****

I was on location again early to get my hair and make-up done. At least I could just sit there waking up but the poor make-up artist and hairdresser had to be switched on! Heath wandered in and greeted us all. His greeting to me was decidedly frosty compared to the day before and we all read the situation. *Great.* The marquee didn't feel big enough for both of us; I was so relieved when he was done and went outside to talk with the director.

Once I was ready, I was dressed in the same silver ballgown with the long train that I wore yesterday. The script required Heath to 'collect' me from my wanders on the moors. I was to join him on the back of his motorbike—lucky it wasn't a fitted dress—and we'd tear off with the storm chasing us across the moors and my dress train billowing behind. It was a lovely day so I suspect they were going to add the storm later.

We did the shots yesterday with Heath looking for me on the moors, riding his bike around in his leathers, looking sexy. Today he finds me, the viewer sees him arriving, then me on the back of the bike, clutching him around the waist, looking at the camera sexily, while he looks straight ahead with a determined and satisfied look and off we go. Sure, happens all the time with passionate couples I imagine.

He sat astride the bike and looked too gorgeous for his own good. The production team put me on the bike, draped the dress appropriately, and placed the train so it would billow as he rode and stepped back. I had to wrap my arms around his waist and do the look.

Our director, Will, stood back and looked at the preview.

'Looks good,' he said. 'Okay Heath, you're going to take off, not fast enough to lose Cathy off the back, drive forward to the turn in the road while we trail you with the camera, then stop and we'll see how that looks.'

'Gotcha,' he said.

Will continued. 'Cathy, you're going to give the camera a look as if you've just landed Heath and can't wait to bed him.'

Every set of eyes pivoted to me, watching for my reaction. Well watch all you like; nothing to see here, no show, move along.

'Got it,' I responded, and wrapped my arms around Heath's leather-clad body. He braced as I did it, conscious of my touch and immediate proximity. He muttered something that I couldn't quite catch but it sounded like, 'for fuck's sake!'

It was agony.

A camera was set up on a car along the side of the road and another camera was fixed to a drone to follow Heath and get the shot.

'Rolling, and in your own time,' Will called.

Heath started the bike and took off, faster than I expected. I yelped and grabbed him tighter.

'Sorry,' I heard him say, his voice carried behind on the wind to me. 'I didn't mean to frighten you.'

This was the old Heath, protective. I squeezed him to let him know I was okay and still hanging on. I focused on what I was supposed to do and we reached the end of the track, Heath slowed the bike down and stopped. A couple of assistants pulled my train in, handing it to me. Heath spun the bike around and we slowly returned to the starting place for another shoot.

'Try and head off a little slower thanks, Heath,' Will joked, and Heath grinned at him.

'Yeah, sorry about that. She's not meant to be tamed … the bike,' he added quickly, seeing the looks he got.

We did the shot another six times until Will was satisfied. Seven times all up with my arms wrapped around Heath.

Agony.

Next shot we were on top of the hill that I stood on yesterday. I changed to another billowing gown and met the crew and Heath on the plateau. I saw Heath appraise me as I walked toward him. With my hair wild in the wind and the dress I was wearing making me look so feminine and ethereal, I think it pained him. He looked away.

For this shot, Heath had to put his hands around my waist and pull me to him; I was to place my hands on his chest, resisting slightly. I could feel his heart pounding, I could feel the heat radiating off him. Neither of us looked at each other until we had to. There was no kiss, that was the scene and nothing more, and if tension and heat could kill, I would have melted.

After Will called cut for the final take on that scene, I almost fell back in my haste to move away from Heath and to breathe again. I'm sure it was obvious to everyone. Heath ran his hand over his face and turned away.

'Brilliant,' Will called, then expanded his comment, 'Great job, everyone. Let's prepare for the next scene'. I imagine he elaborated by including everyone in his praise so it didn't look like he was capitalising on our distress.

I breathed out and then sat in the fold-up chair that was pulled out and set up for me. My hair and make-up were retouched. In this scene, Heath had to look across the moors and I had to cling to him from behind like I was a needy bitch, and he ruled the world. *Whatever.* Again, I had the skirt billowing, the train flying, my hair flowing, so dramatic.

'Okay, places everyone,' Will called once I was touched up.

I stood behind Heath as he stood arms folded, looking over his domain, and I didn't touch him until Will called 'Ready'.

I pressed against his back; my arms wrapped around him. For just a moment I felt him weaken, his frame shuddered just a little.

'For the love of God,' he muttered, then righted himself and stood stiff as a board as he did his best to forget that I was clinging to him in our special place. We waited while they righted the shot, the lighting, the wind direction … everything they could do to delay the shot, or so it felt.

We weren't miked up and no one was immediately near us when Heath said: 'Are we truly over, Cathy? Is there no hope for us? Just tell me yes or no and I'll get out of your life forever.'

I pressed my forehead against his back and breathed too quickly. I recovered myself to answer. 'You could have asked me that at home last night and saved us both the anguish today,' I said. 'We were over the moment you got engaged to Isabella.'

'Not the moment you told me you wanted out or kissed Edgar?' he hissed, through clenched teeth. He kept his voice low so the conversation was only heard by the two of us.

I made a scoffing sound. 'You know Heath, you call Edgar stuck-up but you stand here so full of entitlement as if you have some rights over me, as if you own me.'

We stopped talking as our lighting guy came over and moved the flecky board so that the lighting was a little more focused on Heath. He moved away and Heath continued.

'Cathy, I am such an idiot. I had this track playing in my head of how I'd return to you, what a reunion it would be and how you would want me after your stint in London,' he said. 'I laugh now at the thought of what an idiot I was.'

His words caused a lump in my throat.

Will interrupted our discussion. 'Okay, last shot for the day everyone, let's try and do it in three takes or less,' he said, challenging us. 'Heath, you're looking out over the moors. Cathy, you are wrapped around Heath like you've just scored him and plan to dominate.'

We both nodded and gave cheerless smiles. Will read our looks and cut short the rest of his banter, stepping backwards and looking at the shot on his monitor for one last time.

Clearly all was not well with his stars on their high perch in the moors.

Let's just get this over with.

I was waiting for Will to call action when Heath said in a low rumble: 'Come back to me, Cathy. I love you more in one day than he could love you in his whole lifetime, and you know it.'

His soft words with their sharp edge hit me hard. I wasn't prepared for this, I thought he had said all he had to say last night.

I released my hold on him and stumbled backwards.

'Don't, please,' I hissed. 'You're engaged. We were family once Heath and not even blood. Now, we are nothing.'

He turned to look at me, stepping out of position. 'Oh, we are family, Cathy. We might not be blood, but we're legally family and you can't divorce siblings. Consider us family for life,' he said, glaring at me with passion.

I stood back from him to have a minute to myself.

'Wait up everyone,' Will said. He came over to me. 'Are you okay, Cathy? Do you need a few minutes?'

I shook my head. 'Sorry Will, just …' my voice trailed as I tried to come up with an excuse, as I blinked back tears.

'Cathy thought she was going to sneeze,' Heath plucked out of nowhere.

I nodded and pinched my nose. 'Sorry Will, I'm okay now, it's passed,' I said, blinking, as though that was the reason for my watering eyes.

'No problem,' Will said. He backed away and returned to his post.

'Thanks,' I mumbled to Heath, even though he started the whole discussion.

Will called out: 'Okay everyone, back in places. Make-up, a quick check of Cathy please.'

I moved back into position, rapidly blinked to clear my eyes, and let them dab some powder on my pinched nose.

'Hold your positions, we're ready now,' Will called, and Heath turned back to stare at the moors. His pose was now perfect given the sting of his words. He looked angry, his jaw was locked, his posture ramrod. He looked like he would have it all if it was the last thing he did on this earth.

Will must have thought so too. He must be rubbing his hands with glee hoping the tension emanating from us would translate on screen.

'Action,' Will called, and I held Heath with the fierce determination that for this last day, on this shoot, on *our* moors, he was mine and never, ever again would I hold him.

*****

RUMOUR FILE: Meltdown on the moors

Rumour has it that the crew working on the new *Wylde* fragrance campaign felt the heat on the moors and it had nothing to do with the weather.

The tension emanating from its leads, *Wylde* girl Catherine Earnshaw, and man of the moment, Heath Earnshaw, was a well-calculated gamble by advertising agency, Nolan & Associates.

Ironically both Earnshaws are engaged to the successful Linton siblings – model Isabella and her brother, director Edgar. Must be something in the water on those moors, they all originated from the area.

Rumour has it that there was much glaring, staring and aloofness between Catherine and Heath but when the scenes demanded contact, the steam was rising. This is one campaign that is going to be very, very interesting.

Add to this that Catherine is tipped to be nominated for a best-supporting actress in the pending BAFTA list and Heath Earnshaw's performance in *The Meaning of Nothing* is tipped to see him get a nod in the best actor category. Edgar Linton should also be up for a director gong.

We might just see the four of them together sooner rather than later – at the award ceremony.

Now that would be hot!

Part 4

Chapter 34 – Reviews and awards

He was everywhere I turned – Heath. With his co-star, Trinity Bailey, or with director Nadim Ramirez promoting their film, *The Meaning of Nothing*. Got to hand it to whoever did their publicity, it was better than the publicist Edgar used for my—our film—*Between Night and Day*. There was award buzz around Heath's film and the reviews were amazing. Despite his dislike for the medium, Heath had no problem shifting from the stage to celluloid. I knew he could pull it off ... be as convincing on screen as he was on stage if he could just get over his impatience and deal with the craft.

Imagine if we were together now reading our reviews. Imagine if we were going together to award ceremonies. I couldn't picture this new us now – would we be competitive or jealous if one of us won and the other didn't? If he won on film and I didn't win, would I be angry given I was the one who wanted film the most? Would it destroy us if I took the award home and he didn't? Would he blame me for pushing him to film and ruining his 'reputation'? It could be an ugly picture or a beautiful outcome – I guess we'll never know now.

I decided not to look at his reviews and then I looked at one and suddenly it was an avalanche, I couldn't get enough. The critics claimed he nailed the portrayal of an artist who murdered his muse when inspiration dried up – I wonder who he was channelling when it came to that twisted thought. I scanned down the reviews picking out the stand-out lines:

Earnshaw makes us love him and hate him as he delivered victimisation and vengeance in equal measure.

A mesmerising lead performance; show this to the jury and the artist would never be convicted.

Harrowing and haunting, Earnshaw's performance will stay with you long after you leave the cinema.

Earnshaw morphed into the character with alarming clarity.

Brilliant and unforgettable, Earnshaw's performance is a stand-out.

I felt a wave of pride and I wanted to call and congratulate him, but I couldn't of course. What would be the point of that? What pain would it cause him and me? I felt relieved and proud, like it or not, I was right. His profile was larger than life, he could command the roles he wanted to do now and draw an audience if he went back to the stage.

All hail, Heath.

*****

It hadn't been an easy few months since our encounter on the moors shooting the *Wylde* campaign. After having a dose of Heath, I had to adjust to a life without him again and purge him from my system. But not before Nelly and I went to the cinema to see his new film. I was so paranoid about being seen that we snuck in at the last minute when the cinema was dark and just before the trailers finished. Shame, because I loved the trailers.

It was so bizarre seeing him on the screen. It was like I didn't know him, as if he had been some poster boy from my teenage years. God, he was wonderful. I was overwhelmed with love and happiness, pride and hate. A heady mix.

I came out of the cinema with a weird sense of 'I told you so'. Nelly and I linked arms as we walked home afterwards. I swore her to secrecy that we would never mention socially that we saw the film, imagine if that got back to Edgar!

'Fuck he was good,' she said.

I looked at her and laughed. Nelly was so lovely and often proper, that any time she swore it always sounded so bizarre coming out of her mouth.

'Well, he was,' she said, justifying her comments.

'Don't I know it,' I said. 'Thank God I'm not judging the best film for this year's award.' I shook my head thinking about Edgar's film amongst the mix too.

We turned into our street and our apartment came into view.

'Are you okay?' she asked.

I turned to look at her. 'Yes, Surprisingly so. All through the film, I felt like I was looking at my high school crush, and I'm all grown up now.'

'Really?' she asked, surprised.

I looked at her. Who was I kidding? 'No. But that's what I'm telling myself.'

She started to laugh and I joined in. *Oh, fuck it.*

After that, my focus was on staying busy. I read through scripts and selected a few I wanted to audition for and let Jaz, my agent, know. I did publicity photos and interviews for the pending release of my romantic comedy film, and I was planning a wedding after all. I wish Mum and Dad were here – I missed Mum so much knowing what fun we would have had doing all the planning together. I felt a huge hole in my heart that no one could fill in her absence.

I ploughed on, and Edgar and I decided on an April wedding and to have an intimate gathering at Thrushcross Grange – well, about fifty people or so. We booked out all available guest rooms in the village for any guests who didn't fit into Thrushcross Grange or Wuthering Heights that weekend. Edgar wanted to look after the catering and wine which was just fine by me, I'd focus on the hair, make-up, invitations, dress, and my bridesmaids – Nelly and my best friend from school, Cassie. I wondered if Heath would come to the wedding on Isabella's arm. What a nightmare.

But I had something bigger to focus on, and Edgar was pretty distracted too … the BAFTA list—the British Academy of Film and Television Arts awards—were announced today, and while Edgar was away for a few days doing some location scouting, Nelly and I were waiting for the announcement. It was a shame Edgar was away because members of the crew of *Between Night and Day* had organised reunion drinks at one of the studio bars and we were all there waiting. It was great to see everyone again.

I was on my second champagne; it was Nelly's idea.

'You need to have champagne before the announcement –

it acknowledges that you are good enough to be considered and that's worth celebrating no matter what happens,' she said.

'Thanks, Nelly. But if it doesn't get announced soon, I'll be under the table and will miss it.'

'If I don't get nominated, I'm going to be super pissed off,' Nathaniel said, sidling up next to me.

'More importantly, if I don't get nominated, it's a travesty of justice,' Niall said.

Nelly and I looked from one to the other and burst out laughing. The guys were support actors who had about two lines each in the whole movie, but because they constantly hung around together and their names were Nathaniel and Niall, no one could tell them apart and they became the two-Ns. They were funny and irreverent and just what every film cast needed. They were on screen for so little time they had no chance of being nominated and they knew it … they were the perfect icebreakers.

Nathaniel nudged me. 'You could lose that director and take me on your arm as your date,' he suggested to me. 'What's he got that I haven't?'

'Fair point,' I agreed and chuckled. 'You're surer than I am that I'm going to be on the list.'

The volume of the television went up to full bore as the hosts of *Insider E-News* came on to share the news.

Everyone was so busy saying 'Sshhh' and 'quiet' that we couldn't hear the television hosts. One of the girls hit a knife against a wine glass and everyone stopped talking at the familiar dinging sound.

Nelly grabbed my arm. 'Here we go,' she whispered. I

think my blood froze because I sat there not able to breathe or move. I didn't realise how much I wanted it for me, Edgar and yes, Heath, and how tense I had been with anticipation. The hosts were raving on about this year's nominees, I suspect they did that every year.

'It's an amazing list this year, Joel, what do you think?' co-host, the very blonde and glamourous Jennifer asked.

'Couldn't agree more, Jen. You've got veterans, newcomers, the unexpected and I'm pleased to say the deserving. Let's begin,' Joel said, and they went live to the BAFTA nomination announcement. As the categories were listed, I tuned in and out, waiting and hearing the nominees relevant to *Between Night and Day* and Heath's film. Then it was one of our categories:

'The nominees for the best film are: *The Missing; Journey of the Soul; Between Night and Day; Cliffhanger;* and *The Meaning of Nothing.*'

All of our team was cheering. Thank God! Edgar's film was listed in the best film category and so was the film Heath was in – a good sign. We had to quieten again for the next category, best leading actress. I was relieved that Holly wasn't with us as she hadn't scored a nomination. Neither did Heath's leading lady … her name escaped me. The host announced the next category of the best lead actor and we all held our breath for Travis from our film. I held mine for Heath but I wasn't going to tell anyone that.

'Nominees for leading actor,' the BAFTA announcer said, and read two names that were huge in the industry and then one I knew intimately. 'Heath Earnshaw, *The Meaning of Nothing.*' I felt every eye turn to me and Nelly and I cheered along with some of the other crew members who knew Heath from his stage work. The fourth name announced wasn't Travis, but the fifth name was!

'Travis Taylor, *Between Night and Day*.' We all cheered and everyone was kissing Travis or patting him on the back including Nelly and me. I was so glad he came for drinks – he had so little ego and this was so exciting. We all gave Tamara—the film's casting director—a huge cheer, she got it right. Two film nominations so far for *Between Night and Day*. I grabbed my phone and glanced at it. I thought Edgar might have texted or called but not yet. He was probably waiting for my category. So was I, it was killing me. And then it came.

The host began, 'the nominees for best supporting actress are: Rachel Sumina, *Cliffhanger*.'

Nelly squeezed my hand; I thought I'd be sick with the tension, the potential embarrassment and major disappointment threatening to erupt. I felt like all eyes were upon me.

'Amee Andrews, *Journey of the Soul* … Julia Vazquez, *You and Me* …'

Fucking killing me. Two to go, two to go …

'Catherine Earnshaw, *Between Night and Day*.'

I think I screamed like a teenager at a concert. Oh My God, I'm a BAFTA nominee! I – am – a – BAFTA – nominee. I don't know who followed me in the announcements but I'm a BAFTA nominee! Everyone was hugging and kissing me and when I surfaced, I thanked Tamara. I tried to rein it in as we listened to the other categories but I couldn't concentrate I was so excited and I had a wave of missing

Mum and Dad again. I wish they could be here to be proud of me, to share in my joy.

It was so exciting and we also got a nomination for best make-up ... there were a lot of very 'tortured' cast members, including me, that needed our make-up team to make us look like the end was near. They earned that nomination. And then the best director category came up and I held my breath for Edgar and silently prayed. The room was still again as we all listened in.

'Nominees for the best director are—'

I didn't have to wait as Edgar's was the first name read and we all cheered again. *Between Night and Day* had done well with five nominations. Heath's film had three including a nomination for the best director category. It was going to be one hell of a night.

I excused myself for a few moments and went to call Edgar to congratulate him and bask in my happiness. What a brilliant day, what a brilliant feeling, there were no words – I wish he was with me. My gamble had paid off – coming to London with Nelly, taking the parts, this was what I had dreamed of. Now I just had the anxiety of waiting for the night and then waiting while the winner was announced for me, Edgar, and for my only living family member – Heath.

Chapter 35 – The relaxation coach

I don't want to sound like a drama queen but I had to get some relaxation help before the award ceremony. I was so nervous and anxious that I wouldn't win; that I would win; that I'd say something stupid; that I would trip over on the way up to get my award; that my real friends would treat me differently after; and new friends would only like me because of my award if I won, and you get the picture, I was overthinking the whole thing way too much!

I mentioned it to Edgar but he shut me down with a kiss and a comment about how brilliant I would be no matter what happened. Okay then, that's that. I vowed not to worry him again with my worry. So, I got a relaxation coach – yes there's such a thing. Jaz, my agent, suggested it and put me on to *Miss Dahlia Krueger, Relaxation Coach to the Entertainment Industry* – that's what her business card said.

I went to her office which was in the same building as Jaz—handy—and I felt automatically relaxed. I kid you not – the office was full of plants. It was a forest ... I had to follow the sound of the waterfall to find the receptionist.

'Just-call-me-Dahlia, darling,' was probably in her fifties with silver strands through her brunette hair, which she

wore up in a bun. Her colouring nicely complemented her flowing red and yellow flower print Kaftan. I felt immediately at home, but that's her job. I also felt rather drab in my jeans, a white T-shirt, a navy jacket, and white canvas sandshoes. I wish I was wearing a flower print and some obvious jewellery like Dahlia.

'Darling, do sit,' she said, as we entered her office and she closed the door. We both sat on a cream leather couch which was so comfy I could have curled up and had a quick nap. I was exhausted from over-thinking.

I had a one-hour session twice a week and I told her all my concerns. Dahlia nodded throughout and had a wonderfully sympathetic look on her face – God she was good.

'Catherine, darling, let's begin,' she said when I finished talking. Spent, I nodded and shut up.

'You are twenty-five and at the start of your career. Your work is done here,' she said, and webbed her fingers, placing her hands on her lap and looking satisfied. I must have looked blank because she continued. 'Being a nominee is an endorsement of your skills. It says to the audience and the industry that this young woman can act. We're noticing her.'

I nodded. 'Right, yes,' I said.

'You don't have to do anything else but enjoy yourself on the night and if you take home the trophy as well, well that's lovely isn't it?'

She said it so matter-of-factly that I laughed. She had a lovely kind demeanour.

She smiled at me. 'Well, we're not saving the world, just entertaining them, darling.'

I conceded and gave her a nod. 'Thank you.'

She held up her hand which I'm surprised she did so easily given the number of rings and bracelets she was wearing.

'I'm not minimising the pressure you are feeling or making fun of you,' she said. 'Of course you are nervous, maybe even terrified, but it is all about perspective before, during, and after the win or event.'

I nodded again, following along. Dahlia, my relaxation coach, continued – I feel the need to say her title again because it was so weird to have a relaxation coach. Next, I'll be hiring someone to give me compliments, good grief.

Focus, I told myself.

Anyway, Dahlia continued addressing my concerns. She had a very good memory given she wrote none of my concerns down … perhaps I'm cliché.

'Darling,' she said, 'I want you to watch this beautiful and talented actress fall at an awards ceremony.' The next moment, she turned her computer screen to face me, clicked on a link on her desktop and we watched as some poor woman stumbled up the stairs.

Dahlia laughed lightly. 'Oh, she was so sophisticated and fun about it, she almost started a trend. She's made it her signature not to take herself too seriously.' She closed the link.

'Got that, thank you,' I said, exhaling with relief.

At my second session which has almost identical to the first but Dahlia wore a blue kaftan, I was told to come with a very brief speech prepared. Dahlia said I should just read it and not feel the pressure to be clever. She asked me how many speeches from winners I remembered from past award nights and there were very few I could recall. So my 'relaxation coach' reinforced to me that no one was hanging off my words. Of course … perspective, good to know.

And then she gave me the best piece of advice yet: 'Darling Catherine, stop thinking about yourself and focus elsewhere.'

There's a challenge and I was up for it. That night when I was sitting on the couch at home with Nelly, I got out my class list from college and I looked up my friends who were studying costume, stage hair and make-up—after all, the BAFTAs were just presentations on a big stage—and with Nelly's help I rang a few of them. I asked if they would do my hair and make-up and of course, I'd pay, but I would also put it out there on social media. They were wild with excitement which relaxed me and made me excited.

'Dahlia is brilliant,' I said to Nelly. 'I can't wait to share the excitement of the night with them because then it is important to all of us.'

'She's worth every cent,' Nelly said. 'How much was she?'

I told Nelly and she nearly fell over. 'Next time, just call me and I'll buy a few cartons of wine … much cheaper.' She gave me a wink and a grin but it was a good fall-back option if I was broke in the future.

Then there was the dress to think of … I'd have to do that awful posing thing again.

'I've heard some nightmare stories,' I told Nelly. 'People who wore dresses gifted to them for the night and then they've torn them or spilt red wine on them and had to buy them for thousands of dollars.'

Nelly nodded. 'I've heard that stuff too. I bet Isabella will be wearing a major label without paying a cent.'

For a moment, and only a moment, I'd forgotten she would be there on Heath's arm and smiling lovingly beside him when the camera panned to him during the award announcements. *Great.*

Nelly grabbed her phone and found Isabella's online accounts. Naturally, she was singing Heath's praises about his nomination and sharing all the reviews, fair enough.

'Here you go, she's well and truly got the dress in hand.'

I leant over as Nelly thumbed through Isabella's images. She was well into planning her BAFTA outfit as Heath's guest and giving sneak peeks of the design and designer. *Sigh.*

'Well bully for Isabella,' I said, being childish. I sat back. 'I'm going to ask Cassie's sister, Sara, to design it,' I declared. Cassie was after all my high school best friend and her sister Sara had a boutique and made bespoke wedding dresses and prom dresses. I had only hesitated because I was a little worried that if it was awful, it might ruin the friendship. Dahlia inspired me to take the gamble.

Nelly's eyes were huge. 'What if it looks like crap?'

I frowned. 'How can it? I'll pick the fabric and agree on the design, and she'll fit me or design it for me and then her business will get a lift too, hopefully.'

Nelly exhaled. 'That is very, very risky, Cathy,' she said. 'Generous but risky. I need coffee before we can discuss it any further.' She leapt up and headed to the kitchen to make two fresh cups. Returning, she sat back down with her iPad under her arm.

'Before you make this decision,' she said, 'let's just check out some of Sara's designs and her website … just in case her style and tastes are a little different to yours.'

'Yeah, good idea,' I agreed. Luckily Sara's website and designs were amazing, even Nelly was convinced and she's a tough judge. The next morning I vowed to ring Sara and see if she was on board to do it.

It was five weeks away and everything was happening too fast. But there was one noticeable black hole in my life. Heath and I had not exchanged one word … no congratulatory text or good luck message even though my finger had hovered on the send button a thousand times. We were now leading separate lives. It seemed impossible.

Chapter 36 – Award night

Tonight was the night – award night. My wonderful hair and make-up friends did their work on me in Edgar's London apartment. They offered to touch him up, so to speak, and he accepted a bit of work on his hair and declared himself perfect. We all laughed, but he was. Sara came to London to fit the dress for me personally ... plus she wanted to see it on and get photos for her website and social media pages. She wouldn't allow me to pay for her labour, only the fabric because she appreciated the plug, so I paid for a hotel room for her and her boyfriend, and her sister – my friend, Cassie, and her boyfriend, who came along for the ride. Why not? They were all going to stay and watch the awards in Edgar's apartment before heading out to party. God, I hope we had something to celebrate. Edgar's place was buzzing before we left; it was so exciting.

Nelly and her guy got dressed with us as well; Nelly had her hair and make-up done after me and it looked fantastic. We all drank champagne but I only had one glass, it was a great night before the night if that makes sense? Edgar was on the outer a bit but he watched with a grin on his face like he was happy to see me happy and be part of the buzz. It was a good distraction so that I wasn't fixating on the awards! Nelly was going on to an industry party while Edgar and I were at the awards but we vowed to catch up after, no matter what the outcome.

When I was ready, dressed in Sara's glittering silver fitted gown, my hair flowing, make-up done and Edgar in a black tux and looking dashing, we declared ourselves ready to go. Edgar, in front of everyone, took my hand and told me I looked breathtaking. Sigh, I would never forget this night. They all wished us luck, I kissed everyone twice, maybe more, and we finally got down to the car. Edgar had organised a driver for the two of us. I don't know where Isabella and Heath were staying but thank God she hadn't stormed Edgar's apartment before the awards.

Edgar held my hand on the drive and I ran through the mantras my relaxation coach, Dahlia, gave me. Something about it only being one night in a long life; how I was one of many tonight and remember to appreciate all the nominees – that was designed to stop me from focusing on myself; to have fun and notice the details to tell Nelly and Cassie – same outward strategy I suspect; it was just acting – the world was not relying on me to do anything more tonight; remember it for what it might be – the first of many; and save the whales … okay, I made that last one up but I'm one hundred per cent for it and it's a good distraction technique.

'Got your speech?' Edgar asked me. A bit late now if I didn't since we were almost there.

I nodded and looked in my small shell-shaped clutch

purse. There it was with my lipstick, powder and a tissue. No comb – I was under strict orders not to touch my hair as the messed-up look was best left alone, apparently.

'Got yours?' I asked, and he grinned and tapped his head.

'Aren't you, Mr Cool?' I teased him.

'Don't tell me you don't know yours off by heart?' he asked, with a raised eyebrow.

'Of course, but I might forget it under pressure,' I said.

He nodded. 'If I forget mine, I'll just roll out every name I can think of from the cast and crew and tell them I love them all. Your name will be first off my lips of course.'

I laughed. 'I better not be … you can't play favourites. You should do it in order of when they came on board for the film! I'd be about twenty-seventh and by then, the big hook will be coming from the side of the stage to pull you off.'

Edgar laughed and then froze as a flash caught us off guard; a photographer had come alongside our window and we hadn't noticed the car had slowed down and we were in the drop-off zone. There in front of us loomed the grand Royal Albert Hall. The driver dropped us in the designated area to do the red-carpet walk. Both of our car doors opened before we had time for a quiet kiss for good luck, but Edgar grabbed me for one anyway. So sweet – more camera flashes.

Then I was on the red carpet – there was so much red carpet; it seemed to go forever and there were stairs and different levels with something happening from the bottom to the top. I wanted to pull a big sign out of my bag that said hi to Nelly, Lockwood, Cassie, Sara and everyone from home, but of course that would be so uncool amongst the glitter set, and it wouldn't have fitted in my bag anyway. I hitched my hand through Edgar's offered arm and we took the walk. We stopped for four interviews along the way with different media outlets, jumped into selfies with fans along the barriers, did our separate posing and I dropped Sara's name and her label, plus plugged my hair and make-up artists' names as well, even though I had shared the details on my accounts with pics before we left Edgar's apartment.

I didn't see Isabella or Heath on the red carpet which was not surprising – it was frantically busy with stars, industry VIPs, reporters, photographers, you name it ... we just moved along with the flow until we found ourselves being escorted to our seats. Wow, that was a whirlwind. Thank goodness some of our cast and crew were around us. If they were nominated, or former winners or partners, they were there, so we had our little posse.

I tried to not look at all the big-name stars around me but I did peek – who wouldn't? Wow! I stopped looking, it made me nervous. I spotted Isabella and Heath seated on the other side of the aisle from us about one row back. She gave us a big smile and waved; Heath gave a barely discernible nod which Edgar reciprocated. Good grief. Isabella looked stunning, but she was a model. Together they looked like a beautiful couple – Heath dark and handsome, Isabella fair and glowing. I turned my attention back to Edgar to focus on us. I am right in the moment, right here and now – more inspiration from my relaxation coach.

And then the night began. I put Dahlia's training to good use and I stayed in the now – I listened to what was said, clapped, laughed, was in awe, tapped along to any entertainment and did everything in the moment so that I wasn't in my head compulsively going through my speech, worrying I wouldn't look happy for the winner if it wasn't me, or fixating on things that could go wrong. It helped because all around me the theatre was full of people and cameras and lights and – okay, back to Dahlia's techniques. Edgar, beside me, looked so cool. I hope I looked like that – a duck, calm on the surface, paddling frantically underneath.

Fortunately, or unfortunately, the first award for the night was for Most Outstanding Film so straight up we would be celebrating or not! The nominees were read: *Between Night and Day, The Missing, Journey of the Soul, Cliff Hanger* and *The Meaning of Nothing*. We gave a loud cheer for our film, of course. Wow, they took so long to open that envelope, then the presenters looked at each and smiled – for the love of God, read it out! I hope I didn't say that out loud, nope, quick check, all okay.

'The winner of the Most Outstanding Film is *The Meaning of Nothing.*' The film Heath was in. We smiled and clapped, as you do, and looked over his way where everyone was hugging and cheering as they were all seated together. The producer along with the director, Nadim Ramirez, who I recognised from the publicity interviews, got up to accept the award and headed to the stage. One down that we didn't win – I hoped that wasn't an omen. We were in five categories, so four remaining to win. Heath's film had three nominations and they had won one, not that I was counting of course.

We could relax during the next few awards as we weren't nominated for them: Best Newcomer and Best Adapted Screenplay and then before I knew it, it was my award.

I wasn't ready. Yes, I was. Okay, I can do this.

Remember what Dahlia said, smile, acknowledge the work of others and remember I'm a small cog in the wheel that gets to be part of the award. Steady breathing, smile. Edgar held my hand and we exchanged smiles.

And then the presenters read through the nominees and showed an extract of each of us in our performance.

'Rachel Sumina, *Cliffhanger.*' Wow, Rachel was good, her extract was brilliant.

'Amee Andrews, *Journey of the Soul.*' Oh God, Amee was so good, look at her go.

'Julia Vazquez, *You and Me …*' My jaw nearly fell open watching Julia, she was brilliant.

Fuck!

'Catherine Earnshaw, *Between Night and Day.*' I know the camera panned to Edgar and I but I didn't see it. I was just smiling nicely, doing my deer caught in the headlights impersonation. They showed the clip of me as Portia with my supporting actor co-star, Kyle Hughes playing Connor. I watched it as though I was seeing it for the first time.

On-screen, Connor laughed. 'Portia! Christ, your parents must have had great hopes for you when they named you that. Look at you now. Go on, take the pills, finish it off.'

I looked up at him—on the screen of course—my drug-wasted face, my eyes dull, my hair stringy and I smiled, this weird feeble smile and then I threw the pills at him. 'You know what?' I said, shaking with the effort of doing that, 'I'm going to stick around to see what happens next.' And then I threw up on him.

Ah, glamour! The audience gave me a huge cheer and

I laughed because it was a bizarre contradiction to us all sitting here tonight so glamorous. And that laugh did me a world of good because it relaxed me, and I realised that I'm here with all my peers and those that I aspire to be as good as just watched my work.

That's something.

The presenters announced the last nominee: 'Emilia Paulson in *About That*'. Oh fuck, Emilia was great too. Well, I was in good company.

'And the award goes to—' Not breathing, not moving …

'Catherine Earnshaw, *Between Night and Day*'.

Chapter 37 – The meaning of everything

I can't put into words what happened next, but it was surreal and it all happened so fast. I looked to Edgar to make sure I had heard it correctly – it would have been so embarrassing if I walked up and it wasn't me that they called. There was no one else called Catherine Earnshaw was there? He stood, pulled me up, kissed me, and everyone around me did the same. Then Edgar gave me his arm and helped me up the stairs—what a gentleman—before disappearing down them again and leaving me there with the presenters to accept my award.

My award. Oh my God.

I turned to see the audience and I forgot to get my speech out of my bag but I remembered it. It was like the director had called 'action' and I was on. I began:

'Words can't convey how thrilled and grateful I am for this award and opportunity, and it is thanks to the bar set by my fellow nominees. My heartfelt gratitude to Tamara Langer for taking a gamble and casting me; Edgar Linton for letting her, and for directing and guiding me through the role; our cast and crew that made me Portia, the wasted, prostitute at death's door'.

Everyone laughed at that. But then I got serious.

'But Portia meant a lot to me. Because everyone in their life—whether they seem to have it all or they have nothing—will at some point be at that lowest ebb because that's life and we're human. So like Portia, please hang in there. Please...' I paused to say the next words slowly and with emphasis, '*stick around to see what happens next.*' I held up the award. 'This happened. Thank you.'

After losing Mum, Dad and Hindley, I knew what low was like and it was super important to me to get that message out. I was just so thrilled I had the chance.

And I was done. I heard the applause as I gripped that award like it was never leaving my hand and I was led backstage for photos. The next few awards came and went, I could see them on the screen in the photo room – Best Animated Film; Special Visual Effects; Outstanding Debut by a Writer, Director or Producer; and Best Supporting Actor – none of which we had nominees in. Then it was the Best Make-up and Hair Award and I kept glancing at the screen while being photographed hoping we would take it out, but we didn't. It went to one of those brilliant period films – so hard to beat them with the big hair and exaggerated make-up involved!

I was supposed to go to the interview room next but I requested permission to return to my seat so I didn't miss Edgar's award. I promised I would come to the interview room as soon as it was announced. It wasn't the 'done thing' but the behind-the-scenes team kindly acquiesced. I snuck back into my seat as best I could and tried to suppress the joy emanating from me, knowing our fantastic make-up artist was seated behind me and didn't win, and that Edgar would be super tense even if he wasn't showing it. I sat close to him, my hand in his. We waited through another few awards: Outstanding Contribution, Original Screenplay, and then it was the Best Director Category.

My breath hitched and Edgar held my hand so tightly I thought he would break my fingers but I didn't want to complain. The hosts ran through the five nominations and Nadim Ramirez was amongst them for Heath's film, *The Meaning of Nothing*. There were two female directors nominated too which was exciting for the industry. Then the envelope was opened and the screen featured the five faces.

'The award goes to Nadim Ramirez, *The Meaning of Nothing*.'

Edgar and I clapped and smiled as you do. I was so disappointed for my guy – my director, he had done such a brilliant job, but so too had Nadim. That film was amazing. I wondered how tonight would pan out now; would Edgar be happy to celebrate with me or too disappointed to party on.

We sat just holding hands, his hand was now loose and we let the night roll on, but there was still one award that could go to Edgar's film – Best Actor for our lead, Travis. Not that I was keeping score, but currently it was two awards for Heath's film and one for our film. The award for Best Leading Actress was next, we had no one in this category since Holly didn't get nominated, but there was some amazing talent in it!

Then our last chance came and Heath's big moment. I kept thinking about how he didn't want to do a film and here he was at the award ceremony – the first of many for his film I imagine. I glanced over at Travis who was carrying all of our hopes for *Between Night and Day* and he gave me a nervous smile. I know it was probably the wrong thing to be thinking—I wouldn't say it aloud of course—but I wanted Heath to win; to be honest, that's all I've ever wanted. I did my best not to glance Heath's way but I'm sure Isabella was offering him plenty of support. Don't be catty, Cathy, I told myself.

The presenters read out the nominations; Travis was second, Heath was read out next out of the five nominees, and we watched their extracts on screen. Heath was so good and the extract they showed from his soliloquy was his best work without a doubt. Travis' clip was good too but not a patch on Heath's, sadly. Then it was announcement time.

'And the winner is – Heath Earnshaw, *The Meaning of Nothing*'.

He had done it. My Heath had done it. I clapped enthusiastically, it was impulsive; and then I remembered Travis and where I was and reined it in. Isabella gave him an enormous showy kiss, well you would, and Heath adjusted his jacket and headed for the stage. Not a glance in my direction, even though I knew a camera was on me even for just a few seconds when his win was announced. Did they seriously think I was going to roll my eyes or freak out? It would be fun to see someone do that and be real though, just once.

I felt a rush of jealousy. I should be with him tonight celebrating his win.

The audience settled as he shook hands with last year's winner, and turned to address us, the award in his hand.

It was quiet as he began.

'I am here accepting this award because of one person only. But now the entire world is a collection of memoranda that she did exist, and that I have lost her. For you, Cathy.'

He pointed his award at me and then Heath walked off stage.

Shit. Hit. The. Fan.

Chapter 38 – The aftermath

When I look back on that night, and when I watch the end of the award ceremony online, which I couldn't do for the first week or so, I am struck by one thing – Heath has a wonderful sense of drama. He might have won the best actor but he stole the limelight from every other winner that night. His speech and the subsequent fallout were the talk of the entertainment media and as they say, he 'broke the internet'.

As soon as the words left his mouth, the cameras scrambled to get our reactions. What a bummer I had returned to my seat as I had to face the music. I thought Edgar was going to implode he went so stiff and his grimace was sharp enough to kill, but he turned to me and put his arm around me and we kissed like he knew he had the prize and Heath had lost me. But don't be fooled because that was all for the public eye and short-lived.

Across the aisle, Isabella was up and striding out before a camera person could even catch up with her, while the director kept one camera on us and one on the audience's reaction, meanwhile the poor presenters were trying to get the audience's attention for the final category. God, what a nightmare. As they moved the awards along, Edgar and I rose and slinked out. I had to go do the interviews that I promised I would do. Edgar told me he would leave the driver for me to get me home, but I pulled him aside for a moment, far from the madding crowd.

'Hey,' I said, getting his focus on me, 'that is not about us, that's about Heath grandstanding. I'm so, so, sorry that our film didn't bag more, it deserved it.'

He nodded, his mouth a straight line.

'Make no mistake, Cathy,' he said, in a low voice, 'I won't be humiliated by Heath, by you, or by anyone else. First, he turns down my movie offer and accepts another, winning the award for them, then he lays his claim on you. He wouldn't do that if you didn't encourage him. Now I know what happened that weekend you shot the *Wylde* commercial together!'

I'm sure my eyes flared red. Now I was furious.

'Lay his claim! Nothing happened,' I hissed. 'I was on the phone to you both nights, he was staying with your sister, Isabella … remember her, the fiancée? Edgar you know I love you; I am here with you—'

'—I'll see you at home later,' he said and cut me off. 'Go party, you've earned your win. We'll talk tomorrow.'

'Well thanks for your support for my award win for *your* film,' I snapped. 'You take the driver,' I said, shaking my head. 'I'll catch up with Nelly and crash at my place.'

I watched him stride off. Thanks for ruining a great night, Edgar. If he had won and I hadn't, I would have thrown myself into the celebrations for his sake and I would have trusted him if an ex got up and dedicated an award to him –maybe, hard to say, *whatever*. But I did win the award for his film. I sent a quick text to Cassie to let her know I was on my way if they wanted to grab a cab and meet me at the industry party. We were catching up with Nelly and Lockwood there and I was going to get Sara, Cassie and their partners in as guests. Plus, I wanted them to hurriedly evacuate Edgar's apartment before he got home! I warned her he was coming home … if they were still watching the awards, she'd know the drill!

I went and did my final interviews which were a nightmare. The publicity team had to keep telling the journalists to stick to questions about the award, not Heath's announcement and when that seemed futile, I was 'released'. I breathed a sigh of relief and took off.

Twenty minutes later I caught up with my friends at the industry party. They were so happy for me, thank God because I had no one else to share the excitement with. Nelly was full of news and told me that Isabella had thrown Heath's ring back at him and she was all over social media already partying and having a big night with her model friends, ensuring she was caught on the arm of someone handsome and successful to help cover up her humiliation. I guess we won't be sisters-in-law now. So sad.

'Wasn't it so romantic though?' Lockwood said, rolling his eyes.

It truly was and I knew that in my heart and soul and every fibre of my being – I've no business being with Edgar Linton. Heath was more myself than I am. I may not be with him every day, but I knew he was out there and there was strength in that. If he were to leave this earth, the universe would turn into a mighty stranger.

I desperately wanted to see Heath, to celebrate both of our wins – imagine if we were together and had both won. I can't begin to think about what the excitement would have been like. But I couldn't see him tonight … not if Edgar and I were to continue as normal despite Edgar's tantrum.

'Where is Heath?' I asked Nelly, and she shrugged. 'Probably out partying with the *Meaning of Nothing* crew and cast.'

I hoped so because turning up where I was wouldn't be the smartest idea or the best thing for either of us.

'Where's Edgar?' Nelly asked.

'He went back to his place.'

'Right,' she said and added nothing more. Nelly was good at diplomacy.

I stayed out and partied for a few hours, but everyone wanted to talk about what Heath said. So after a while, I left my friends to carry on and I got a taxi and went back to Edgar's apartment. On the way, I grabbed my phone and checked out the banter online – the discussion teetered between people feeling sorry for Edgar, thinking Heath was the ultimate Romeo or feeling humiliated for Isabella. No one seemed to worry too much about me – fair enough, *I have a BAFTA!* But it was amazing how polar opposite peoples' views were … Heath, Edgar and I varied from victims to villains. Then I found *Entertainment Weekly's* piece that went up online about an hour ago – well two pieces. One was the serious article by Bonny Hawkins with all the award information and my name in there – *yes* – the second article was from their '*Rumour File*'. I took a deep breath and began to read.

Entertainment Weekly

RUMOUR FILE: Winning actor hijacks the BAFTAs!

It was a night of nights for the stars and even the critics agreed that the academy got it right with their award list. But one actor stole the show and not for his film performance (although he took home that award too).

The award of the night for *Best Showstopper* must go to Heath Earnshaw … STOP … it's a three-way tie between Heath Earnshaw, Edgar Linton and Catherine Earnshaw.

While Heath Earnshaw is known to love a bit of classic theatre, be still my beating heart because Mr Earnshaw just delivered the ultimate live love ode to the nation – a declaration of his pain having lost the love of one fellow award-winning actor, Catherine Earnshaw.

Keen to show he was the one that got the prize, despite not winning the best director category, Edgar Linton – smooth as cream – gave his woman a passionate kiss and the woman in question, Catherine Earnshaw, was glancing around for the exit doors.

Ah love, ain't it grand? By the looks of Heath Earnshaw's fiancée's Instagram account, that engagement ring is no longer on Isabella Linton's finger, and we've got our spies out to see if Catherine is still sporting her engagement ring to Edgar. Watch this space.

*****

Just great, I groaned. If Edgar hasn't read this, Isabella will be sure to point it out. The driver pulled over, and I paid and thanked him. I said a quick hello to Edgar's doorman in the foyer, who told me I looked lovely – bless him, and I rode the lift to Edgar's apartment and let myself in. Edgar was sitting in the lounge room with a scotch. His jacket and bow tie were draped over a chair, his shoes nearby on the floor. It looked like he had worked his way through the bottle.

Like a good girlfriend, I went to him, slipped off my coat, bag and shoes, and slipped onto his lap, but he wasn't in the mood for comfort or reconciliation. He got up, lifted me off and then it began – an ugly tirade full of implications that Heath wasn't good enough and I had lowered Edgar's standards by associating with Heath. What the hell? He ranted on about the need for him to vet who I see!

'I've tolerated that you wanted to keep up your acquaintance with that miserable, degraded character,' he said, and I felt myself arc up, 'I acquiesced, foolishly.'

'Oh Edgar, how good of you to allow me to have my own choice of friends, until now,' I said, glaring at him. 'May I remind you that it is not me that retains that friendship, but rather your sister who is engaged to him.'

'Well, you can be sure that will be over now too. He is no longer welcome into our home, even if they reconcile.'

I shook my head. 'Good luck with that. I think that will be Isabella's choice, not yours.'

He refilled his glass, moved to the window where he looked out over the heart of London, and then turned to me. I wondered how long he had pondered asking me this question or if it was the alcohol talking.

'Will you give up Heath or will you give up me? You can't have us both at the same time, and I require to know which one of us you choose … now.'

I think my jaw dropped open because I had to gather myself before I spoke.

'Edgar, except for the *Wylde* girl commercial which you supported me doing, I have had no contact with Heath,' I said. I rose and moved towards him at the window. 'I love you. I chose you the day I first kissed you. What would you have me do to prove it? I told you I haven't been leading him on.' I pointed to my handbag on the couch. 'Take my phone now and check my calls, check my messages, I have nothing to hide,' I said and gave a casual shrug.

He glanced at my bag, sorely tempted I imagine but did not move. This should have been one of the happiest days of my life but it was spoiled by both of these men, by their petty jealousy, egos, and hatred of each other.

'You forget,' I said, 'that despite all this, he is family. I've grown up with Heath, he is my stepbrother. That's why he feels the loss so keenly. He is the only family I have left and I am the same to him. I am denying us both any contact because it is easier that way, and because I am with you.' I put extra emphasis on the last four words.

He shook his head.

'Make a choice and choose which one of us it will be,' he said as if I had not spoken at all or he disregarded my words as inadequate.

I was angry now. If he didn't trust me, what difference would it make for me to choose him?

I moved to the couch, slipped on my shoes, and my coat

and grabbed my bag. I turned back to Edgar. 'Well, if I cannot keep Heath for my family and if you persist in being unfairly mean and jealous when I have done nothing to break your heart, then I shall have neither of you and break my own heart,' I said.

I went to the door but he did not call me back or try to stop me. He let me walk away.

Chapter 39 – The Screen Test

Heath did not contact me which was to be expected. He had declared his love on a public stage. The next move was mine and I was in limbo. It was ten whole days after the award night before Edgar contacted me and wanted to talk. Ten days! He didn't apologise but said he might have "been harsh in the passion of the moment". Uh-huh, you think? But those ten days of torment and self-analysis gave me perspective.

My BAFTA got me through – it gave me strength and confidence, and belief in myself. I had never had that before and I kept busy to minimise the pain. The first few days every time the phone rang or a message alert came, I grabbed it with hopeful expectation that it was Edgar wanting to reconcile. I sent him messages and called, asking to talk with him … I couldn't just leave us hanging like that.

Were we together? Did we have a future or was it over? I found not having the closure hard to manage. I wanted to hear the words that we were done, or make that decision myself after speaking with him. But by the time he made contact ten days later, my pain levels had started to diminish, I was angry, I was over the drama. I was sick of looking like a tortured soul. My head and heart were out of the *'please-call-me-and-want-me'* stage and I was beginning the *'I-loved-him-once'* and *'he-never-even-said-goodbye-the-bastard'* phase.

But I couldn't help thinking this was my reckoning – I was being punished for past mistakes. For a while I thought I deserved this pain; that I had put this whole cycle in motion and betrayed my own heart when I first denied myself Heath. I had been given a great love, more than most people ever experienced and I threw that away, dismissed Heath for a more handsome face, a different flavour. Then I sailed along, taking Edgar for granted.

But I knew that wasn't quite true. I deserved the punishment for Heath but I can honestly say in all good consciousness that I never betrayed Edgar. I consulted him on the *Wylde* girl commercial and I never encouraged Heath.

I gave Edgar my heart and he took it and pinched it to death; and flung it back at me. So, I dusted it off and put it back in place, straightened up and carried on. And then he called.

*****

When Nelly arrived home, I was in the kitchen doing my make-up because the light in there was better than anywhere else in the house. She dropped her bag on a chair, flicked on the kettle and offered me a mug of tea which I turned down.

'You're really going to meet with him?' Nelly asked,

incredulously. She had just returned from seeing our agent, Jaz, and brought home the news that my *Wylde* perfume commercial was releasing this weekend.

'Oh goody,' I said with a groan, and then I couldn't help but laugh. 'Why not? Heath and I running around the moors clutching each other. Let's just put more fuel on the fire.'

Nelly grinned. 'The agency director must be wetting himself with delight – they couldn't buy this kind of publicity. Anyway, don't avoid the question. It's taken Edgar ten days to call you and then he beckons and you run over. What the—'

'—because there is no pride in love,' I interrupted her.

'Oh wow, that's good. Is that a Catherine original?' she asked, pulling her teabag out of the cup, and taking a seat to watch me in action.

'No, Mum used to say it all the time. It is good though.'

'Mm,' she agreed. 'I must use that. Do you think you will reconcile? Do you want to?'

I finished applying my mascara and then looked over at her. I was strong most of the time but when I thought about Edgar and I never being together again, never making love or being in each other's arms afterwards, I felt raw. I couldn't imagine not going to his place or sneaking out to restaurants together. I wish my partners didn't have profiles so I wouldn't hear about them or see them in my circle … there's no escaping the hurt. Nelly was lucky that her guy was 'normal'. I loved Edgar. I loved Heath. I hated them both at the moment.

I answered Nelly. 'It would be easy to go back to him, especially if he missed me and was happy to see me.' I bit my lip momentarily as I thought. 'He was humiliated by it all; he probably didn't know how to handle it. Besides, I would love to ease the pain,' I said, and subconsciously rubbed my heart.

She nodded. 'I get that.'

'Anyway, I agreed to meet with him; I owe him that much. We love each other, we're engaged.'

'If you need me to meet you there or somewhere afterwards, call me,' Nelly offered.

I rose and leant down to give her a quick grateful hug and then I went to get changed.

*****

I spent a lot of time dressing and making sure I looked my best … this was make-or-break and I wanted to look good either way. Edgar didn't offer to send a car or his driver for me as he had done in the past, so I took the train – this BAFTA actress can't afford to throw too much money away on taxi fares, my *Wylde* girl payment hadn't come through yet! I watched people around me, it was so bizarre that everyone else looked normal. Are they dealing with stuff too and you can't tell or was everyone else happy and had their life in order? My stomach was churning with the stress and I felt a little weak. I saw fellow passengers glancing at me and looking away, not sure if I was *that* girl. After all, would she be taking public transport? I got off at the station near Edgar's apartment and walked the short distance.

Let's get this over with; I don't want to be this person – all the time with the thinking. Even when I promise I'm not going to think about it anymore, I'm thinking about it. I greeted the doorman and went upstairs. I still had my access keys, but I didn't let myself into his apartment, I knocked and waited.

Deep breath … I was ridiculously nervous.

The door swung open and I knew as soon as our eyes met that his pride had got the better of him. There was no warmth there towards me. Heath would have grabbed me and forgiven me for anything and everything. Edgar was like ice.

'Cathy, come in,' he said and walked away leaving me to close the door. He looked like he hadn't suffered at all these past ten days. He looked calm and rested; expensive. 'Would you like a drink?' he asked, picking up his glass of scotch – his favourite poison.

'No, I'm fine, thank you.'

He sat on the couch and I sat opposite. It was crazy, like an audition. So I rose and came over and sat beside him, turning to face him. The muscles of his countenance tightened; I can only imagine the conversations that he and Isabella had shared about Heath and me since the award night.

I took a deep breath. 'Edgar, what's going on?' I asked, and studied him. 'You know that was all Heath's doing. You know in your heart of hearts that I have been nothing but loyal to you.'

He was frosty, there was a distinct wall between us. I always thought that we were like safe ships in the harbour, attracted to each other because it was easy. There was never the passion I had with Heath, but Edgar and I got on and we laughed, loved and were comfortable. I was impressed by him and respected him. Is that so bad?

He cleared his throat. 'It's not what you have done Cathy, it is what you haven't done,' he said, his chin up, his fingers tapping the side of his glass with arrogance and impatience. 'When we were having breakfast the morning after our engagement and I asked you to sell Wuthering Heights, you wouldn't even consider it. You intended to maintain that connection with Heath forever.'

I laughed, surprised. 'Edgar, that is my family home. Besides, your sister was engaged to Heath. I think the connection was going to continue regardless of what I did. He was going to be your family, your brother-in-law.'

'I would have disowned her if she did marry him,' he said. 'I just expected it to fall apart before I had to advise her of my intentions.'

I think my mouth fell open. 'What? But she loved him?'

He shrugged. 'Well that problem is gone, isn't it? Except for your connection. While you share Wuthering Heights with him, and while you are in my life, so by default is he,' he said, so haughtily.

I could hear Heath in my head calling Edgar a privileged twat. *Leave me alone Heath.*

I waited for a beat, thinking. If he could disown his sister, the closest relative he had in the world, he would have no problem replacing me. I confess I was thrown; I had placed such faith in Edgar's stable love that I was delusional.

Edgar continued. 'Loyalty is everything to me, Cathy. I love you, and the woman I marry I will love for life. There will be no one else. I don't ask for much in return,' he said.

'But you are asking me to do something I don't want to do – to give up Wuthering Heights ... something that is part of who I am as much as you will be part of my future.'

He swallowed and thought about my words.

I kept going. 'I find it so odd that you of all people, Edgar, would be so insecure about a man you believe is beneath you. A man you called if I remember correctly ... a miserable, degraded character. You could, of course, think of it as winning, that Heath had lost me to you – you are the victor.'

He scoffed. Clearly he had considered that argument but perhaps thought he was the prize, not me.

I sighed. 'Edgar, just because he wasn't ready to do a film when you offered him the part, is not a slight on you. Heath is worthy of anyone's regard. Couldn't you have tried to be a friend, tried to like him?' I asked.

Edgar's voice rose. 'I welcomed him at my home, I offered him a drink. His replies were nothing more than a grunt. You brought him into my life, our life, Cathy. You can take him out of it again.'

His face said there was no compromise; he needed me to sell Wuthering Heights as a show of loyalty and if I did, we would be fine, we would go on.

Edgar strode to the table and refilled his glass.

'Heath knew that what he was saying at the award night was disrespectful to me and you, and humiliating to my sister,' Edgar snapped.

I had to concede he had a point there. 'Yes. But I had no control over that, and I did warn your sister about him,' I reminded Edgar.

He nodded, granting me that small concession.

'Regardless, Cathy, I've given this a lot of thought over the past week and that is the only way I can go forward in this relationship. The choice is yours,' Edgar finished.

That was it—he had found my Achille's heel—the weakness that would lead to our downfall – my home, my vulnerability. There seemed little point in continuing this talk; everything had changed and we couldn't get back to being good together. He had been publicly, even nationally humiliated by someone he considered not worthy and, in his mind, I had allowed it.

I would not sell Wuthering Heights for Edgar or anyone. What would he ask of me after that? Someone who loved me would not ask that of me.

We were over.

Unlike Heath, I knew Edgar would not chase me all over the country. His love for me was conditional, Heath's love for me had no boundaries, he would have taken me back in whatever form I came to him. Edgar could not celebrate my victories but chose to blame me for what had befallen him. His determined request would eventually extinguish my love for him, once I recovered and anger took over.

I slipped my engagement ring off and placed it on the glass coffee table beside me. Next to it, I placed the key to his apartment.

'I understand, Edgar, what you need from me,' I said, softly, 'but I won't part with Wuthering Heights.'

He glared at me; I don't think he expected that response, not for a moment. I suspect he thought I would do whatever was required to keep him and to marry him.

'Thank you,' I said. 'Thank you for your love and our good times together. Please don't be a stranger if we meet in the future, I love and respect you.'

I stopped talking because I couldn't speak anymore. The lump in my throat was huge, I was on the verge of tears but I wanted to end as I began the relationship, admiring him.

I left. It all seemed so futile over so little. Maybe it always was.

Chapter 40 – Three months later

It was surreal and after all the drama and excitement had settled down, I found that I was Catherine Earnshaw, a single woman, an award-winning actor, a friend, stepsister, daughter, and a college graduate.

I originally came to the city to challenge myself and to stand on my own two feet but I went from Heath to Edgar, both of them boosting my career. So for the past couple of months after that night with Edgar, I was just me. I went out with Nelly and her man, and my friends; I worked with Jaz—my agent—on potential projects; I did interviews as organised by the publicists to promote my two films that were currently screening; I prepared stock standard answers to the Heath and Edgar question … something about respect and awe for their talents, blah, blah, blah; and I privately regrouped.

It was impossible to avoid information about Edgar and Isabella, but not so hard with Heath as he kept well away from social media. I knew the Lintons—Edgar and Isabella—were both seeing someone else or several someones. Edgar's actions really cut me. Before I would even consider another relationship, I needed that time to recover.

I had a BAFTA – did I mention that? I still couldn't believe it. I looked at it all the time like it wasn't quite real. It made me stronger, I was moving forward. Heath had one too. Ah, Heath. *Miss you, love you, want you, hate you – no, not so much hate now.*

Then, I did something that I knew would make me happy and it was something that I knew Nelly wanted to do as well. Hopefully, Lockwood could wrap up his work gig and join us. We wanted to work together, so what was stopping us? Well money, but hey, there were ways around that. Nelly and I came up with the plan over a few drinks at our favourite pub and in the cold, hard sobering light of morning, it still had legs! Luckily her guy—who had a brain for figures—thought it was feasible too, and that gave us wings.

I wanted to stage *Les Miserables* – not the musical, the drama. I wanted to play Fantine – the pretty, poor and abandoned young mother who becomes a prostitute to support her illegitimate daughter … yes, another tragic character but a wonderful role. Nelly wanted to direct or co-direct and we wanted Lockwood as stage manager. With an award behind me and some funds in the bank thanks to my two films and *Wylde* commercial, I was happy to also co-produce and put up a sum of money as an investor.

Nelly and I met with our agent Jaz, and with Tamara—whom we hoped might cast talent for us—to discuss who might be interested in backing and staging the production. We didn't care if we started in a small theatre in the backwater, but Jaz wouldn't have that. She said it wouldn't be good for my career now, and it had to be staged in the West End – a small theatre – and then it could go on the road for a season. To say Nelly, Lockwood and I were beside ourselves with excitement was an understatement. Even our BAFTA-nominated hair and make-up colleague was keen to come on board with us – she wanted some stage make-up practice after working in the film industry for the last year.

Jaz organised a lunch with a producer and a financier friend of hers, along with Tamara, Nelly and me. Having Jaz and Tamara supporting us gave us cred. It had been at least eight years or more since *Les Miserables* had been on stage so it was due back. The backers were interested and liked our enthusiasm. They liked the networks we had and the possibility to draw a crowd given the recent hype and my award. Plus, with my films both out there at the moment – I was in people's faces one way or another. No one mentioned Heath or Edgar. The irony wasn't lost on me that I was keen to go back on the stage; Heath would be smirking.

A few days after our meeting, Jaz called and said the backers would give us the green light if we were open to two conditions. Hell yeah, we were open to anything – it was going to be another milestone, another step in our careers. Nelly and I went in to meet Jaz and hear what we needed to do to secure the deal. We spent our cocktail hour the night before thrashing out what we thought the deal breakers would be and I thought it might be that we needed more experience or star power. It turned out it was a little of both.

Back in Jaz's office, and doing our best to look professional, I took a breath before Jaz delivered the ultimatum; the producer and financier would back our London season and consider touring us depending on the London success if Nelly worked with a co-director who had a little more experience and could guide her. Basically, if she was happy to be the first assistant director. That was fair enough as she didn't have a lot of runs on the board and Nelly agreed, happy to have the experience and the credit. So far so good. They were fine with Lockwood as the stage manager as long as he hired experienced stagehands, especially stagehands who had worked on productions of *Les Miserables*.

The second condition was all about the casting of the lead male role – Jean Valjean. He was a convict, hero and Fantine supporter, and he had to be a known name for the deal to be done. Our backers had a name in mind.

Nelly and I exchanged glances and Jaz said she would give us time to think about it, but that was not necessary, we agreed we were happy with both conditions if the lead male actor agreed to sign on the dotted line. We thanked Jaz and went away to work on the requests. We wanted to make this happen.

That night, I stood on the balcony of my and Nelly's apartment. I drank in London, the cool night air, and all the possibilities ahead. I took a deep breath and finding the name and number on my phone that I had not called for over a year, I rang with an offer – the part of Jean Valjean opposite my role of Fantine in *Les Miserables* to open in London's West End.

Heath answered straight away.

The End.

Also by Ally Adams:

The Dark Moors (*Paranormal romance – for lovers of powerful vampires, moody werewolves and dark romance!*):
Three truths could be said of Catherine Earnshaw:
1. She loves Heath, always has, always will.
2. She thinks she might love Edgar too – he's everything Heath is not.
3. On her 21st birthday, she will become a vampire.
Inspired by Emily Bronte's Wuthering Heights.

THE SPIES IN LOVE SERIES (*Contemporary romance*):

My Boyfriend the Spy:
Matilda Martin is having a life change – new job, new city, and a new dating outlook. She is over men and too busy to date. Adam Cahill is tall, dark, handsome and a spy. According to his ex-girlfriend, he is "as much fun as a crisis meeting". Adam has given up on finding love – he's focusing on his career. Luckily Matilda's been assigned to his next project since neither of them is bound to be interested in each other.

I Spy My Guy:
Irish-girl Orla Murphy is a romantic – books, films, real life – she believes in love; she's just got to find it. Accepting a one-year contract to work in Washington DC as a translator, Orla leaves her Dublin hometown for a new start. Nick

Hughes is 100 per cent work-focused, especially after his last relationship exploded, along with his heart. He's made it clear he's not interested in romance, no matter who might catch his eye. When Orla finds several old notes written by a child in her library copy of 'Anna Karenina', she decides to track down the owner and give them back. She soon discovers that the owner has been missing for decades and is filed as a cold case. Suddenly Orla finds herself with a mystery, the notes open up a whole new angle to the case, and Nick is assigned to work on it. Now they'll have to see each other every single day!

THE SAINTS SERIES (Contemporary romance):

Team Lucas
Just let me get my fill of you and I'll deal with the fallout if it happens… when it happens.

Mia Carter never thought getting suspended from her part-time job for having attitude could be the best thing to ever happen … maybe. When Lucas Ainswright—one of the world's biggest sporting stars—needs a minder, it just so happens that attitude is needed to keep Lucas in line. Now Mia's job is to manage the sporting world's bad boy and keep him at the top of his game for the season. Game on!

Team Tomás
Tomás Carrera has had to be responsible all his life. Growing up with a single mom and as the eldest of five siblings, Tomás

missed out on a childhood of his own. Now his superstar soccer status has provided for his family and allowed him to let his hair down… and that's just what he's doing. Signed to the Santa Ana Saints, Tomás is catching up for lost time with fast women, a fast Ducati motorcycle and a bevy of adoring fans. That is until he loses his heart to Alice and is torn between wanting her and his independence.

Team Niklas

In his hometown of Berlin, Germany, Niklas Wagner is a superstar and when the Saints' pay the big bucks to sign him up and bring him to Santa Ana, California, Nik takes a shine to his new life. When he meets the Saints' media officer, Sasha Saxon, sparks fly, literally. But Sasha is not your average girl—by day she is a journalist who looks after the media for the national champion soccer team and at night she designs for her fashion label. She had big dreams and they don't include a boyfriend. Nik has never had to chase the girls, but now he has met his match—Sasha is about to lead him on the biggest chase of his life.

Team Alex

He's tall, dark, handsome and athletic and just that little bit mysterious. He's also over women, big time. A star of the Saint's team, Alex Renwick – nicknamed 'The Russian' – has had a high-profile relationship with a Hollywood director's daughter for years, and now that it is over, he just wants to focus on his sporting career. Carly Brooker's professional sporting career as a basketballer with the Suns is about to end due to injury. To mask the pain, she throws herself into developing her role as a sports reporter. There's just one problem, she needs a date for the Suns' Ball where she will announce her retirement. When these two sporting hotshots meet, they are more than a good fit; they are made for each other... if they can just file away the doubts they carry and find a way to be together.

Acknowledgments:

Thank you for reading and hopefully enjoying my star-crossed lovers based on my favourite novel, *Wuthering Heights*. I have long held a passion for the moors and for Emily Bronte's powerful classic novel. If you would like to read more of Catherine and Heath but with a twist... they are vampires, then try my novel, *The Dark Moors*. The power and moodiness of the moors lends itself so perfectly to a generation of dark spirits.

Thank you to Penny Clarkson who tirelessly proofreads my work and it is all the better for it. And thanks to Simona Moroni for the constructive read-through and feedback.

I look forward to connecting with you on Facebook, Bookbub, TikTok and Goodreads. And finally, thank you to all my favourite romance authors whose works keep me inspired and challenged!

About Ally:

I am an Australian journalist and writer, postgraduate qualified in Literature and Communications, with a diploma in Counselling! I've been so lucky to have worked in television, print newspapers, magazines, radio and online media. Now I just love writing at my home desk overlooking the park with my favourite romance programs streaming in the background and my beloved Boxer, Hastings, on the couch nearby.

Connect with Ally:

TikTok: @authorallyadams
Website - www.allyadamsbooks.com/
Facebook - https://www.facebook.com/allyadamswriter
BookBub - https://www.bookbub.com/authors/ally-adams
Instagram: https://www.instagram.com/allyadamsauthor/